FRENCH SUMMER

LISE GOLD

Copyright © 2018 by Anne-Lise Goud

All rights reserved.

No part of this book may be reproduced in any form or by any electronic or mechanical means, including information storage and retrieval systems, without written permission from the author, except for the use of brief quotations in a book review.

For Sophie and Gemma
Who found a new home
But more importantly, a home with each other

Home -- that blessed word, which opens to the human heart the most perfect glimpse of Heaven, and helps to carry it thither, as on an angel's wings.

— Lydia Child

1

Nathalie was welcomed by a warm breeze and the smell of freshly cut grass when she exited the arrivals hall at Nice airport. Her tired, sore eyes scanned the area, searching for car rental signs. It had been a long flight from Chicago, with a tight stop-over in Paris, forcing her to sprint towards the gate, arriving just before it closed. Following the arrows along the parking lot, she smiled and sighed at the sight of the palm trees that surrounded the modest airport, and the flower beds with bright pink oleanders on the roundabout, leading to the motorway. Nathalie stopped for a moment, rolled her shoulders and leaned onto her baggage trolley, which was stacked three-high with cases. Her feet were killing her in the high heels, still swollen from the flight. She wasn't looking forward to driving in a strange country, and the stories she'd heard about French traffic hadn't exactly boosted her confidence either. But there was something about the unknown that made her smile, despite her nerves. She was in France, of all places.

She picked up the keys to her Mercedes, bought herself a coffee and waited in the carpark for assistance with her baggage. Three staff members and a security guard stared at her blankly while smoking a cigarette in the shade of a tree. When no one moved a finger to help her, she reluctantly opened the trunk and loaded the heavy cases into the car herself. *Fine. I guess service is not a thing here.*

"Could you please point me in the general direction of Valbonne?" She asked the security guard, after rolling down the window by the gates of the parking lot. He frowned and waved a dismissive hand.

"No Anglais," he said, stubbing out the cigarette on the sole of his shoe.

"Valbonne?" Nathalie tried again. She held up the printout with the directions the caretaker of the estate had sent her, after strict instructions not to rely on her satnav in the mountains. The man took the piece of paper from her and read the address out loud, wiggling his well-groomed mustache. Then he nodded and pointed towards the third exit on the roundabout, holding up three fingers.

"Merci beaucoup," Nathalie tried. She blushed in embarrassment when he grinned at her poor French, while checking out her breasts. *So much for French charm.* She could feel sweat dripping down her back as soon as she drove off, and it wasn't just from the heat. Nathalie rarely drove herself. Back home in Chicago, she took cabs to work or used the company driver. *Come on, Nat. You can do this. You're heading in the right direction, that's a start.*

Nathalie's vacation to France was the most out of character thing she'd ever done. She rarely took vacations and when she did, she had always traveled with Jack, her ex-husband. She had pictured herself arriving at the airport, flaunting her white and navy striped boat-neck top and oversized shades, speaking French fluently. Instead, she was still in her pant-suit and she couldn't remember anything from the intensive French classes she had taken in the past weeks.

Nathalie struggled to get off the roundabout with all the cars zooming past. Her hands were shaking on the steering wheel, clamping onto the leather when cars sped past her on either side. *I should have taken my jacket off.* She felt clammy and warm, and was on the edge of a panic attack as she double checked the exit number on the directions lying next to her in the passenger seat. Finally, she exited the motorway onto a quieter road that took her through smaller towns and villages. She allowed herself to relax a little bit, and opened all the windows, letting in the scent of lavender fields, bakeries, and a faint hint of the ocean that lay behind her. Most villages were small and sleepy, with ivy-covered stone houses, colorful flower beds, small boutiques and family-run grocery stores. One blended into another as she followed the only road that would lead her to her destination. The instructions the caretaker had given her were clear, and she only had to stop once to double check that she hadn't gone too far wrong. Driving through a sweet little town, lined with garden centers, she pulled over and opened a pack of cigarettes, leaning out of the window as she lit one. There was no phone ringing, there were no urgent matters, and nowhere to be apart from wherever the hell she wanted to be. For some reason she felt more accomplished driving in France on her own, than she ever had building a successful global company from scratch. She watched herself in the side view mirror as she blew out the smoke, smiling at her own rebellion. She hadn't smoked in a while.

Not since Jack, her ex-husband quit two years ago. She had agreed to give up too, to make it easier for him. But Jack's opinion didn't matter anymore, and as soon as she'd landed, and spotted the slim, French cigarettes, the craving had returned. Nathalie pulled up her shades, wiped the mascara stains from underneath her eyes and secured the loose locks of blonde hair that had fallen out of her bun. Watching the locals walk by, she felt out of place in her big, flashy car and business attire. Some older ladies stared at her, suspiciously. Others, mainly men, smiled or winked when they passed. She had packed casual clothes, but it hadn't felt right to wear them at the airport in Chicago, and so she had put on a suit one last time.

Nathalie looked down at the piece of paper in the passenger's seat. *Watch out, the next part will be steep and narrow*, the directions told her. *Be careful in the bends.* She threw the cigarette stub into her half-empty coffee cup, took a left turn and braced herself for a bumpy ride. Although she'd read about driving in rural France, nothing could have prepared her for the spiraling sandy road that felt more like a rollercoaster, winding up and down around the mountains. The Mercedes was nothing short of impractical in the sharp bends, and too large to let other vehicles pass, but it had been the only automatic available. Nathalie was used to comfort, with all the business travel she'd been doing throughout her career, and she never shied away from an upgrade. This time around however, her choice of comfort was down-right silly. The TV screens in the back were of no use, and the drinks cooler in between the two front seats couldn't help her either as she clumsily reversed into someone's drive to let a truck pass, almost taking down a fence in the process. But the view was breathtaking. Hills and valleys stretched out in front of her with only the odd church tower here and there, marking a village. The bright-green from the forest roof, the wild river and the sun-baked farms with cows and pigs lazing on the surrounding land was something she could get used to, and Nathalie stopped several times to take it all in. She felt calmer already. Wherever she would end up, it was bound to be secluded.

2

Lena washed her hands, shook them off over the ceramic kitchen sink and ran them through her short dark hair before drying them. She'd been working on the garden designs for one of her new clients, when the buzzer for the gate went off. Most landscape architects used computers nowadays, but she liked to work the old-fashioned way, with thick cream paper, a good pencil, a ruler and a piece of charcoal. She was just getting into the flow, jotting down ideas, and didn't like to be interrupted. *She's early.* Unfortunately, it was time to switch into social mode. She pressed the button below the buzzer to open the gates, took a sip of her coffee and checked herself in the mirror, smiling back at her reflection. Nathalie Kingston would only be her third tenant, and she wanted to make a good first impression. Lena was wearing her usual meet-and-greet outfit, consisting of navy shorts, a white shirt and suede navy loafers. It was casual, but still smart enough to look like she'd made an effort. Finding tenants had been easy, but she was still growing into her role as a hostess, and her nerves played up when she stepped out of the pool annex and into the garden. Her correspondence with the new tenant had been short and to the point. Miss Kingston didn't beat around the bush. She had made it clear that she needed a quiet place to herself to spend some time over the summer. She'd enquired if there was a village nearby where she could get groceries and had offered to pay upfront. Ten minutes after Lena's first reply, she'd sent proof of the transaction and that was that.

Lena watched the Mercedes enter the driveway and chuckled. *Why would anyone choose a car like that?* It was big and impractical in the mountains, not to mention impossible to park anywhere in the village. She had emailed the tenant to let her know that she was welcome to use one of the cars at the property, but the woman had insisted on hiring an automatic. *Typical lady boss. Just had to do it her own way.* She walked over to greet the tenant when the car came to a halt at the end of the driveway. The blonde lady stepping out struggled to get a grip on the pebbled driveway with her high-heeled shoes. She was tall, but still slightly shorter than Lena, and was terribly overdressed in a fitted black pant-suit with a white blouse underneath. Her hair was pinned up, and she smiled nervously as she swung her purse over her shoulder. *Seriously?* Lena tried to wipe the amused grin off her face and forced herself to look the woman in the eye, instead of at her cleavage. The top four buttons had come undone, or maybe she'd just been warm during the drive, Lena thought, casting a fleeting glance over the edge of the woman's bra.

3

Nathalie stepped out of the car and held on to the roof when one of her heels sank into the driveway. She looked over the garden of *Villa Provence*, steadying herself. The name had been carved into a stone sign, cemented into the wall next to the front gate. She would have missed the subtle sign, if it hadn't been for the directions that told her it was the first gate after three deep potholes in the road, which she couldn't have missed if she tried. Although she had paid a hefty price for the villa, it was much grander than she had expected it to be. But then again, she wasn't in Cannes or St Tropez, where a premium rental came at a ridiculous price. The driveway was long, with a beautiful stretch of well-maintained garden, reaching towards the ivy-covered walls that surrounded the estate. The two-story house was big, but had lots of character, with its stone exterior, bright blue shutters and flat roof. It was quiet. Very quiet. *You wanted peace, now you've got it.*

"Hey, I'm Lena Delano." A young woman with a soft American accent held out her hand when Nathalie had finally found her balance. "Welcome to Valbonne."

"Thank you," Nathalie said, somewhat surprised at seeing the caretaker. From their correspondence, she had imagined her a lot older, but Lena looked around her own age. She had short black hair, dark eyes and features, and was tall and athletic. Her smile was genuine, and the dimples that appeared when she smiled, gave her a certain charm. "It's beautiful here." Nathalie shook Lena's hand, then stretched her back, taking her time to look out over the estate that would be her home for the coming months. There were fruit trees as far as she could see, and a subtle pool that blended in with the natural beauty of its surroundings. Behind the pool, there was another building with the same stone exterior and blue shutters. *A guest house maybe?*

"I'm glad it's to your taste." Lena gestured towards the main house. "Come on, let me show you to your room so you can freshen up. You must be tired from the long journey. After that, I'll give you the tour of the house if you have any energy left." Lena smiled as she lifted Nathalie's luggage out of the car with little effort. Nathalie threw one bag over her shoulder and dragged another suitcase behind her, following Lena over the terrace and into the kitchen. The kitchen was rustic but equipped with modern appliances. The old exposed brickwork brought character to the dining space that consisted of an old wooden table with matching chairs, and blue patchwork pillows on the seats, matching the pot of lavender on top of the table. The focal point of the kitchen was a black Aga, with on top of it a big pan, simmering on a low heat. Above the wooden worktop on either side, various shades of blue tiles covered the wall around the windows that looked out over the garden and the pool.

"I made some food," Lena said. "It's self-service here,

unless you request otherwise, but I thought you might be tired today so there's coq au vin and fresh bread if you get hungry." She winked. "I also put a bottle of rosé in the fridge in case you feel like a drink. The grocery store closes in twenty minutes, but we can go there tomorrow if you like."

"Thank you, that's very kind," Nathalie said, gazing over the selection of fresh herbs, growing in the alcoves in the wall behind the table. "I just can't get over how pretty this place is."

"Good. It's always a relief to know my guests are happy with what they've booked." Lena opened the kitchen door and stepped into a long, dark hallway, with doors on either side. "I would recommend this room for you," she said, opening the first door on the right. "There are towels and toiletries in the bathroom." Nathalie stepped into the spacious room and sighed as she put her heavy bag down on the floor. The bed was made up with fluffy pillows and yellow bedsheets. A modern painting of two naked women, entangled in an embrace, hung above it in an ornamental frame. Next to the bed was an antique nightstand with a bouquet of white roses sitting on top, elegantly displayed in a rustic looking jug. The yellow chaise longue at the bed-end matched the comforter and the carpet on the tiled floor. Lena wheeled the other suitcases in and opened the heavy linen drapes, exposing the French doors facing the terrace, with behind it the pool.

"The key is in the door. Make sure you put the mosquito cover on after sunset, or you'll be in trouble tonight." She gestured towards the frame that was leaning against the wall.

"Great. I'll remember that." Nathalie opened the bathroom door and switched on the lights. "The room is gorgeous. The owners have done an amazing job." She turned back to Lena and looked down at her pant-suit and high-heeled shoes. "I'll have a shower and get changed. I don't think I'll need a suit around here."

Lena laughed. "I can't believe you're still walking in those shoes after the journey you've just had." She lingered in the doorway. "Anyway, I'll be in the kitchen for a little while, finishing off the food. Come and find me if you want me to show you around."

NATHALIE OPENED THE FRENCH DOORS, allowing a breeze into the room. In front of her was the sunny terrace, where a cast iron table and chairs stood amongst flower pots and birdfeeders. A little further down the terrace, just in front of the kitchen door, was an outdoor dining area, seating twelve. Ivy grew up the trellis against the walls and over an arcade that led to the swimming pool. Behind that were the mountains. She could see a church in the distance, and some townhouses, scattered along the top. It was certainly idyllic; the advert hadn't lied about that. She kicked off her shoes and shivered with pleasure at the feeling of her bare feet on the cold tiles. Then she took off her suit and searched for a kaftan in her luggage.

4

"I'm sorry I've kept you waiting," Nathalie said as she walked into the kitchen with a towel wrapped around her wet hair.

"Don't apologize, there's no need to rush." Lena smiled. "That's what you're here for, right? You said you wanted to take it easy for a while?" She gestured towards the garden. "Well, you've got it."

She got up from her chair and beckoned Nathalie to follow her back into the hallway. "Come on, let's do a quick tour of the house first."

They entered the living area that was situated on the back side of the house.

"There is a front door," Lena said, "but you'll see that you won't use it very much. In France, especially around here, we like to use the kitchen door. The gate and the kitchen door both open with a code, so you won't really be needing keys either. I live in the annex in the garden, and I'm usually here at night. There is an alarm system, if that makes you feel safer, although I've never used it myself." She pointed at the mosaic-tiled fireplace.

"The fireplace works fine, and there's wood underneath the coffee table. Just give me a shout if you want it on, I'll show you how to light it. It will be too warm this week, but occasionally, it gets chilly at night."

"Thanks." Nathalie looked around the room. It was cozy, almost farm-like. The two deep dark leather couches were placed in front of the fireplace with a rustic wooden coffee table in front of them. There were cowhide rugs throughout the room, and plants. Lots of plants, in pots, or hanging down from the ceiling in crochet baskets. It looked like one of those houses in interior magazines, Nathalie thought. The modern, abstract paintings in neutral colors complemented the rustic décor. They were the only reminder that she hadn't traveled back in time. There was no TV, and no music system. Nathalie imagined herself reading here at night, with the candles lit, and a glass of good French wine. "Show me no more, I'm happy as it is," she said.

Lena laughed. "We're not done yet. There are two more bedrooms downstairs, besides yours. You're in the biggest en suite. I call it the yellow room. The blue room is next to it, and the pink room opposite." She pointed towards the end of the hallway as they walked back. "The wet room is over there, with all the facilities you'll need to do your laundry. You'll find the towels in there too. If you want, I can arrange for one of the local cleaners to do your laundry for you."

"No need," Nathalie said. "I'll be fine."

Lena smiled. "Okay. Let me know if you change your mind." She pointed to the door next to the laundry room. "There's a pantry over there, but you might not need it since the kitchen has a lot of storage space. Upstairs are four more bedrooms, also marked by color, but you'll see that when you have a look around. Two of them have a small balcony overlooking the garden. Please feel free to switch rooms if you prefer one of those." She shrugged. "It's all yours for the coming months, so do whatever you like."

Nathalie followed her back through the kitchen and out onto the terrace, where the roses were in full bloom. Trees provided shade throughout the neatly kept garden and the white linen used to create a canopy over the seating area, gave it a bohemian feel.

"I assume there's a gardener here?" she asked. "It must be a lot of work to maintain a place like this."

Lena held up a hand and chuckled. "That would be me." She gestured towards the neatly trimmed lawn. "I love yard work, so it's not a chore. I spend about an hour out there each day, usually in the early morning. It relaxes me. We've got a great irrigation system in place, so I don't need to water the plants. That saves me a lot of time."

"Wow. People must be lining up to hire you." Nathalie regarded Lena, who smiled proudly. Her dimples were cute, and she found herself staring at her for just a moment too long. They crossed the lawn and walked over to the pool, which was the only paved area surrounding the estate, apart from the terrace and the narrow path towards it. There were wooden sun loungers with thick, white foam covers and matching coffee tables. The navy tiles that lined the pool made it look deep and cool.

"The pool is serviced every two weeks," Lena continued. "I'll give you a heads up before they come in. It only takes about an hour, so you might want to cover up during that time." She grinned. "The working-class Frenchmen tend to be a bit flirtier than their American equivalent, but it's all light-hearted and I'm sure you'll get used to it."

Nathalie dipped a toe into the water, bent down and checked the pool thermometer. It was a perfect twenty-five degrees. "The owner must either have really good taste, or a very expensive decorator."

"I'll make sure to pass on your comments," Lena said. "This is the first year it's being rented out after the renovation. You're only the third person to stay here so there shouldn't be any problems with the boiler or electricity." She pointed to the pool annex. It looked quite spacious from the outside. The baskets underneath the three windows were filled with lavender, and just like the main house, half of the façade was covered in ivy. "I live there. If you need anything, anything at all, just knock. I'm usually around." There was barking coming from inside the annex.

"Do you have a dog?" Nathalie asked.

"Yeah. I kind of forgot to mention that in my emails." Lena grimaced. "I left him in there, in case you're allergic or scared of dogs. Not everyone appreciates pets on their holiday. Do you mind if I let him out?"

"No, not at all." Nathalie smiled. "Please, I love dogs." She bent down to greet the black and white terrier when Lena opened the door. He was barking in excitement, wagging his tail and jumping up at her whilst licking her face. "Oh, look at you. You must be the cutest little thing I've ever seen!"

Lena laughed at his antics. "His name is Gumbo. My grandfather named him that, after his favorite dish. I think he likes you, Nathalie."

"Nat. Please call me Nat," Nathalie said, petting Gumbo.

"Okay, Nat. I'm glad you don't mind having a dog around. I'm going to take him for a walk now." She gestured to Gumbo. "There's more than enough space for him around here, but he's bored of the garden. Aren't you Gumbo?" Gumbo ran inside and brought back a tennis ball that he dropped in front of Lena. "I'll leave you to it, unless there's anything else you need from me?"

"No, I'm good, thanks." Nathalie stood up and took a step back. "I can feel my jetlag kicking in. I think I might try some of that delicious food you made and have an early night." She looked at her watch, surprised to see that it was only six p.m. The sun was still up, but her body felt like it was midnight. Lena laughed.

"You have a good rest. Give me a shout if you want me to show you around the shops tomorrow." She waved as she walked towards the gate, the little dog tearing around her like a maniac.

5

Nathalie looked at the clock on her nightstand. It was only seven in the morning, and she was wide awake. Not that she ever slept late back in Chicago. She was always up early, even on weekends. But she'd expected to sleep longer without an alarm clock, and the prospect of a busy day ahead. The bed was incredibly comfortable, with its firm mattress and crisp sheets, and the room was much cooler than she'd expected it to be. She got out and opened the drapes to let the sun in. Then she searched for a book in one of her suitcases that was still unpacked and got back into bed. She couldn't remember the last time she'd read anything apart from emails, contracts, financial reports or strategic plans. It was strange, not having a reason to get up in the morning. She held her breath, waiting for the panic to kick in, and exhaled deeply when it didn't. *I'm fine. Everything's fine.* She took another deep breath and settled into the thriller, which made her forget about her lack of purpose for a while. Still, an eerie feeling of restlessness stabbed at her, just as she was starting to relax. She thought of her apartment in Chicago, that was now up for sale, and couldn't help but wonder how the company was doing. What decisions were being taken without her? Had her successor been appointed yet? *Stop thinking about things that don't concern you anymore. That's behind you now. You're here to figure out what you want to do with your life, so go figure it out.*

Great. She'd only been here one night, and she was worried about the company already. She sat up in bed and peered out through the French doors, trying to ignore the thoughts that were poking their way through her consciousness. Lena was cutting the hedge behind the terrace. Nathalie could see the concentration on her face, as she worked methodically, taking a step back to inspect her work every minute or so. There was something very attractive about Lena, Nathalie thought. The short, shaggy black hair, and the deep dark eyes, not to mention her amazing smile. But there was also a hint of boyish mischief in her demeanor; the casual way in which she moved and her chilled attitude.

Lena stood up and looked in the direction of Nathalie's bedroom, as if she could feel a pair of eyes on her. In a reflex, Nathalie turned her head back to her book so fast, that she pulled her neck, groaning in pain.

"Fuck!" she said, just a little too loud. Gumbo, who was sniffing around the terrace, heard her and before Lena could get a hold of him, he'd sprinted towards Nathalie's bedroom, jumping up against the glass doors. Nathalie rolled her shoulders, stood up and opened the doors to let him in.

"I'm so sorry," Lena shouted from behind the hedge. "Did he wake you? Wait, I'll come and get him." Gumbo however, had other plans. He managed to jump onto the bed via the chaise in no time and settled on Nathalie's pillow as if it was the most natural thing in the world. Nathalie laughed at Lena's mortified expression.

"It's okay," she shouted back. "I feel kind of honored he wants to come into bed with me."

"Are you sure?" Lena took a couple of steps towards her, but kept her distance when Nathalie got back into bed. She swallowed at the sight of her crème-colored, silk nightgown. "He's not allowed into the main house, he knows that. I have no idea why he thought it was okay to…"

"I'm sure." Nathalie interrupted her. She smiled, looking down at Gumbo, who was pretending to be in a deep sleep.

"Alright then," Lena said, returning to the hedge. "But please kick him out whenever you want." She waved a hand. "I don't mean literally kick him out of course… Just give me a shout."

"Sure, but I really don't mind him being here," Nathalie said, giving her a thumbs-up. She fell back into her pillow and giggled when Gumbo moved closer, licking her face.

6

Should I leave her alone? She said she needed some time to herself... Lena watched Nathalie as she was lying by the poolside. Relaxing wouldn't be the right word to describe the scene. She was nervously looking at her phone every ten seconds, then slamming it back on the table next to her, closing her eyes shut for a while before repeating the ritual again and again. She was gorgeous though, in her white bikini. Her blonde hair was pulled back into a knot and her skin was shimmering from the sunscreen. Before Lena was able to think it through, she found herself walking up to her.

"You okay there?"

Nathalie lowered her shades as she looked up. "Yeah, I'm good." Then she laughed and held up both hands. "Actually, it's completely alien for me to be doing nothing. It feels weird." She nodded towards her phone. "I'm used to getting over two hundred emails a day and non-stop phone calls. I think it might take a while before I stop obsessing over my phone."

"Okay." Lena smiled. "Why don't you switch it off, or

leave it in your room?" She decided not to inquire about Nathalie's life. It was too early, and she didn't want to come across as nosy, even though she was dying to know more about her.

Nathalie rolled her eyes. "That would be the obvious thing to do, wouldn't it?" She picked up her phone again, switched it off and put it in her bag. "There. It's off." She chuckled. "So *now* what do I do?"

"Now you relax." Lena pointed to the chair next to Nathalie. "May I?"

"Sure." Nathalie stole a glance at Lena as she sat down, crossing her long, toned legs. Something stirred inside of her when Lena's eyes fixated on hers with the most intense stare. Her long lashes fluttered against the sun as she spoke.

"I'm going to teach you to relax," Lena said matter-of-factly. "Close your eyes and keep your head turned up to the sun." She did so herself, and Nathalie followed suit.

"You're not going to make me meditate, are you?"

"There's nothing wrong with meditation." Lena's voice wasn't accusing. It was calm and kind of soothing. "It serves its purpose from time to time." She placed a hand over Nathalie's in between them. "I used to suffer from anxiety and it's helped me a lot, so give it a shot, okay?"

"Alright." Nathalie closed her eyes again and sighed at the feeling of Lena's hand on hers. It was nice. Oh God, was she really this desperate for human contact? Had she been so lonely that she'd forgotten what it felt like to be touched, even in the most casual of ways? *I'm pathetic.*

"Now concentrate on the mattress and how your body sinks into it," Lena said. "Feel the surface beneath you as the sunbeams warm your toes. Wiggle them, tense them, then relax them one by one. Feel the heat of the sun on your feet."

Nathalie relaxed her feet and followed Lena's instructions as they slowly worked their way up her body, limb by limb. She tensed, then relaxed, allowing the sun to warm her. Her breathing became slow and steady, and to her surprise, she was starting to feel calmer.

"Focus on your breathing," Lena continued, "as you relax your chest. Breathe in deeply, soak up the sun's energy and breathe out while you sink deeper into the mattress. You're heavy now, but it feels good. Can you feel it?"

"Uhuh." Nathalie didn't want to ruin the moment by speaking. She felt warm and fuzzy, although she wasn't sure if that was down to the meditation, or because of Lena's hand on hers and the surprising appreciation she felt at the closeness to another human being. "I feel great," she mumbled.

"Good." Lena's voice was soft now, almost whispering. "Now open your eyes and look around you. You're awake but your body is calm. Listen to the birds, smell the summer in the air and be aware of everything around you. The sound of the soft whistle in the trees, the breeze on your skin and the scent of lavender and rosemary."

Nathalie opened her eyes and turned to Lena, who was facing her. She indulged in losing herself for a moment, wondering why looking into Lena's eyes was so soothing. They were both quiet, and it felt like the most natural thing to lie next to her, even though she was practically a stranger.

Lena smiled. "Did that help?"

Nathalie nodded. "Thank you. You're good at this."

"No problem." Lena stood back up, breaking the contact. "Glad to be of help. And if you feel like it's all nonsense, please tell me to stop bugging you with it. I just know that it worked for me. But then again, there's never any harm in trying, right?"

Nathalie realized she had a big grin on her face. "So true," she said. "I think I could read something now. I might even be able to concentrate." She searched for her book in her bag while she watched Lena walk back to the lawn where she'd been trimming the edges. She loved looking at her.

7

"Want me to take you to the shops?" Lena bent over Nathalie's car as she opened her window, trying to get some relief from the scorching heat. Even the thin summer dress seemed too much for the French sun, and she turned on the air-conditioning in an attempt to cool her skin from the leather seat, burning into her back.

"Thanks. But I'll be okay." Nathalie leaned out of her car and pointed at the map on her phone. "I think I've figured it out. Anyway, it's not like I'm in a hurry." Lena nodded, shaking the soil off her fingers. She'd been doing yard work the whole morning, despite claiming that she only spent an hour there each day.

"I don't want you to think that it's any trouble for me, because it's not. It's my job, you know. To make sure you're comfortable."

Nathalie smiled. "Don't worry about me. It's very kind of you to offer, but the sooner I manage to get around by myself, the better. I don't like being dependent on people."

"Okay." Lena took a step back, allowing Nathalie to

reverse. "You've got my number if anything goes wrong. Don't hesitate to call." She winked, and Nathalie felt a strange sensation in her belly when their eyes met. It came out of nowhere and made her break out in a cold sweat. *What the hell was that?*

"I will," she said with a nervous giggle, steering the car out of the driveway.

NATHALIE WAS STILL TRYING to figure out what had just happened to her as she drove down the hill. Because really, nothing had happened. So why was she feeling like she'd just been in a car crash? Where did all this adrenaline come from and how had Lena managed to stir it up? Nathalie wasn't uncomfortable with her presence. On the contrary. She liked having someone around, even if it was just to say good morning and have a fleeting conversation to make sure her vocal cords still worked. But for some reason she couldn't explain, she also felt slightly nervous around Lena. Lena had a certain air about her, some kind of natural and relaxed way of being that she wasn't used to. It was admirable, and charming. Nathalie had spent hours wondering what Lena thought of her, and for that, she was angry with herself. So far, she had gone through life with ease, never intimidated by anyone. She'd built professional relationships with CEO's and investors and was known for being a great social asset to the company she'd built with her ex-husband. So why did a caretaker make her feel this way? She turned into the parking lot of the supermarket, relieved that she'd found it without driving around in circles. *See? You can do this.* Since resigning from her job, even the smallest of things had seemed hard. A simple conversation was like climbing a mountain, without a business purpose to fall back on. What the hell did people talk about when they were simply hanging out? She could ask about people's children, but she didn't have any of her own, and she couldn't relate to the sleepless night stories. She couldn't talk about hobbies, because she didn't have any of those either. Things like sports, movies or even music were alien to her. Small-talk used to come easy when she could talk about work but lately, she even struggled to stammer her way through the checkout at the local grocery store. Her job was all she had known for far too long, and she had given it all up in the hope of finding herself, only to discover there was nothing but a sad, boring creature underneath the corporate shell, desperately searching for her own personality. *Stop it. Stop the negative thoughts. Remember what Doctor Kennedy said. Think positive.* Unfortunately, her attempts to positive thinking didn't get her a parking space, and she drove back out through the barriers, looking for a free spot along the main road that led into town. She wasn't the only one with a parking problem. Creeping behind three other cars, she finally managed to find a space that was big enough in front of the bank. Nathalie got out of the car and stared at the parking meter. It was in French. *Of course it's in French. What did you expect?* After examining it closely, she concluded that there was no hole to put coins in, no slot for her card, and that she had absolutely no idea what to do. She randomly swiped her credit card over the screen and poked at all options listed, hoping for a miracle, but nothing happened. She waved at an old lady, who was carrying her groceries towards her car.

"Excusez-moi, Madame. Could you please help me?" She asked, putting on a pleading tone. The lady stopped and looked at her with a friendly frown on her face. She said something in French that Nathalie didn't understand. "I'm so sorry, I have no idea what you're saying. Do you speak English?" she articulated, as if speaking to a child. The lady put a bag down and held up her hand in an apologetic gesture. Then she opened her trunk and started loading her groceries without giving Nathalie a second glance.

"Great." Nathalie looked around, searching for help in the near distance. There was no one, apart from a man at the bus stop opposite the church. Nathalie opened her mouth to call for help, then gave up when a bus pulled in to let him on. *Never mind. I'm sure the car will be fine.*

Half an hour later, Nathalie came back out with five bags of groceries and a bunch of long-stemmed red roses clenched between her teeth. She didn't usually buy flowers, but it seemed appropriate now, and the simple purchase had put a smile on her face. She put the bags down, noticed the yellow wheel clamp around her tire and let out a deep sigh.

"Fuck." She bent over, tugged at it and kicked it, but it wasn't going anywhere. *So much for independence.* She searched for her phone in her purse and called the number listed on the side of the clamp, but all she got was a monotone zoom. She tried again, without the net-number, but it didn't seem to work from her American mobile. "Great. Just great." She put the groceries in her trunk, opened the driver's door and searched for her cigarettes in the front compartment. Then she sat down on the pavement, leaned back against her car and lit one, closing her eyes in frustration.

8

"The French aren't very lenient when it comes to parking offenses," Lena said as she got out of the car. "Drunk driving is fine, but a parking violation is unforgivable in this part of France. I still haven't figured out why, it's not like there's a shortage of space." She opened the trunk to Nathalie's Mercedes, took out three bags and headed for the kitchen.

"I wouldn't have known what to do without you," Nathalie said as she followed her inside. "I didn't want to call you, but the language..." She sighed. "I felt helpless and I don't like it one bit."

"You'll get used to it. The helpless part of it, I mean." Lena smiled. "But hey, that's what you've got me for. You're on holiday after all." She laughed. "Imagine living here without speaking French. It took me at least two years to find my way around the various systems, and I didn't even have to pay the bills back then." She placed a hand on Nathalie's shoulder. "Hey, don't let it discourage you. You're not the first tourist to get a wheel clamp. The economy thrives on it in high season. That's why they're able to pay gardeners like me a good salary to make their precious roundabouts look like a scene from a Disney movie." Nathalie laughed.

"It's good to know my money is going towards a good cause." She sat down at the kitchen table and held up a sticky cardboard box, containing melted ice cream. "Okay, maybe I do need your help. If you could just explain the basics to me, like parking meters, certain road signs, and help me get a French phone number and things like that." She looked up at Lena, who was busying herself with the coffee maker. "So, if you're still willing to help a stubborn woman out, I'd be grateful."

"Anytime," Lena said, pouring them both a fresh cup of coffee. She handed one to Nathalie and raised herself onto the kitchen counter. "First lesson starts tomorrow. We're going to cover road signs, parking meters, coffee orders and standard bistro menus." She held up her cup. "You'll need to know how to order a coffee, because surely, there can't be anything more important than that."

9

"Hey. I'm sorry to disturb you." Nathalie held up a bottle of rosé when Lena opened the door. "I was wondering if you'd like to join me for a glass." She bit her lip and winced. "I totally understand if you don't hang out with guests, but I thought I'd ask anyway. I won't be offended if you want to be alone."

"Sure." Lena gave her that broad smile again, making Nathalie's insides flutter. "I would love to have a drink with you." She gestured towards the modest terrace in front of the annex. "My place or yours?"

Nathalie laughed. "Yours is fine." She sat down on the bench next to Lena's front door and put the bottle on the table in front of her. Lena went inside and came back with two wine glasses, a tumbler full of ice cubes and a bowl of olives. Her oversized sweatshirt was barely covering the white boxers she was wearing underneath.

"Please don't mind my outfit," she said. "As you can probably imagine, I don't really bother with my appearance here after hours."

"Of course. Please don't apologize." Nathalie rolled up

the sleeves of her button-down striped shirt, suddenly feeling overdressed. "It's nice not having to worry about that."

"Yeah." Lena looked her up and down, finally resting her gaze on Nathalie's gold watch, as if trying to gauge her. "So, tell me, what brought you here if you don't mind me asking?"

Nathalie sighed and held out her glass for Lena to fill it. "Oh, I don't know. Everything, I suppose. Work, life, divorce…" She put some ice cubes into her glass and dropped two into Lena's glass too. "I was married. My husband… I mean my ex-husband and I had a company together. We specialized in renewable energy, providing factories with solar panels that made certain parts of their production process environmentally friendly. My husband was the brains behind the company, I oversaw the accounts, PR, and the financial side of it." She paused and looked up at Lena. "For the past seven years, I was the CFO. It's a big company now, with offices in eleven different countries. My ex-husband bought me out after our divorce last month, and so here I am, taking a break."

"I'm sorry to hear that. What happened?" Lena asked.

Nathalie leaned back and put her feet up on a stool, making herself comfortable.

"I'm not sure. It all happened so fast." She sighed. "I mean time… It went by in a blink. We met in college, at a demonstration. I don't even remember what it was for." She laughed, thinking back to her college years. "We were idealistic once. We wanted to create a better world, be a part of something greater than ourselves. It was the only thing we had in common, but it held us together. We started from a cheap office we rented on the outskirts of Chicago. We worked day and night, and celebrated each milestone. We were so passionate back then." Nathalie took a moment as she stared into blank space. "But as the years passed and the company grew with wealthy investors and government backing, it was just as much about money as it was about making the world a better place, perhaps even more so. We lost sight of our dream, and with that, we lost sight of each other, I suppose. Before we knew it, twelve years had passed, and wealth had changed everything. We were working sixty-hour weeks and barely saw each other, apart from in the boardroom."

"It must be hard when you suddenly realize that," Lena said.

"Yeah." Nathalie nodded. "A year ago, Jack, my ex-husband, confessed that he'd been having an affair for over two years, and he told me he wanted a divorce." She shrugged. "It came as a total surprise, but looking back, I don't even blame him that much."

"Really?" Lena frowned. "Did you not feel hurt? I mean, he was your husband, after all."

"Of course I felt hurt." Nathalie took a long drink from her rosé. "But we'd lost the connection we once had." She shook her head and rolled her eyes. "My husband fell in love with his secretary. I know it's a cliché, but the fact that I worked so hard that I didn't pay attention to what was happening right under my own nose, was worse for me. Our working relationship was great, so I felt betrayed because he'd lied to me. But regarding our marriage, I think that was over a long time ago."

"So what happens to the company?" Lena asked. "Your life's work?"

Nathalie shrugged. "I asked him to buy me out. We're in the process of finalizing it as we speak. I'm not going to lie, it was a difficult decision. Jack and I had a long talk." She held out her glass for Lena to refill it. "It was hard to let go of something I'd spent half of my life building, it still is. But it didn't feel like a partnership anymore so in the end, I managed to put a proposal together that would give me financial freedom without putting the company in any real danger." Nathalie looked down at her knees, deciding to be completely honest. She felt comfortable talking to Lena and it felt good to finally open up to someone other than her psychologist. "I thought it would be a positive thing," she said, "starting over fresh. I mean, I'm only thirty-five. I figured I had the world at my feet. But it wasn't like that. Within days, I realized I was alone and without a purpose, even without friends. I'd been neglecting my personal relationships and stopped making time for birthdays or get-togethers. I even forgot to send my childhood friend a message after she'd given birth to her first child because I was preparing for a big pitch. Needless to say, she stopped calling me many years ago. So, after my first two weeks at home I felt like I was going crazy. That's when I decided to go away for a while."

Lena nodded. "Why France? Why here?"

"No idea. I've never been to France before, but I've always been intrigued by this country so it seemed like the natural thing to do. I'll have a good chunk of money soon, and no idea what to do with my life. Add to that, all the time in the world to think about what I *do* want to do, and here I am." She laughed. "I'm sorry for pouring my heart out like this. It's not something I normally do. And I don't want you to think that I'm bored and lonely and that I'll be at your doorstep every night."

"Hey, I never thought that." Lena nudged her. "But I wouldn't mind if you wanted to. It gets awfully quiet here sometimes. If you want peace, you certainly managed to find the right place." A sleepy Gumbo came out of the house. He sat down by Nathalie's legs and looked up at her.

"Hey Gumbo. Do you want to sit with me?" Nathalie patted her knees and smiled at him. Gumbo's tail started wagging and he jumped onto her lap, settling into a comfortable position. She stroked him until he closed his eyes. It was nice to have a dog around. She'd always wanted one, but never had the time to take care of anyone other than herself.

"And you?" Nathalie asked, turning to Lena "What's your story? You sound like you're from New York, but your French is fluent too, at least from what I gathered when we picked up my car."

Lena shrugged. "Yeah, I'm from New York, but I've been living in France for quite a while now. I take care of the property and do some landscaping a couple of days a week." She smiled. "I run a landscaping company, but it's mostly management, so now and then, I like to get my hands dirty. I'm lucky to be in the position that I can plan myself in on the sunny days and the fun projects."

"Wow." Nathalie cocked her head. "You must be busy." She studied Lena, trying to imagine her running a company. "You seem so chilled."

Lena laughed. "I only work when I want to, and I run the business from here. I have great freelancers who work for me, so that means no obligations towards others, and no stress."

Nathalie nodded. "Sounds like you've got it all figured out."

"I'm not sure about that." Lena divided the rest of the wine over their glasses. "But I'm getting there."

"Are you in a relationship?" Nathalie asked.

Lena shook her head. "No." She opened her mouth to

continue, then decided against it and stood up. "More wine? I have another bottle in the fridge if you like. It's a local one, very nice." Nathalie waved a hand. Her head was already spinning from the half bottle she'd consumed.

"No thank you. I think I need my bed so I won't keep you up any longer, I'm sure you've got better things to do."

"Don't worry about that. I don't do anything at night, apart from a bit of work and reading." Lena hesitated. "I'm going to the local market tomorrow morning. Would you like to join me?"

Nathalie put down her glass. "I don't know. I don't want to impose. I'm sure I'll be able to find everything by myself."

"Nonsense." Lena put a hand on her knee. "It's my job. I'm just lucky to have someone as nice as you, staying here. It makes it a pleasure. And besides, I need to teach you the basics, remember?"

"Alright then, I would love to." Nathalie held her breath, looking down at the hand that was still resting on her knee.

10

"Morning!" Lena waved at Nathalie from the poolside. She was scooping a net through the water, picking out the leaves that had blown in overnight. Nathalie waved back as she walked out onto the terrace and sat down with a coffee and her book.

"Would you like a coffee?" she shouted.

"No thanks, I've already had four." Lena laughed. "I'm buzzing right now, so I'd better not."

Nathalie watched her work in the morning sun, swiping the net from one side of the pool to the other. She tried to concentrate on the new book she'd bought at the airport but found herself distracted by Lena's presence, once again. She was statuesque, with toned arms and legs. She was attractive, natural and easy to talk to. Nathalie continued to find herself worrying about what Lena thought of her, but most curious perhaps, was the strange feeling that spread throughout her core, each time Lena looked at her. She flipped the page and forced herself to concentrate on the story, but instead, her eyes kept wandering off to the poolside, where Lena was bending over, emptying the net into a wheelbarrow. When she stood back up and rolled her shoulders, her t-shirt crept up, exposing her belly. Nathalie stared at her flat stomach, trying to ignore the funny sensation she felt at the sight. Looking at Lena had become her new favorite pastime, and although she had no idea why, she was pretty sure she could easily spend hours on the terrace while Lena was working. *Stop looking at her. You're going to freak her out.*

"Hop in!" Lena beeped the horn and opened the door to the Porsche convertible. Gumbo was in the passenger seat, his tongue hanging out, and his eyes wide in excitement.

"Are you serious?" Nathalie brushed the top of the red door with her fingertips, before getting in. "Do the owners let you drive this?"

"All part of the package, Nat." Lena winked. "Beats your corporate rental, doesn't it?"

Nathalie settled into the low seat with Gumbo on her lap, looking over the dashboard. She was pushed back into her seat when Lena stepped on the gas and headed towards the gate. Out on the road, Lena waited for the gates to close and put on her shades before taking a right turn, speeding up into the hills. Her outfit hadn't gone unnoticed. She had changed into jeans and a thin, grey t-shirt that hugged her in all the right places.

"You look like you were born driving this," Nathalie shouted over the noise of the roaring engine. "I don't think you have any idea how cool you look."

Lena turned to her and arched an eyebrow. "Well, I don't think you have any idea how great you look in it either, with your blonde hair blowing in the wind."

Nathalie laughed and suddenly realized she was blushing. It had been years since anyone had complimented her, even though it came from the caretaker, who was clearly biased and possibly hoping for a good review. She turned her gaze towards the mountains on one side of the road, then shifted her eyes the valley on the other. The sun came out from behind one of the fleeting clouds, creating a spectacular pattern of shadows and highlights over the green and yellow hills. Lena took a turn and drove down a narrow road, slowing down as she went through the bends. Every now and then, a car would come from the opposite direction, forcing her to reverse into the roadside to let it pass. She was a good driver, Nathalie noticed, handling the car like a pro in the sharpest of bends.

"Lesson one," Lena said, waiting for a car to pass. "When you're driving in the mountains, the car going uphill always has the right of way."

"Thanks. I'll remember that." Nathalie winced. "I hope I didn't upset any of your neighbors."

"Don't worry. The people here are friendly. If they don't recognize your face, they'll assume you're a tourist and forgive you." Lena waved back at the other driver, who thanked her for letting him pass. "Lesson two. Always thank the person who lets you pass. Wave, smile, it doesn't matter as long as it's obvious." Just as she was about to take the next bend, another car came out of nowhere. Lena was quick to step on the break and laughed at Nathalie's startled expression. She was holding on to the side of the door, her eyes wide. "And lesson three, always have your foot on the break."

The brick townhouses along the hill were beautiful and old. Some were overgrown with ivy, others were surrounded by generous gardens, blessed with the most gorgeous wildflowers. The names of the properties were carved into wooden signs or painted on the fences.

"That's the mayor's house," Lena said, pointing at a large cast iron fence at the bottom of the road. "He's got a pretty nice place." She nodded towards the house opposite and grinned. "And that's where the local parking officer lives, in case you feel like toilet papering his garden tonight."

Nathalie laughed. "I think I'll pass on that. I'm sure he could make my life a living hell around here, forcing me to cycle into town instead."

LENA PARKED the car behind the village church. Gumbo jumped out as soon as she turned off the engine, ready to mark every pole and plant nearby. Nathalie looked around the medieval village and smiled. The colors, the cobbled streets and the light that hit the sun-kissed buildings in the most perfect way would have made a nice postcard. She could hear the market noise as she followed Lena through the narrow, cobbled alleyways that led into the town center, where three and four-story houses shaded the streets below. They were painted in stone and pastel shades, but their shutters and flower baskets gave them all their own colorful personality. There were news-stands, small coffee shops and a bakery underneath the old apartments. Most of the business owners seemed to know Lena, as they waved at her when they passed. Nathalie took pictures of the pastel colored facades against the blue sky, the pink and green macaroons in the bakery's window and the rusty shop signs that looked like they had hung out front since the beginning of time. They walked in a slow pace until they reached the *Place des Arcades*, the main village square. Framed by picturesque arcades, small shops and terraces, it was the heartbeat of the town. In the middle of the busy square was the market, stocked with traditional Provencal produce.

"This is everything I hoped France would be and more," Nathalie said, looking over the market stalls that were stocked with fresh fruit and vegetables, bread, meats and cheeses, olive oils and condiments, and a variety of homemade delicacies to take away.

"So, you like our little town?" Lena asked.

"Like it? I love it!" Nathalie let her eyes wander over the selection of olives in front of her. Large, small, stuffed or marinated in black, green, red and yellow varieties. "Educate me," she said to Lena. "What should I get?"

"Ah." Lena smiled. "I'm glad you asked me." She pointed to the red olives in an herby marinade. "You need to get some of these to start with. They are home-grown, from a neighboring town, and they're very punchy." She ordered a box from the lady in the stall and turned back to Nathalie. "Do you speak any French at all?" Nathalie shook her head.

"Not a word." She shrugged. "I did a speed course before I came here, but my mind seems to go blank each time I'm under pressure to say something."

"That's okay," Lena said. "We can practice together if you want to learn. Privately at first, if you're shy." She smiled. "Then, after a while, you can practice in supermarkets, cafés and restaurants. Trust me, you'll know the basics before you go home." They heard Gumbo bark at the man behind the meat stall and laughed when he jumped up and caught a piece of sausage that the man threw for him. "That's Gumbo's best friend, as you can probably imagine," Lena said, waving at him. "We call him Monsieur Steak, but that's just between Gumbo and me." She winked at Nathalie and handed her the olives. "Oh, and you'll have to get some of this rosemary bread." She tore a piece off from the sample loaf and handed it to Nathalie.

"Mmm..." Nathalie nodded. "This is good. Yeah, I'll have one of those." She pointed to the bread and paid the stall holder. "What's this?" She asked at the next stall, hovering over a selection of jars with red checked fabric draped over the top.

"These are homemade sauces and tapenades." Lena picked two and added them to Nathalie's shopping bag. "I think you should get the aioli and one of the caper and anchovies tapenade. Believe, me, you'll be coming back for more. They're both delicious with bread, meat or fish. Just don't kiss anyone after you've eaten them," she joked. Nathalie listened to Lena's conversation with the stall owner while she paid. Although Lena was American, she spoke French with the ease and flair of a local, joking and laughing as they said goodbye. The language sounded like music to her ears, especially when it was Lena talking. Nathalie followed her to the next stalls, where they got fresh garlic butter, a couple of artichokes, a bag of large, ripe tomatoes and a bottle of olive oil. They passed through one of the arcades into another narrow street full of small, specialized shops that sold souvenirs, soaps, candles and flowers. It was such a contrast to the big, American supermarkets Nathalie was used to. She'd run in and out once a week, throwing the same things into her cart without even thinking about it. This was fun and exciting.

Lena insisted on carrying most of the bags so that Nathalie could look around and inspect the selection of hand-made soap bars. She picked them up one by one and smelt them.

"Is this what you use?" she asked, holding up a bar of lavender soap.

Lena frowned. "Yeah, it is, actually. Not that exact one, but similar." She cocked her head with an amused smile. "So, you know what I smell like, huh?"

Nathalie blushed. "I guess so." She put the bar back and picked up another one, pretending to be interested in the label. "You smell nice, that's all. I recognized the scent right away when I walked in here."

"Well, thank you," Lena said. "It's good to know I smell nice, I had no idea it was noticeable." She turned to Nathalie. "I happen to know what you smell like too." She leaned in closer and closed her eyes as she inhaled Nathalie's scent.

Nathalie's heart started racing when she felt Lena's breath on her neck.

"What do I smell like?" she asked in an unsteady voice.

Lena straightened her back and faced her with a smug look.

"Argan oil. I suppose that's what you use for your hair. Then there's a hint of a classic perfume. You don't use much but it's always there, and if I'm not mistaken, it's Chanel. It's nice." She put down the bags and leaned in again, taking another deep breath against Nathalie's skin. "There's also a hint of cucumber. Is it your moisturizer, maybe?" Nathalie's reaction was nothing short of fascinating. Her cheeks were rosy and her lips parted, staring up at Lena with a look she couldn't quite comprehend. "And right now," Lena continued, lowering her voice, "I'm also smelling a hint of panic, although I'm not sure why." She took a step back, giving Nathalie space, and picked up the bags with a nonchalant smile.

Nathalie shook her head as if waking up from a daydream. *She's on to me.*

"I have to disagree with the panic," she said, trying to

calm her nerves. "But you're right about the rest. Well done, Sherlock." She put her shaking hands behind her back and tried to steady her breathing as she followed Lena out of the shop.

"Can I buy you lunch?" Nathalie asked when they headed back to the main square with shopping bags full of food and trinkets. "Or are you busy? I can make my own way home if you need to go…"

"No, absolutely not. I would love to have lunch with you." Lena beckoned Nathalie to follow her to one of the cafés and secured a table underneath a large, white parasol. "But I won't allow you to pay. Your welcome lunch is on me." She pulled out a chair for Nathalie. "Madame" She gesture to the chair.

Nathalie giggled. "Thanks."

A server walked over to their table with a bottle of cold water, two glasses and a basket with bread and butter. A smile broke out on his face when he saw Lena, and he yelled something in French, making wild hand gestures, before kissing her on each cheek.

"Alain, this is my friend Nathalie," Lena said. "Nathalie, meet Alain. He's the owner of this place." Nathalie stood up to shake his hand but was surprised to get two kisses instead.

She laughed. "I still need to get used to the intimate greeting."

"Ah oui, ma belle," he said. "We love kissing in France." He handed them both a menu, exchanged some words with Lena and winked before heading back inside.

"He thinks you're beautiful," Lena said. "I told him I agree."

Nathalie blushed again and looked down at her menu, avoiding eye contact.

"You people are pretty straightforward, aren't you?"

Lena shrugged. "If it makes you feel uncomfortable, you'd better get used to it. We are much more open than most Americans, if you don't mind me saying. We're more intimate and honest too. It's important that you learn how to take a compliment, especially from sincere people like Alain and me." She cocked her head. "I say *we* because I feel French too. There's not much American left in me apart from a slight accent, I'm afraid."

"Okay." Nathalie chuckled. "Thank you for the compliment." She finally looked up at Lena, summoning the courage to speak her mind. "Then I'm sure you won't mind me saying that I think you're gorgeous too." Her eyes widened at her own words that had just slipped out of her mouth.

Lena laughed at her flushed state. "Thank you," she said, studying the menu with a smirk on her face. "Now, would you like me to order for you?"

"How long have you lived here?" Nathalie asked a little later, sipping on her wine.

"Eighteen years." Lena said. She frowned, calculating in her head. "Or it might be nineteen by now, I'm starting to lose track of time. I moved here from New York when I was seventeen, and I never looked back."

"That's very young to move so far away," Nathalie remarked. "Do you mind if I ask why?"

Lena refilled their glasses. "It's no secret. I moved to France to live with my grandfather after I had a big fight with my parents. He lived here, in Valbonne."

Nathalie nodded. "Is he still around?"

"No. He died a couple of years ago." Lena avoided Nathalie's eyes, but managed to paint on a smile. "So, how are you finding it so far?" she asked, changing the topic back to Nathalie. "It must be strange making a shift from being in a high-powered job in Chicago to doing absolutely nothing in a sleepy village in France."

"Yeah." Nathalie paused, pondering over the question. "It's definitely a change. I'm still feeling stressed about the fact that I don't know what to do with my life, but I've got to be realistic; the answer is not going to magically appear before me. I'm lucky that I don't have to worry about my finances right now. It buys me time to figure things out, although the future is always in the back of my mind, and I'm not quite sure how to shake that off." She scooped some salad on to her plate. "This was a good call, though. France, I mean." She took a bite of her steak and closed her eyes in delight. "It's like I've been neglecting my senses and I'm slowly getting them back. This morning, for example. I really appreciated my coffee. Normally, I would have made a double espresso at seven in the morning, knocked it back, and rushed to the office through heavy traffic, only to arrive for a three-hour meeting in a soulless office." She smiled. "Today, I got out of bed, put on my robe and made myself a coffee. Nothing fancy like the machine I have at home in Chicago. Just a plain old simple filter coffee." She waved a hand. "Sorry, no offense to your coffee maker. Anyway, I took it outside, along with my book, where I could smell the roses on the terrace and the rain in the air from the night before. I really savored my coffee, smelt it as I drank. I don't really know how to explain this, but it's almost like I've been switched off for years and my body is slowly coming back to life. I'm starting to see what's around me, I hear sounds I didn't hear before, I smell things I've never smelt before…" She looked around the square and nodded towards the other tables with diners. "Look at them. They're not focused on their smartphones. They're not rushing the server to bring their lunch over, or eating it as fast as they can because they have meetings to attend. They're talking, laughing, sharing and drinking, and it's a weekday!"

"I like that you see that." Lena leaned in over the table. "Some people are so busy climbing the career ladder that they forget how to live. I'm glad you're starting to relax." She raised her glass. "To your time here in France, Nat. You're here for a reason, so make sure it counts. And never, ever forget how you feel right now, in this very moment, because you look pretty happy."

"Thank you." Nathalie clinked her glass against Lena's. Lena was right. She was happy.

11

It was pitch-dark as Nathalie bent over her steering wheel, struggling to see the bends as she drove back home after a long day of sightseeing. Early afternoon, she'd driven to Grasse, where she'd walked for hours, visiting the perfume museums and the historic city center. After that, she'd treated herself to a three-course meal in a family-run fine dining restaurant. Feeling accomplished, and strangely independent, she was on her way home with a boot full of souvenirs, all windows wide open and the radio on. The only thing missing was light. The lack of street lights in the valley hadn't bothered her before but now, she was wondering if she'd ever be able to find her way home. She drove slowly, checking each bend and corner. She saw the gate to the Mayor's house and thanked her lucky stars for the sign that she was still on the right road. *Almost home now.* She stepped on the gas, suddenly more confident, when the car drove over something, bounced up, and came to an abrupt halt. She instinctively checked her nose and her forehead, both having been smashed into the steering wheel on impact. She wasn't bleeding, and apart from a throbbing pain between her eyebrows, she was pretty sure she was alright. *What was that?* Her heart raced as she tried to catch her breath, opening the door with a trembling hand. *I didn't hit anyone, did I?* It took a while for her eyes to adjust to the dark, but she realized what had happened soon enough as she stepped into a flower bed. Nathalie sighed in relief. She was on a roundabout. The back wheels of the car were off the ground, still spinning. Using her phone as a torch, she stepped down and walked around the car to inspect the damage. The car seemed fine, apart from the fact that the back had been lifted off the ground. She took a stance behind it and tried to push it up onto the roundabout, so she'd be able to drive it off, but it was too heavy. Out of breath, she sat down on the stoop, hoping for another car to pass. Ten minutes passed, then twenty. *Damn it. If only I could get some help...* When she tried to call the roadside assistance number on her keychain, she got an answering machine with menu options in French. After listening to it five times, and trying every available option without success, she gave up. Looking down at her phone, she sighed as she dialed Lena's number again.

"What happened here?" Lena laughed as she stepped out of her car.

Nathalie shrugged. "Honestly, I have no idea how I got up there. It was so dark and I..." She shook her head. "I'm sorry for calling you this late. I feel incredibly stupid and I hate it that you have to see me this way. I've never needed help, not from anyone. And now I'm calling you for the second time this week."

"Hey, it's not a crime to need help from time to time." Lena held up a hand. "We all do, sometimes."

Nathalie grimaced. "I know. But I feel incompetent and silly, and it's so frustrating."

"You're not incompetent." Lena closed the distance between them and took her into a tight embrace. "Come here."

Nathalie sank into Lena's arms and closed her eyes. It was an instant comfort that seemed to mellow her mood within seconds. It wasn't like her, allowing someone she barely knew to take care of her. In fact, apart from her parents, people rarely attempted to hug her. It felt so good.

"It's only a roundabout," Lena continued. "And you're okay. That's the most important thing, right?"

Nathalie bit her lip, looking at the crushed flowerbed. "Was that one of your creations?" she asked, assessing the damage.

"Yep." Lena chuckled. "But they'll grow back. They always do." She let go of Nathalie and bent down to look underneath the car, before inspecting the back. "Shall we try and lift it together?"

Nathalie walked around to the back of the car and rolled her shoulders, still sore from her previous attempts.

"Sure. Let's do this." She watched Lena roll up the sleeves of her shirt and marveled over her muscular biceps. It wasn't the first time she'd noticed Lena's arms.

"Okay, I'm going to count to three," Lena said. "Give it all you've got."

After three attempts, they managed to lift the back of the car onto the roundabout. Nathalie jumped in to put on the hand-break so that it wouldn't roll back.

"Yay, we did it!" she yelled as she stepped back out.

Lena laughed. "You're cute when you get excited."

"Cute?" Nathalie's face pulled into a smile. She was still flushed from the hug and on a bit if a high, despite her earlier frustration. "I guess there's a first time for everything. No one's ever called me cute before."

"Oh yeah? What *do* they call you then? Back home?"

Nathalie thought about the question, leaning against the car door. "I'm not sure. I don't socialize much because I'm always working." She shook her head. "I mean I *was* always working. But I'm sure they had a lot to say about me behind my back, at least in the office."

Lena laughed. "I find it hard to imagine you as the ladyboss. What were you like at work anyway?" She cocked her head, arching an eyebrow.

"I don't know." Nathalie shrugged. "Work is work. I didn't beat around the bush, but I also didn't raise my voice at people and was never rude so overall, I think I was okay. I wasn't friends with my staff either, never. I liked my people to be efficient, I guess. And to think for themselves, come up with solutions instead of problems. That's not too much to ask, is it?"

"Nope. That sounds perfectly reasonable." Lena sat down on the edge of the roundabout and Nathalie took a seat next to her, exhausted from the lifting.

"Thank you again for coming to the rescue."

Lena put an arm around her shoulder and pulled her in. "No problem, it's my pleasure."

Although it was only a friendly gesture, Nathalie seemed to lose all train of thought as she rested her head on Lena's shoulder. Her scent, her warmth... *What the hell is going on with me?* Her heart was beating in her throat and she couldn't seem to decide whether to stand back up or not. In need of something to do, she searched for the pack of cigarettes in her purse and lit one. Lena watched Nathalie blow out the smoke before she took her wrist and directed her hand towards her own lips, taking a long drag. The silence wasn't uncomfortable, but it felt loaded, somehow.

"I didn't know you smoked," Nathalie finally said. "Would you like one?" She took another drag, for some reason eager to put her lips where Lena's had been.

"No thanks. I don't really smoke anymore, it's just an old habit." She turned to Nathalie and shot her a grin. "Does it sound crazy if I say that I enjoy sitting here with you? On a roundabout, late at night?" She looked out over the dark, quiet road in front of them.

"No." Nathalie shook her head. "As a matter of fact, I like it too. We should do it more often." She laughed, leaning into Lena. The physical contact was addictive now, and she felt herself craving more, although more of what, she wasn't sure.

Lena reluctantly stood up when she heard a car approaching. "I'd better move my car out of the way before someone gets hurt. Follow me, it's much easier when someone's driving up front. Are you going to be okay getting down?"

Nathalie nodded. "I'll be fine."

Lena winked as she opened the door to her Porsche. "I'll see you at home then. Nightcap?"

"Yeah." Nathalie smiled. "A nightcap would be nice."

12

Lena peeked through the drapes of her bedroom window. Gumbo was standing on his tiptoes, barely reaching the windowsill. She gave him a push, allowing him to sit on top and lean against the cool glass. They watched Nathalie cross the pool area and drop her bag onto one of the sun loungers. She dipped a toe into the water, testing the temperature before she took off her robe, tossed it behind her and dove into the pool in one fluid motion.

"You like her too, don't you, Gumbo?" Lena laughed at Gumbo, who was staring in Nathalie's direction, following her every move. She propped her chin on his head and watched Nathalie reappear, Gumbo's wagging tale tickling her chest. "Yeah. I know. She's pretty, isn't she? But guess what? Mummy can't have her because she's a paying guest. And besides, I don't think she's interested in me." She sighed dramatically. "Nathalie doesn't like the ladies, I'm afraid. She might be a bit curious though, I'm not sure yet. She does seem to get a bit flustered by my harmless flirting." She placed a kiss on top of Gumbo's head. "Anyway, it doesn't matter, she's a no-go." Gumbo turned his head and gave her a clueless look. Lena chuckled at their one-sided conversation. "What do you think? Should we go and say hello?" Gumbo jumped back onto the bed and barked in excitement. "Of course, you want to go. You think everything's a great idea, don't you?" She laughed at his hysterical enthusiasm and went into the kitchen to make herself a strong cup of coffee.

"Good morning." Nathalie's face broke into a huge smile when Lena and Gumbo stepped out onto the terrace.

"Hey. How are you today?" Lena sat down with her newspaper, trying to act casual when Nathalie stepped out of the pool in her white bikini. She was starting to get a tan now, Lena could tell by the white line below her bikini bottoms as Nathalie bent over to greet Gumbo. She squeezed the water out of her long hair before she dropped down on her bed, facing Lena.

"I've been wide awake since seven." Nathalie dried her hands and held up her book.

"I've almost finished this one already. I think my body is worried about missing out on sunshine. It's like I'm drawn outside as soon as I open my eyes." She pointed to her face. "And I'm finally starting to get a tan, even a couple of freckles. I haven't had a tan in years."

Drawn by the word 'freckles', Lena stood up from her bench and walked over to Nathalie. She kneeled down, studying her cheeks.

"Yeah, you are getting freckles. It's really cute." She grinned, unable to take her eyes off Nathalie's face. "I've always been a sucker for freckles." *Stop it, Lena. Don't push it.*

She shook her head, as if cursing herself. "I'm sorry, I didn't mean to..."

"No, it's fine." Nathalie felt herself go warm at the compliment.

"Do you have any plans for today?" Lena asked, in an attempt to casually steer the conversation in a different direction. She returned to her coffee and her newspaper, propping her feet up on the table as she sat back down.

"Yeah, I do." Nathalie turned on her side and steadied herself on her elbow. "I'm going to attend a watercolor course in town. I think it's in that little gallery just off the square."

"Gallery Valbonne?" Lena asked. "Marie-Louise's gallery?" Her expression changed as she mentioned her name.

"Yes, that's the one," Nathalie said. "Why? You seem worried."

Lena shook her head. "No, not at all. I think it's a great idea." *As long as you don't talk about me.* She managed a smile. "Marie-Louise is a lovely lady. She used to teach at the art college in Nice, but she's retired now. She's quite eccentric, it should be fun."

"Okay, great." Nathalie searched for the sunscreen in her bag and put some on her face. "I have absolutely no artistic talent in me, but it seemed like such an appropriate thing to do whilst I'm here in France, so I signed up for it before I came. Thought it might be fun to try something new."

"Absolutely. And who knows? You might discover you have a hidden talent." Lena nodded in the direction of the village. "Do you want me to drive you there? Or do you want to borrow the Porsche? It'll be difficult to park yours near the gallery."

Nathalie shook her head. She didn't want to take another favor from Lena. Not after the roundabout incident.

"Thank you for the offer, but I think I'll walk. It's not like I'm in a hurry, and it's not that far, is it?"

"Are you crazy?" Lena laughed. "It's not far, but with the hills, it might take you close to an hour. And in this heat?"

"I don't mind the heat." Nathalie shrugged. "I need sun and I need exercise, and this way, I'll get both."

"Alright, suit yourself." Lena drank the last of her coffee and took her cup into the annex, returning with a dog lead. "Gumbo and I are going for a walk. You've got my number. Call me if you change your mind." She waved without looking back, leaving Nathalie to stare at her behind. Nathalie only turned back to her book when Lena was out of sight. She'd been unable to keep her eyes off her lately. Lena was stunning in every way. Nathalie took a deep breath, trying to focus on anything but her unconventional fantasies that, as of today, apparently involved Lena minus clothes. *Jesus woman, get a grip.*

13

"Alors. Thank you for coming everyone. Please take an easel and a palette, fill your jar with water and follow me into the garden." Marie-Louise opened the door to the storage room, waited for her students to gather their utensils and led the way outside through her gallery and her kitchen. The voluptuous older lady, with a strong French accent, strutted around in a floral dress and a bright yellow kimono-style jacket with tassels hanging down from the sleeves and the hem. Her white hair was fastened into a big knot, topped off with two taxidermy parrots that made her head look like a bird's nest. She walked barefoot, not in the least bothered by the pebbles on the path that led them to a charming courtyard where Nathalie and her four fellow students set up in a semi-circle around her. There was a pond with waterlilies and goldfish, pink flowers in the beds along the white walls surrounding the patio, and a large apple tree where parakeets were sitting on different levels of the branches, chattering away. Nathalie tried to guess their teacher's age, but it was hard to tell with all the work that had gone into preserving her face. She looked at the other people on her course and felt nervous as she struggled to secure the easel at the right height. Everyone seemed to know what they were doing, apart from her. After the introductions, she'd learned that their group consisted of Brenda and Samantha, a mother and daughter from the UK, who were vacationing together, an American man in his late fifties called Graham, and a young French girl named Cherie, who didn't speak much English.

"Here, let me help you with that," Brenda, the mother in their group said. She loosened the screw on the back of the easel, lifted the board and secured it at Nathalie's eye-height.

"Thank you." Nathalie smiled at her. "I've never done any of this before, I'm sure you can tell."

"Don't worry." Brenda went back to her own easel. "Samantha and I aren't exactly professionals either. We've all got to start somewhere, right?" She looked around the courtyard. "It's beautiful here, isn't it? So idyllic... and the light is perfect for painting." She pointed out the shadows on the white walls.

"Well spotted, Brenda," Marie-Louise said. "We're going to start here because we have the perfect mix of light, water, shadow and color. They're all the basics you need to understand before we head out to the coast or into the fields." She looked around the group and smiled. "There is no need to be nervous. Art is a beautiful thing. It's meant to bring joy and expression to your life, so please stop worrying if you are." She opened a bottle of red wine next to her easel and poured six glasses, which she handed out to everyone, including the young girl. "Let's have a drink to loosen up during our first class. Don't beat yourself up if you don't like your work, all you need to do is try, and try, and then try some more. You'll get better eventually. There's no judging here." She raised her glass and took a sip. "Watercolor is not about perfection. It's about expression, and expression leads to inner calm. You might not understand what I mean right now, but hopefully, you will soon. Now, have any of you ever done this before?" She nodded towards the girl. "Except for Cherie here. She's been taking my course since she was nine, so please don't compare yourself to her." Brenda and her daughter Samantha raised their hands.

"We've done a couple of workshops," Samantha said. "We love painting, don't we, Mum?"

Her mother nodded. "It's the only thing we can do together without arguing."

"Excellent," Marie-Louise said, laughing. "If you two don't mind, I'm going to start with the basics." She picked up a pencil and held it up to the group.

Two hours later, Nathalie stepped back from the easel to inspect her work, chuckling at her lack of talent. She had enjoyed it though and felt excited at the prospect of coming back twice a week. The relaxed atmosphere and the friendly people in the group made her feel like she was part of something, and she hadn't felt like that in a while. At work, she had always been the leader and was never part of after work activities, like the weekly happy hour, teambuilding events, or birthdays. She wasn't a member of a gym, or a book club either. Even in her marriage, the sense of partnership had faded when she and Jack stopped spending quality time together.

"Great use of color," Marie-Louise said, pointing to the purple shadows on the pink flowers Nathalie had attempted to paint.

"Thanks," Nathalie said, trying to imagine anything

good about the work she'd been slaving over. She looked at Cherie's painting and decided it was a masterpiece; the girl clearly had talent.

"Brenda, that's a lovely representation of water ripples." Marie-Louise pointed at a section on Brenda's paper.

"Really?" Brenda smiled proudly, then looked over to her daughter, who was struggling to finish the same section.

Marie-Louise tapped Samantha on her shoulder. "Don't rush, Samantha. That's a really good start. You don't need to have it finished today. Take a picture of the pond on your phone and finish it when you're home. There's never any rush."

"Sure." Samantha sighed. "I've never painted water before. It's really hard."

"Everything comes with practice," Marie-Louise assured her. She walked over to Graham, the only man in their group, and smiled. "I think you might have some natural talent in you, Mr. White."

Graham stepped back and shook his head, stroking his long, grey beard. "I don't see where you're coming from, but I'll take your word for it, Ma'am."

Nathalie laughed at his reply. "Marie-Louise is right," she said. "I can't believe this is your first time. It looks right, somehow, although I wouldn't be able to tell you why."

Marie Louise nodded. "Abstract expressionism," she said, "is never a true representation, but rather a bigger picture, if you will. It steers you away from pointless details and allows you to express how the light was when you painted it, how you felt that day."

Nathalie studied her painting again, with more appreciation this time, and decided she liked her new hobby.

14

"Santé." Lena raised her glass and clinked it with her friend's. Alain downed his beer in one go and put his glass back on the table with a smack, gesturing to his server for another.

"Heavy day?" She asked.

Alain chuckled. "Heavy day... not so much." He gave her a smirk. "Heavy night, more like it."

"Ah." Lena shot him a skeptical look. "So who was it this time? The new waitress from the bar next door?" She nodded in the direction of the woman who had been keeping a close eye on them, ever since Alain had finished for the day. He was a good-looking man, but Lena also knew that anyone aware of his reputation would steer far away from him.

"No." Alain looked up and winked at the woman. "Although she is pretty hot. I might ask her out some time." He smiled when she gave him a playful wink back and followed her with his eyes until she disappeared back inside. "No, last night's conquest was a tourist. She's staying in the guesthouse in town. We met in the Orangerie, had some drinks back at my house and then..."

Lena rolled her eyes. "Jesus, spare me the details. No one is safe from you."

Alain shrugged. "Hey, we had a great time. Those English girls love themselves a French charmer." He chuckled. "How's your American lady by the way? She's cute."

"She's not *my* American lady," Lena said, giving him a warning look. "And you're not going anywhere near her either, understood?"

Alain took his second beer from the server and smiled. "Wouldn't that be up to her, Lena?"

Lena shook her head. "No, it's not up to her. Not if I can help it. I'll make sure she's never within talking distance of you ever again if you have your mind set on her, so you can forget about asking her out. She's better than..."

"Better than me?" Alain finished her sentence.

Lena thought about it. "Yeah. She is better than you. Too good to be in your bed, anyway."

"Oh la la..." Alain nudged her. "I think someone's got a little crush..."

"Shut up." Lena laughed. "I do *not* have a crush on her. I've only known her for a week, and besides, she's not my type." She sighed as she cooled her forehead with her beer glass. A smile played around her mouth. "Okay, maybe I like her a little."

Alain sat back and shielded his eyes from the setting sun, that was leaving a yellow glow on the old buildings surrounding the square.

"Aha! I knew it." He gave her a mocking look. "I knew it, I knew it, I knew it. As soon as I saw you pulling out that chair for her, I said to myself: 'Alain, if you want to ask her tenant out, you'd better be fast, because Lena is working her magic again.'"

"I was just being nice," Lena said in defense.

"Yeah, well there's a reason they call you *Magic Lena*." Alain cocked his head. "You know that's what they call you, right? *Magic Lena*?"

Lena shook her head. "No. Who calls me that?"

"Are you serious, Lena? You don't know? Your own staff calls you that!" Alain couldn't stop laughing at her ignorance. "They told me that every time you do the gardening for some hot housewife, then boom! All of a sudden, the wife decides she wants to divorce her husband. Just like that." He snapped his fingers. "Bernie told me it's happened twice now. First Christine Delevoire from across town, and now Farah, the glamorous lady who comes here for lunch after the market on Fridays. She finalized her divorce last month." Alain's eyes narrowed. "Is that why you don't do private yard work anymore?"

"Great." Lena sighed. "So, my own staff has a nickname for me now? And what kind of bullshit is that about the divorce? I didn't know anything about that."

"Is it true though?" Alain asked. "Did you get involved with them?"

"I suppose I might have had a certain connection with some of my clients," Lena said, staring into her glass. "But I had no idea about the divorces."

"Have you seen them since?" Alain raised an eyebrow.

"No." Lena held up her hand and gestured for another beer.

"So, you slept with them, messed with their heads, and then walked away, leaving poor old Bernie to pick up the job where you left it? Why the hell are you judging me for sleeping with tourists, Lena?" He laughed.

"I never messed with their heads," Lena said. "We had an agreement, it was nothing serious. Things just got a bit complicated when I found out they knew each other. I saw Farah and Christine having lunch together one day, so I decided to withdraw myself from the pool of private customers. You know, in case they started 'sharing secrets'. Thought it might hurt my reputation." She shrugged. "Look, I'm sorry Farah's marriage broke up, but it's not like she wasn't in it for the money in the first place. Why else would a beautiful thirty-something marry a sixty-year-old bald guy with a weak bladder?" She pointed an accusing finger towards Alain. "So don't you go telling me I broke up their marriages. I was just a distraction to them, maybe even an excuse to talk themselves out of it." She shrugged. "Anyway, I think I'm done with all that now. The whole affair thing is getting boring."

Alain almost choked on his beer. "Are you telling me you're ready to settle down?"

Lena laughed. "I wouldn't go that far, but I think I'm ready to date someone who's available and uncomplicated, yeah. It's been, what... three years since Selma left?" Lena tried to act casual, but in truth, she knew all too well that it had been two years and eleven months since the woman she thought she'd grow old with had left her for someone else. And ever since that day, she'd been trying to fill the void with meaningless encounters, telling herself that she was fine on her own, that she got what she needed without the drama.

"Do you still miss her?" Alain asked.

"Of course not." Lena snorted. "But I am angry with myself for wasting that much time on a relationship that was never going to work out in the first place." She shook her head and shot Alain a questioning look. "Hey, where's this seriousness coming from? Can't we just have a beer and talk nonsense?"

Alain shrugged. "Sure. Just trying to be a friend."

15

Nathalie got up from the terrace table and took her empty coffee cup into the kitchen, where she made herself another one. She was already halfway through her second book and had started to master the art of relaxation. It was a sunny day, and although it was only nine in the morning, the temperature was rising fast, leaving her sweating, even in the shade. She poured herself a generous amount of coffee from the filter machine and grabbed a bottle of cold water from the fridge, before heading to the pool.

"Hey there." Lena smiled at her from the annex terrace, where she was reading the morning papers. Gumbo came tearing up at Nathalie, greeting her with his typical enthusiasm.

"Morning." Nathalie waved at her before kneeling down to greet Gumbo. "You don't have to put the towels out for me, Lena. I can get them myself." She cocked her head, shielding her eyes from the sun. "I'm sure you've got better things to do than looking after me."

"Don't worry about it," Lena said. "How many times do I

have to tell you, it's my job. Just enjoy yourself." She held her gaze as Nathalie took off her robe and lowered herself into the pool, shivering when the cold water hit her chest. *She's so fucking beautiful.* Nathalie dipped under and swam over to the edge where she came up, facing Lena.

"I feel bad, though," she continued, rubbing the water out of her eyes. "I've noticed you don't use the pool while I'm here. Is that because you're not supposed to? Because I don't care if you do, I'd be happy to share."

"Come on, Nat. I'm the caretaker." Lena laughed. "I can't just go splashing around here, it's unprofessional. Have you ever seen resort staff jump in the pool when you were on vacation?"

Nathalie laughed. "I wouldn't know, to be honest. I can't remember the last time I went on vacation. But it would make me feel better if you did. It's not like the owners are going to turn up out of the blue, right?"

Lena looked down at her paper, avoiding Nathalie's eyes. "No. But that's not the point. I have a job to do here and besides that, I couldn't care less about the pool. I go to the beach with Gumbo every other day, and believe it or not, I actually prefer salt water to chlorine."

"Yeah, but still..." Nathalie stroked Gumbo, who was standing at the edge of the pool. "I don't see you as the caretaker. You feel more like a friend to me. I feel comfortable around you. Is it weird that I say that?"

Lena smiled and shook her head. "No, it's not weird. I like you too, and I like spending time with you."

"So, what's the problem then?" Nathalie knew she needed to stop going on about it. She didn't want to come across as annoying, but she was desperate to make a point.

"You really won't let it go, will you?" Lena stood up and rolled her eyes. She took off her t-shirt and her shorts, leaving her in a pair of white panties and a matching sports bra. "Alright, if it makes you happy…"

Nathalie stared at Lena wide-eyed from the pool as she walked towards the edge and dove in. *My God, that body…* Nathalie was unable to keep herself from following Lena with her eyes.

"Happy now?" Lena asked when she resurfaced, swimming towards Nathalie. Nathalie felt her insides flutter at the sight of her wet hair, and the water dripping down her face.

"Yeah. I'm happy now," she stuttered.

"Good. Because I aim to please." Lena propped her elbows on the poolside next to Nathalie and gave her a broad grin. "So, you don't remember the last time you were on vacation?"

Nathalie shook her head. "Honestly, no." She winced, digging through her memory. "The last time was in college, I think. I went to Cancun with some friends. After Jack and I got married and started the company, we couldn't afford to go on holiday. We were a start-up, desperately scraping together any funding we could get for our first production run. Later, when the company started doing well, we didn't have the time. So, I guess it's safe to say that it's been a while."

"That's sad." Lena cocked her head with a mocking smile. "And I mean super-sad. Poor little rich woman."

Nathalie laughed at Lena's sarcasm. "I know. Poor me. What about you? When was the last time you went away?"

"Six months ago," Lena scratched Gumbo behind his ear. "Gumbo and I went to visit friends in Spain. We drove there. It was fun, wasn't it, Gumbo?" Gumbo showed his appreciation for involving him in the conversation by jumping up and barking at nothing in particular.

Lena sighed and looked up at the sky. There wasn't a cloud in sight. "Spain is lovely but I'm always happy to come back. I love it here this time of year. It's not unbearably hot, but it's warm enough to sit outside in the evening. The garden's in full bloom, and you can smell the lavender and the roses in the air. Plus, the area isn't overrun with tourists yet. You chose a good time to come here."

"Yeah, I did." The hairs on Nathalie's arm rose when she accidentally brushed against Lena's hand. "What have your other tenants been like?" she asked, trying to shift her thoughts from Lena's half-naked body beside her.

"What do you mean?"

"I mean, were they nice? Were you close to them?"

Lena arched an eyebrow. "I'm not sure where you're going with this but no, I wasn't close to any of them and that was fine with me."

"Okay." Nathalie cast her a teasing smile. "Does that mean I'm your favorite tenant ever?" She wiggled her eyebrows.

Lena turned and swam towards her. The look on her face was mischievous, almost flirty, Nathalie thought. She loved the way Lena looked at her.

"Even if I told you that you were my favorite tenant," Lena said, "I've only had two other couples here before you, so there'd be no need to flatter yourself." They both laughed, and Lena swam closer to Nathalie until she could reach the floor. She leaned against the pool's edge next to her and crossed her arms as she noticed Nathalie's broad smile. There was something about Nathalie today that was different. She joked a lot more, and her playful demeanor seemed out of character for her. If Lena didn't know better, she'd almost think Nathalie was being a bit flirty too. She decided to push the boat out further, just to test her theory.

"They were both couples," she continued. "The first were married with a young kid, the other without. They did their thing, were out for most of the day, said good morning and goodnight and that was about it. They kept to themselves, didn't get wheel clamps, didn't get stranded on roundabouts, and they certainly weren't as intrusive as you." She winked. "They didn't ask me to join them in the pool in my underwear, that's for sure."

Nathalie giggled. "That's not fair. I never asked you to jump into the pool in your underwear. That was your idea."

"You didn't seem to mind though." Lena kept her eyes fixed on Nathalie, a small smile playing around her mouth.

Nathalie took a step towards her, holding her gaze too. *Is she flirting with me?* She held her breath, waiting for Lena to close the distance between them. Adrenaline shot through her while they faced each other in some kind of weird chemistry stand-off that turned Nathalie on like nothing else ever had. Without exchanging a single word, their looks said it all. *Oh my God, she is flirting with me.*

Lena was the first to break the spell. As if waking up from a daydream, she suddenly shook her head and waded back to the edge, where she pushed herself out of the pool. She seemed confused, or frustrated, Nathalie wasn't sure. But it was clear that it was no time to ask questions, so she pretended she hadn't noticed the sudden shift in Lena's mood.

"I'm sorry. I forgot I have an appointment in town." Lena grabbed a towel from one of the sunbeds and turned at the door. "Have a nice day, Nat."

NATHALIE GOT out of the pool after Lena had left and lowered herself onto a sunbed. Still shaking from their encounter, she folded her hands behind her head and looked up at the two lonely clouds above her. One of them had taken on the shape of a heart, expanding as it drifted over her. She was almost certain that Lena had been flirting with her and couldn't help but wonder if that was the reason she had left in a hurry. *Why am I so obsessed with her?* Sure, Lena was stunning, but Nathalie had never been attracted to a woman before. Still, she found herself waiting for Lena to come home whenever she left, and she was dying to know where Lena was going and who she'd be with each time she drove off in that flashy car. For days, Nathalie had felt like a confused teenager. Insecure one moment and bouncing off the walls another. She hardly recognized herself from the stern woman she had been, only weeks ago. She laughed and joked, was able to relax, enjoy the sun and the food without feeling guilty about doing nothing at all now. Why had she always been so serious? Somehow, between getting married at a young age and building a multinational together with her husband, she'd lost herself along the way. She'd lost the woman who loved to take the time to eat and drink, who loved to laugh and explore, and had become boring and predictable instead. She'd lost the curiosity she once had, and with that, her sexuality. *Maybe that's why Jack left me for his secretary.* It had been a long time since Nathalie felt attractive, but in the past week, she had looked at herself in the mirror with approval and confidence. Feelings that were long lost were coming back tenfold. She'd started to appreciate her body more, her face, and her smile. But she wasn't sure if that had something to do with the effect of being in France, or the fact that she had stopped thinking about work. Or maybe, just maybe, it was because of Lena's delightful presence.

16

Lena drove as fast as she could on the narrow mountain roads. Gumbo was in the seat next to her, his head peeking over the passenger door, catching the wind as they drove. She was angry with herself for getting close to Nathalie. For finally giving in to the desire she felt, each time she looked into those blue eyes. Women were everywhere, and she had no problem catching their attention, so why was she all over the only person she wasn't supposed to get close to? *My straight, newly divorced tenant of all people...* She took a left turn onto a private road, leading up to a modern mansion that overlooked the coast of Cannes.

"Yes?" a woman's voice said over the loudspeaker.

"It's me, Lena. Are you alone?" Lena looked up into the camera on top of the gate. There was no answer, but the gate buzzed and opened seconds later. The garden was still in good shape, Lena noticed, as she drove up towards the house. Apart from the conifer next to the kitchen. That one could do with some trimming to create more light on the patio. She parked her car next to a brand-new white Bentley and opened the passenger door first to let Gumbo out.

"Lena!" Beth, the lady of the house, came rushing towards her, dressed in a gold sequined bikini and a transparent white wrap with a long tail that was flowing behind her in the wind. She wore black shades that covered almost half of her face, and her chestnut hair hung loosely around her shoulders, framing her delicate face. She was carrying a large cocktail, and by the looks of her, Lena thought, it wasn't her first of the day. "I didn't expect you, Lena. You didn't tell me you were coming." Beth bent over to greet Gumbo. "Hey little man. Your friend is in the kitchen. Go and say hello to Rufus." They watched Gumbo sprint into the house, only to run back out seconds later with a Chihuahua chasing his tail.

"Sorry. Is it a bad time?" Lena asked. "I should have called first."

Beth shook her head. "No. Not at all. Bruce is away for work." She pursed her lips and frowned, trying to remember where her husband was holding up these days. "Shanghai, I think, but it could be Hong Kong. I'm not too sure." She took Lena's hand. "It doesn't matter where he is. What's important is that he's gone, and I haven't seen you in far too long. You never returned my calls. That man you keep sending over to trim the hedges... Bernie? It's not the same, Lena. I've missed you."

"Yeah. Sorry about that. I've been busy with other projects, so I've had to hand the private work over to Bernie," Lena lied. *At least Bernie isn't aware of my history with this one.*

"Well, you're here now, that's all that matters." Beth pressed her lips against Lena's, and Lena kissed her back, digging her nails into Beth's bottom as she drew her closer.

To her surprise, she didn't feel aroused. There was no spark, no anticipation and no overwhelming need to rip her clothes off and consume her body. She kissed Beth harder, trying to feel something but there was nothing there. *Fuck.*

Lena took a step back and shook her head. "I'm sorry Beth, I don't think I can do this."

Beth shot her a confused look. "What, Lena? What's the problem?"

"I..." Lena paused. "I don't know." She whistled for Gumbo and opened the door to her car. "I shouldn't have come here."

17

"Hey." Nathalie opened the kitchen door to find Lena with a big bunch of roses. "Here, these are for you." She handed them to Nathalie.

"For me?" Nathalie smiled in surprise.

"I always make sure there are fresh flowers," Lena said, "but since you won't let me change the bedsheets or send someone in to clean the house for you, I didn't have a reason to let myself in."

Nathalie opened the door wider and stepped back so Lena could enter. "Thank you. But you didn't need to do that. And you know I don't mind it if you let yourself in, it's just that I happen to like cleaning and doing the laundry. I've always had a housekeeper, but there's no excuse now." She held up the book in her hand. "All I do is read, paint, swim and sleep. I've almost finished this one and it's the last one in my bag."

"You're really getting into reading, aren't you?" Lena tried not to stare at Nathalie. She was wearing her robe, and the faint contour of her nipples underneath indicated that she wasn't wearing any underwear.

"I am." Nathalie sighed. "I could read on my laptop I suppose, as I don't have an iPad, but I'm used to the paperbacks now, and I like them. I went into town today, but I didn't realize it would be so hard to find English books around here."

Lena took the book and studied it. "So, you like crime stories?" Nathalie shrugged. "I don't really know what I like, I've never taken the time to read before. All I know is that I've enjoyed every book I've read so far, and they were just random picks from the airport, so I guess that means I like reading in general."

"It's never too late to discover new passions," Lena joked. "You could try the international bookstore in Nice. They're pretty good. Or you could borrow some of mine? I'm not sure they'll be to your taste, they might be a bit..." she paused. "Different?"

Nathalie shook her head. "Oh please, I don't care, I'd love to borrow a book, at least until I've bought some more. I'm panicking already, just at the thought of having nothing to read in bed tonight." She bit her lip, leaning against the kitchen counter. "Would you mind if I came over to take a look at your books?"

Lena laughed. "Jesus woman, you sure seem desperate for reading material." She turned back towards the door. "Give me a minute, will you? My place is too messy to let anyone in right now. I'll bring a couple over for you." Nathalie folded her hands in front of her chest in a grateful gesture.

"Thank you so much, Lena. I promise I won't drop them in the pool." She pointed to one of her books that was drying on the radiator.

Lena waved a dismissive hand as she headed towards the annex. "Don't worry, I'm not precious about them."

A LITTLE LATER, Lena was back with a pile of books that she dropped onto the kitchen table. She sat down and nodded when Nathalie held up a bottle of wine and two glasses.

"Thank you. I could do with a glass. It's been a long day." She pushed the books into Nathalie's direction. "These were the only ones I could find, stowed away in a box under my bed. I tend to give them away or lose them after I've read them." Nathalie poured two glasses of red wine and put a chopping board with fresh rosemary bread and a bowl of olive oil in between them. She picked the books up one by one, studying the front and the back.

"Sorry," Lena said, referring to the third book that Nathalie picked up. "That one wasn't supposed to be part of the selection." She laughed. "I must have forgotten I had it, I just grabbed whatever I could find." She studied Nathalie's face as she read the blurb. Nathalie's cheeks went rosy when she realized it was a lesbian romance novel.

"Oh," she said, laughing. "I didn't see this one coming."

Lena took it from her. "Forget about that one. It's not for you."

Nathalie stood up and snatched the book back from Lena's hands. "No, I want to read it. Why not?" She put it back on top of the others. "I'll read them all, if you don't mind. Nothing wrong with broadening my horizons a bit."

"Whatever rocks your socks, Nat." Lena popped a piece of bread into her mouth, amused at Nathalie's unease.

Nathalie broke off a piece too and dipped it into the olive oil. "Just curious," she said with a mouthful, pointing at the book in question. "Is that your... thing?"

Lena grinned. "My thing?" She picked up the book and

gave Nathalie a teasing smile. "You mean this?" There was a pause. "Yeah, I guess you could say that's my *thing*." She articulated that last word, mocking Nathalie's nervousness about the subject.

Nathalie sighed and rolled her eyes. "Stop making fun of me, Lena. You know very well that I was asking you if you were..." She paused and laughed. "Into women." She nodded, relieved that the question was out of the way. "Are you into women? Not that it's any of my business," she hastily added. "I'm just curious, that's all." Lena smiled, and Nathalie felt herself turn crimson this time.

"Yes, I'm into women," Lena said. "And I'm surprised you didn't know. Apparently, most women know within a matter of seconds."

"Right." Nathalie giggled. "I guess I'm not most women then. Although I did wonder... There's something about your energy..." She shook her head. "Never mind."

Lena sank back in her chair and cocked her head. "No, you've said it now, so I want to know. What about my energy?" She arched an eyebrow.

"Nothing." Nathalie grimaced. "I'm saying all the wrong things tonight. Jesus, it's like I've got verbal diarrhea. It just keeps coming out." She sighed. "I used to be so diplomatic at work, but it's become clear to me now that I haven't had much practice in casual conversation." She laughed. "Okay, let me just approach this like I would in a board meeting, otherwise I'll get all giddy." She buried her head in her hands, avoiding Lena's gaze as she spoke in a business-like manner, cringing at her tone of voice. "I got this strange energy from you that I've never felt with anyone before. Maybe you were being flirty, or maybe I got it all wrong. If I did, I apologize for making assumptions." She took a deep breath, lowered her hands into her lap and straightened her back, facing Lena.

"You weren't wrong." Lena lowered her voice and shot her a mischievous grin. "I might have flirted with you, but it won't happen again. It's unprofessional and besides, you're very much straight so it's pointless, right?"

Nathalie stared at her for a moment, processing her words. "No, it's fine. I feel flattered and I don't mind, but I'm not... I mean..." She looked up to the ceiling for help, but there were no clues carved onto the wooden beams. "Are you seeing someone?" *That's better, Nat. Change the subject. Well done.*

Lena shook her head. "No, not since last time you asked."

Nathalie nodded. "Of course. We had this conversation already." She poured them both another glass of wine, trying to get a grip on her thoughts. "Is it hard for you to meet women around here? I mean, it seems pretty remote, and most people who live here are either families, or seasonal visitors, right? I can't imagine there being much of a scene around here?"

"No, it's not hard, believe me," Lena laughed. "You don't need a scene to meet women. But finding someone who matters is always hard, I guess. Not that I'm looking." She took a long drink from her wine. "I was in a long-term relationship. Selma, my ex and I, were together for ten years before we split up a couple of years ago. She's French, but she moved to New York for a job. I had no intention of going back there and she had made up her mind before we'd even discussed the subject, so that was that. We tried the long-distance thing for a while but, needless to say, it didn't end well."

"I'm sorry," Nathalie said.

"It's okay," Lena cast her a sad smile. "Maybe I was inflexible. Maybe I should have gone with her, but something inside me told me that it wasn't going to last anyway. And I was right. Three months later she called me to tell me she'd met someone else, someone more suited, to use her exact words. But I don't regret staying here. I love France. This is my home now, and I have no intention of leaving. Not ever, and not for anyone."

"I can understand why you love it so much," Nathalie said. "I've only been here for two weeks, and I feel sick at the thought of going home."

Lena nodded. "I'm guessing that's not because you don't like Chicago, though. Or because you love France so much. I think it's because you'll be going back to your old life after this, and you've got no idea what to do with it." She raised her glass. "But hey, as I said, that's why you're here. To figure out what you want to do. And if you don't, that's fine too. At least you had some fun along the way."

"I suppose you're right," Nathalie said. "I'm not passionate about Chicago though. I studied there, met Jack, got married and stuck around. But it doesn't feel like home, it never has." She paused. "I don't think I've ever lived somewhere where I felt like I belonged. My parents are from a small town in Louisiana, and although I lived there until I was seventeen, now I feel like a stranger each time I visit them."

Lena was unable to hide her surprise. "You? A Southern belle? Wow, I like that. I usually spot them from a mile away, but with you, I would have never guessed. You don't even have a twang."

Nathalie laughed. "Let's just say I left for University and

found out pretty soon that people don't take you seriously when you have a Southern accent."

"That's rubbish," Lena said. "There's nothing cuter than a Southern accent."

"Yeah well, try it in a debate with twenty cocky students. Anyway, I have no plans on moving back to the South either, but I might go and see my parents for a couple of weeks. I feel like I've been neglecting them lately." Nathalie took a sip of her wine, finally relaxing. "So, what about your parents? Are they still in New York?"

Lena shook her head. "To be honest, I have no idea. I haven't seen or spoken to them since we had the fight before I moved here."

"What were you fighting about?" Nathalie decided it was okay to ask questions. Lena had been curious about her, and now it was her turn. There was a pause.

"The day I turned seventeen, I'd finally worked up the courage to tell them I was gay," Lena finally said. "I'd been brooding over it for months, trying to figure out the best way to break it to them gently, because I knew it was going to upset them. They're very religious, my parents, and although my mother never went to church until she met my father, she turned out to be even more devout than him. Anyway, after a lot of shouting and crying, it was her idea to send me to one of those Christian summer camps where they try to brainwash your sexuality out of you. I'd heard about these places and I had no intention of going. Besides, I didn't believe there was anything wrong with me, so I called my grandfather and he bought me a ticket to France. I was angry and hurt and to me, it was the best way of getting back at them. My grandfather from my mother's side was a sinner in their eyes too, you see. They'd broken off all contact with him after my mother walked in on him and his 'special friend' François in the bedroom in a rather compromising position." Lena laughed. "She decided to let herself in, even though she only had the key to his place for emergencies. Until this day, we still don't know what she was doing there. My grandfather was hurt by her reaction, and when she hadn't come round after a year, he decided there was nothing left to keep him in New York. That's when he moved to France to spend the rest of his life with François, who lived in a villa not far from here. We'd always been close, my grandfather and I, and I knew I could count on his help when I called him."

"You were lucky to have him," Nathalie said. "Did you miss your parents?"

Lena shrugged. "Sometimes. I wondered how they were, if they missed me, or thought of me. But they never called, even though they knew where I was. It didn't really upset me though. Coming here was such a breath of fresh air that I was desperate to leave my past behind and move forward. My grandfather sent me to a local French class and I did yard work for his neighbors to make some money. I realized I loved landscaping and got better at it. A year later, I started my own company and used my earnings to pay my way through a part-time landscape architecture design course."

"Is that when you met Selma?" Nathalie asked.

"Yeah. I met Selma when I was doing her parents' garden. She was studying finance in Nice at the time. She was out and proud and I'd never had a serious girlfriend, so it was a big deal for me. When she graduated, we got a place together and she managed to work her way up from an accountant to head of finance at a big firm in Monaco. Selma was always ambitious, and I admired her for that. I just never thought she would put her career before me."

"I'm so sorry. That must have been hard for you," Nathalie said.

Lena smiled and stood up, finishing her drink. "It was, but I'm over it. Anyway, I should get going. I've got a meeting to prepare for tomorrow." She winked as she turned by the door. "Enjoy the book."

18

"Busted."

Nathalie lowered her novel, meeting Lena's amused smirk that was aimed right at her.

She was standing over her by the sun lounger, hands on her hips. "How do you like the book?" she asked.

Nathalie chuckled, feeling caught in the act. She hadn't been able to stop reading since she'd started Lena's lesbian romance novel, and she was secretly loving every single page.

"Busted indeed, I didn't hear you coming." She took off her shades and sat straight up, facing Lena. "I have to admit, it's pretty good."

"Right?" Lena laughed. "And what exactly do you like about it?" She looked at Nathalie, who has now hiding her grin behind the cover.

"I don't know, it's romantic. I'm hoping for a happy ending."

"And the sex scenes?" Lena sat down beside her, checking what chapter she was on.

Nathalie blushed. She was already three quarters

through the book and had read a certain scene over and over again. She grinned. "They're kind of hot. And I mean, really hot."

"So, you like that, huh?" Lena laughed. "Is it safe to say you might have a new found passion for lesbian fiction?"

Nathalie shook her head. "I don't know... maybe? I can't seem to stop reading it, so I can see why you like it."

"Why I like it?" Lena looked at her with a mixture of surprise and curiosity. "What I'm intrigued by, is why you like it. Because last time I checked, you were straight, Nat."

Nathalie blinked against the sunlight, hardly able to hide her embarrassment.

"True," she said. "I don't know. Maybe I'm somewhere on the spectrum? Isn't that what they say? That most women are a little bit bi-curious?"

"That is what they say." Lena leaned back and put her feet up. "Is that a recent thing you've discovered about yourself? About being on the spectrum? Or am I being too presumptive now?"

"I'm not sure," Nathalie answered honestly. "It's something I've been asking myself since I've had too much time on my hands, I suppose."

"Have you ever felt anything for a woman?" Lena asked. The question was loaded, but she said it in such a casual way, that it didn't seem like a big deal.

"No. I don't think so." Nathalie lowered the book and turned to Lena. "But I've never been head over heels with a man either. I loved Jack, but it wasn't love at first sight. It grew, and I cared for him. That was all."

Lena frowned. She seemed to process the information before asking the next question.

"Have you ever kissed a woman? In college, or on a night out?"

"No, never." Nathalie shook her head. "What's it like?"

Now it was Lena's turn to laugh. "It's nice. Sensual. Not much different from your encounters with men, I assume. It just happens to be my preference."

"How did you know it was your preference?" Nathalie put the book down, focusing on their conversation.

"I don't know. Attraction is attraction. You either want someone or you don't, I really believe it's that simple. I've always found women far more intriguing than men. Both on a sexual and an intellectual level. That doesn't mean I don't like men, I just prefer them as friends. Women are sensual and seductive, but they can also be strong and fierce. I like how they look; I love their curves, their skin, their smell and their voices." She hesitated but couldn't resist teasing Nathalie. "I love how they sound when I pleasure them."

Nathalie's face took on a whole new level of crimson. She let it sink in and nodded in a cool manner, pretending she wasn't affected by Lena's words, and that it was the most normal thing to talk about.

"Do you date a lot?" she asked. She felt surprisingly aroused by their conversation and intrigued by the fact that Lena had finally started to open up to her.

"You're mighty curious all of a sudden, aren't you?" Lena teased her. She decided to be honest. "No, I don't date. I just have arrangements, if you don't mind me calling it that. But I've broken off most of those arrangements lately."

"Right." Nathalie was surprised at the jealous stitch she felt when she imagined Lena with another woman. "So... multiple arrangements. My God, you're a popular woman." She winced. "I need to ask you one more question, if you don't mind my curiosity. Were they gay or straight?"

"Straight-ish," Lena said. "Most of them were married to men." She had no idea why she was being honest about her bad behavior, especially to Nathalie, who had been cheated on herself. But she wanted to tell her the truth. There had been enough lies. Practical lies at first, but now that they were becoming friends, she had to be open about her lifestyle.

"I see." Nathalie said, staring at the pool. "So how did you get them into bed?" She chuckled. "I'm sorry. More questions, I know."

"It didn't happen like that," Lena said. "It was more like a natural evolution of circumstances." She held up a hand. "Hey, as I said, attraction is attraction, no matter where you are on the scale. Sometimes, it just works."

"Right." Nathalie thought about that, then shook her head. "I can see why you're popular with straight women." She held up the book in her hand. "The main protagonist in this book is a bit like you. She's a tomboy; confident and attractive. It's a sexy combination the way the author describes her."

Lena laughed, shaking her head. "Be careful not to read too many of those books, they might send you over the edge. Although I'm flattered you think I'm attractive."

Nathalie blushed. "Yeah, well, we've already established that." A loaded silence followed, and she struggled to find words to break it. There was so much she wanted to ask, so much she wanted to know. She felt flushed by their conversation but couldn't seem to stop herself from probing.

"So, how is your watercolor course going?" Lena asked, easing them away from the topic.

"It's going," Nathalie said, relieved that Lena had taken charge. "Let's just say I haven't been blessed with natural artistic talent."

"Are you sure?" Lena turned her way and lowered her shades. "You seem like a woman who can take on anything.

Can I see your work? I mean not now, you don't have to get up or anything, I'd just like to see it sometime." Nathalie got up from the sun lounger and put on her robe. She needed an excuse to splash some cold water on her face because right now, she was on fire.

"No, I'll get it. But I'm warning you; once you've seen it you can't make it unseen, so don't come running to me when you can't sleep at night." She walked back to the house, leaving Lena waiting by the pool. Lena followed her with her eyes until she disappeared into the kitchen, the corners of her mouth pulling up into a tiny smile. *I wonder what that cute ass would feel like in my hands.*

"Okay, here we go." Nathalie rolled out the sheet of paper and took a dramatic stance, holding it up before Lena. "My latest masterpiece." Lena studied the work and tried not to laugh.

"It's very abstract, for sure," she said. "What's that in the middle of the bouquet? Is it a potato? I mean, I knew Marie-Louise was a bit eccentric, but I didn't imagine her putting potatoes in her practice bouquets..."

"Shut up." Nathalie's gave her a playful slap on the shoulder. "That is not a potato. It's an artichoke. Can't you tell?"

Lena shrugged. "Sorry... It's brown and it's got a lumpy shape, so I just assumed."

"Don't mock my work, Lena. I'd like to see you try your hand at this art stuff. It's harder than you think."

"I know," Lena said, laughing. "Been there, done that, gave up. I was only joking. You're actually not bad for a beginner. Keep up the good work and I might ask you to do a commission for me one day."

Nathalie rolled her eyes. "Keep on making fun of me and I might do you one." She sat down on the edge of Lena's sun lounger. Her thigh brushed against Lena's calf as she turned towards her, sending shivers up her spine. "So, remind me what you're doing today?"

"I'm driving to Monaco," Lena said. "Gumbo and I are staying the night there; my client's representatives are taking me out for dinner. We'll be back tomorrow lunchtime, but it looks like, overall, it's going to be a long-term project. I'll be there on and off for the coming weeks."

"Some rich family who needs a new lawn?" Nathalie asked.

Lena smiled. "Yeah. Something like that."

19

"Samantha and I are going for a drink on the square," Brenda said to the group as they finished off their paintings. "Would any of you like to join us?" Nathalie looked up from her still-life and put her paintbrush back into her jar.

"Sure. That would be nice." She smiled and turned to Graham, Cherie and Marie-Louise.

"Yeah, why not?" Graham said. "Just one though. I need to drive back to Cannes." Marie-Louise shook her head.

"Maybe another time for me. I have some work to do in the gallery. Cherie is going to help me, I've taken her on as an apprentice." She winked at Cherie, who had just finished the most beautiful looking painting of the pond. The ripples on the water surface were exquisite, and she had gracefully accepted the compliments they had given her.

"Okay, just us English speaking folks then," Brenda said cheerfully. "I can't wait to have a drink."

It was quiet on the now sleepy Valbonne Square. The lunch

shift was over, and there were only a couple of tables remaining, with groups of people finishing off their bottles of wine in the afternoon sun. Nathalie and her fellow students sat down around one of the front tables, shaded by a big parasol. She waved at Alain when he came out.

"Bonjour, Nathalie. How's my favorite American doing today?" He cast her one of his most charming smiles, scratching the stubble on his chin.

"I'm great, thank you." Nathalie looked up at him. "And you, Alain?"

Alain looked around the group and rested his eyes on Samantha. "I can't complain. Not with all these beautiful women on my terrace." He shot a fleeting glance at Samantha's low-cut top before turning back to Nathalie. "What can I do for you?"

Nathalie gestured to the others. "Don't worry, we won't bother you with food. Just a bottle of rosé would be great."

Alain winked. "Only the best rosé for you, ma belle."

Brenda and Samantha giggled.

"I see you've made friends already. He's cute. Tall, dark and handsome," Brenda whispered. "And I think he likes you."

Nathalie shook her head and slouched, stretching her legs out in front of her.

"I'm not so sure about that, Brenda. I've got the feeling Alain likes anything with a pulse. Besides, I think I've had enough of men for the time being." She turned to Graham. "So, tell me, Graham. What's your story? Are you married?" she asked. She knew nothing about him, other than that he was from California, which she had only guessed by his accent.

"Yeah. I'm married," Graham said. "My wife and I are renting a place in Cannes for the summer."

"Oh, how romantic," Brenda shrieked. "I wish I'd meet a man who would take me to Cannes one day."

Graham grinned. "Romance is dead, Brenda. No need to be envious. Our therapist thought it might be a good idea if we went away for a while and spent some real time together. I suppose it's the last chance to save our marriage. We both retired early and realized we couldn't stand being around each other all day. All we did was fight." He laughed. "And now we're here, still fighting, just a little less."

"Was your wife not interested in doing Marie-Louise's course?" Samantha asked.

"Not really." Graham grimaced. "She's more into shopping. And that's an expensive hobby, especially when staying in Cannes." He thanked Alain, who brought over their bottle in a cooler and filled up their glasses, before taking a long drink. "But hey, if it makes her happy... Anyway, Doctor Chuckabee - that's the name of our couples' therapist - claims it's good to partake in activities separately. That way we'll have something to talk about when we see each other again." He paused and thought for a moment. "I'm not sure if we're talking more now, but I must admit, I do like being away from her twice a week." He laughed. "I'm trying to convince her to join a tennis club or take cooking classes, so she can meet other people too, maybe make some friends." He shrugged. "So that's me. What about you guys?"

Samantha put a loving arm around her mother. "Mum is a cancer survivor. We've come here to celebrate that she's been given the all-clear."

"Congratulations," Nathalie said. "That's great news."

Brenda nodded and raised her glass. "No more chemo for me. I just want to have a good time now, enjoy life to the full, and spend as much time with my daughter as possible. We've both taken a sabbatical from work. Samantha is a store manager and I'm a primary school teacher. We're staying in a guesthouse just outside town." She beamed. "Nothing as fancy as Cannes, but it's wonderful there. We're both single and we've been saving up for years, so now seemed to be the perfect time to live our French dream for a while. We go out into the fields to paint every morning when the sun comes up and we just love it, don't we Samantha?"

Samantha smiled. "Yes, it's wonderful. I don't think I ever want to leave again." She turned to Nathalie. "And you? What are you doing here? Apart from painting?"

Nathalie took a sip from the cold rosé. "I guess you could call it a sabbatical too. I just got divorced and I'm taking a break from work, to figure out where to go from here. I only signed up for the watercolor course, so I'd have something to do. I've never considered myself artistic, as you can probably tell by the fruits of my labor." She held up the cardboard tube that contained her paintings. "I'm a perfectionist, and it's really hard for me to try my hand at something I'm not naturally good at. But I have to admit, I'm enjoying it."

"Good for you," Graham said. "And don't beat yourself up about your work, you're already improving. Haven't you noticed?"

"Yeah," Brenda chipped in. "Your first work looked like a murder scene, but now you can tell they're flowers you're painting." They all laughed, and Nathalie rolled her eyes.

"Thanks guys. How about another bottle, huh?" She turned to call Alain, when her eye caught a glimpse of a dark-haired woman. Her heart skipped a beat. *Lena?* She was talking to a woman at one of the tables by the restaurant entrance. The young lady was a tourist, Nathalie guessed. She was holding a map over the table, and Lena was kneeling down beside her, pointing out different places.

They seemed engrossed in conversation and were laughing a lot. Lena raised her hand and called for Alain to bring them two coffees. Alain shook his head and laughed.

"Nathalie?" Nathalie turned back and looked at her fellow table mates. "Are you okay?" Samantha asked.

Nathalie nodded, forcing a smile on her face. "Yeah, I'm good," she said, trying to keep her cool. "Just someone I know. I'll go and say hi later." She felt sick at the sight of Lena, clearly chatting up the girl, who seemed to welcome her advances. She couldn't help but look over again, as Lena sat down opposite the woman at the table. The red-headed tourist was cute. Too cute.

"Another bottle, Nathalie?" Alain put down a cooler with fresh ice and a bottle of rosé. He nodded towards Lena. "She's working her magic again." He sighed. "Magic Lena. I don't know how she does it, but she's ruining my chances with anyone who comes near her."

"Yes, it seems to be working," Nathalie said, taking a long drink from the wine that Alain poured for her. "She's the caretaker of the estate I'm staying at," Nathalie explained to her new friends.

"And she loves the ladies," Alain added before he moved on to the next table, producing a check from his apron pocket.

"You're staying at an estate?" Brenda asked curiously. "What does that mean? Is it a big villa with a large plot of land, like in the UK?"

"Yeah." Nathalie shifted in her chair. "Villa Provence. It's a ten-minute drive from here." She wasn't sure if she was comfortable talking about the eight-bedroom house she'd rented. Not with two people who had been saving up for years to stay in a guesthouse.

"So, you're there on your own?" Brenda was on a roll

now, apparently fascinated by how the other half lived. "All by yourself in a massive house?"

"And what about the lesbian caretaker?" Samantha whispered, looking over at Lena. "Is it weird having her there?"

"No, it's not weird." Nathalie laughed. "Lena is lovely."

Lena turned at the sound of her name. There was a hint of panic on her face when she saw Nathalie. "Hey you! Were you talking about me?" She said something to the woman opposite her, got up from her chair and walked over to Nathalie.

"I might have." Nathalie kissed her on both cheeks. She could have sworn Lena was uncomfortable, the way her eyes shifted from Nathalie to the mystery woman and back. "Glad you made it back from your trip. I was just telling my friends from art class how lovely you are." She gestured towards them. "Lena, meet Graham, Brenda and Samantha. Guys, this is Lena."

Lena relaxed a little and greeted them with her effortless charm before turning back to Nathalie. "So, how was class? Did you draw any more potatoes?"

Nathalie nudged her, laughing. "Ha ha, very funny". She nodded towards Lena's table. "How was Monaco? And more importantly, who's that? Are you on a date?" She tried her hardest to sound chirpy, even though she felt sick at the sight of them together.

"A date? Oh God, no." Lena's cheeks turned rosy. "I just came to drop something off for Alain's accountant."

"Oh." Nathalie frowned. "And is that Alain's accountant? She looks lost."

Lena put her hands in her back pockets and chuckled.

"No, that's not the accountant. That's Nora. Nora's a

tourist. She asked me for directions, so I'm helping her out, giving her some tips on where to go."

"That's very nice of you." Nathalie tried her best not to sound sarcastic. There was an awkward silence, and the otherwise chatty Lena seemed desperate to get away from the conversation.

"Well, I'll leave you guys to it," she said. "Nice to meet you all, have a good day." She turned back to Nathalie and hesitated. "Do you need a lift home, by the way?"

"No, I'm good. I drove here," Nathalie lied, glancing at her second glass of wine. "You take your time. I'm going to do a bit of shopping, I'll see you later." She winced at the lie that had slipped from her tongue. Why had she said that? If Lena came home before she did, the car would be there in the driveway. *Why did you lie about that, you idiot?* She tried to let it go, focusing on the conversation that had now turned to French food, wondering how fast she could get out of there.

20

"I'm sorry Nora, I have to go. I've got work to do." Lena got up from the table and put some money into the folder. "It was nice to meet you. Enjoy your stay. And don't forget to go to Gourdon, it's a really nice little town."

"No, please. Don't worry, I'll get this one," Nora said. She stood up too when Lena didn't answer and ran after her, writing her number down on their check. "Here. This is my number. Call me if you want to go for a drink, I'll be here for a couple of days." Lena took the piece of paper and gave Nora a flirty smile, just to make sure they were on the same wavelength. Nora didn't flinch. Instead, she took a step closer and bit her bottom lip as she looked up at Lena in a seductive manner.

Lena nodded slowly. Yep. They were definitely on the same wavelength.

"Thanks. I think I might do that." Then she turned and walked away to look for Nathalie, tucking Nora's number deep into her pocket. *She might still be here.* It bothered her that Nathalie had seen her talking to another woman. Sure, she had been flirting with Nora. She was single, and there was no reason why she shouldn't. *Why do I care what Nathalie thinks of me anyway?* Lena scanned the shops but couldn't find her anywhere. She tried the parking lot too, but Nathalie's car was gone, and so she got some groceries from the market and walked back to her car. She felt like a hypocrite for trying to hide her flirtations from Nathalie. She should have just admitted it, but instead, she'd come up with some lame excuse. When it came to women, Lena never gave things much thought. She just did what felt right, and mostly, whatever the hell she wanted to do. But having Nathalie in her life confused her, made her overthink her every move. *It's because you like her. And she might even like you back.*

Driving up the hill, Lena slowed down when she saw something along the side of the road. At first, she thought it was a wounded animal, but as she came closer, she realized it was a woman, lying on her back, covering her face with her hands. Lena stepped on the breaks immediately and jumped out of the car with her phone in one hand, ready to call an ambulance. The woman was covered in dirt, but the designer purse left no mistake about her identity. *Oh God, Nathalie.*

21

Nathalie panted, resting her hands on her knees. It was an intense hike up the hill, especially when trying to break a world record. Each time she heard a car coming, she dove into the overgrown roadside, terrified Lena would see her. She was furious with herself for refusing the lift, and especially for telling Lena she'd taken the car. Back home, she rarely made mistakes like this. She was sharp, to the point, honest, and had an almost photographic memory. No one had ever been able to fool her at work, especially not with excuses, but now she was fooling herself. Nathalie felt like she was slowly losing her grip on the control she'd never failed to let go of. She felt vulnerable, insecure, and above all, very, very confused about the recent events with Lena that had her doubting her sanity. She heard another car approaching and jumped behind a bush, failing to notice the ravine behind it. The hill was steep, and despite her best efforts to grab on to anything in sight, she'd slipped and rolled down until she finally hit a tree.

"Fuck!" she screamed, when a jolt of pain went through

her ankle. She sat up, inspecting her surroundings. The recent rainfall had turned the hill into a slippery slope, and she was coated in mud. She hadn't fallen far down, but the landing against the tree had seriously hurt her ankle. She tried to stand up and cried out again when she put her weight on it. Nathalie groaned in agony, sat back down, and examined her arms and legs. They were covered in scratches, and her wrist was bleeding. At least she still had her purse, clenched in one hand. Her tube with paintings was gone. It had rolled all the way down into the river and was now making its way towards the next village, where some kids would find it and laugh at her clumsy attempt to paint a pond. She turned herself onto her hands and knees and started making her way back up towards the road, crawling and pulling herself up by the low hanging branches. She was out of breath by the time she rolled herself onto the asphalt, staring up at the sky. Her white jeans were green and brown now, and the fabric was ripped at one knee. Her leg was bleeding too, but it didn't look like a serious injury. Another car approached, but this time, she refused to go back into the undergrowth. It couldn't get any worse than this. *If that's Lena, I must have done something to deserve it.* Nathalie was beyond shame when the car came to a halt next to her, and the voice she was dreading to hear echoed through the valley. She covered her face with her hands.

"Nat! Are you okay? What are you doing here?" Lena got out, ran around the car and kneeled down beside to her. "What the hell happened?" She glanced at Nathalie's purse. "Were you robbed? Attacked? Please say something!"

"I'm okay," Nathalie said in a shaky voice. "Nothing like that, it was just an accident." She sat up, too mortified to meet Lena's eyes. "Please just take me home. I don't want to talk about it."

Lena lifted her up and helped her into the car. "Do you need a doctor? And where's your car?"

Nathalie shook her head. "I'm fine. The car is at home."

"Are you finally going to tell me what happened?" Lena asked as she put her first-aid kit on the kitchen table. Nathalie felt slightly better after a shower, but she was still too embarrassed to tell Lena the truth.

"I saw a squirrel."

"Okay," Lena gave her an amused smile. She sat down and lifted Nathalie's leg on to her lap. Nathalie shivered when her hand stroked the skin around her knee. It wasn't the pain that caused the goose bumps to appear on her thigh, and she hoped Lena wouldn't notice. "So, you jumped down into the ravine to catch the squirrel, so you could what... eat it? I told you I would cook you dinner if you wanted me to." Lena squirted some disinfectant onto a cotton pad and carefully cleaned the wound, holding the leg in place with her other hand.

Nathalie let out a chuckle. "Something like that."

Lena gave her a curious look. "Why did you tell me you took the car?" she asked, pulling a Band-Aid out of the box. Nathalie closed her eyes, frantically searching for an excuse. *Think Nathalie, think.*

"I didn't want to ruin your date," she said. *Good one!* "You two seemed to be hitting it off, so I didn't want you to leave, just because of me."

"So, you jumped into the ravine when you heard a car coming? That's silly. Besides, I already told you, it wasn't a date," Lena said, still smiling. Nathalie shifted her gaze to her dimples, and her mouth. Lena was biting her lip in concentration as she secured the Band-Aid. "I was just being nice to her."

"Right," Nathalie said with a sigh.

Lena let go of Nathalie's leg. Then she took her hand and studied her scratched palm. "I think there's a thorn in here. Will you let me take it out?"

Nathalie nodded. Everything hurt, but at least her ankle wasn't broken. It was swelling up, but she'd been able to get in and out of the shower and wobble around, leaning on an old walking stick she'd found in the hallway.

"Can I ask you something?" Lena kept her eyes fixed on Nathalie's hand as she disinfected her palm and tried to get hold of the thorn with a pair of tweezers.

"Sure." Nathalie's heart was beating rapidly. *She's on to you, you idiot.*

"Why am I getting the feeling that you're judging me for flirting with that woman earlier today?"

"So, you admit you were flirting?" Nathalie regretted the words as soon as she'd said them out loud. "I mean, not that it's any of my business, of course," she hastily added. "And no, I'm not judging you. As I said, I didn't want to break up your conversation with the beautiful lady you seemed so captivated with, so I decided to make my own way home. But by then I'd already lied about the car, so I couldn't ask the others for a lift either and I didn't want you to see me when you drove past." She winced when Lena got hold of the thorn and pulled it out.

"There," she said. "Better?" She took Nathalie's hand in hers and stroked the sore skin.

Nathalie held her breath as a jolt of electricity shot through her core. She waited for it to pass, but Lena kept on holding her hand and rubbing it, until finally, she let go.

Lena raised her head with a smile as if nothing had happened. "Yes, I was flirting with her," she said. "So, I'm going to ask you again. Why does it bother you? I didn't mean for you to see it, but you were clearly upset."

"Do you flirt with a lot of women?" Nathalie asked, avoiding her question.

Lena looked at her intently. "Yes, I do. I'm single, it's not a crime."

Nathalie nodded, brooding over her next question. "How do you know they're into women?"

Lena laughed, shaking her head. "Haven't we already had this conversation? It's not like that. They don't have to be gay, I'm pretty sure Nora wasn't. It's honestly not hard to charm a woman, and I can tell when someone's interested." She looked into Nathalie's eyes and held her gaze. "You just have to be super confident, it confuses the hell out of them. Then, as soon as you leave, they come running after you and give you their number." She held up the piece of paper with Nora's number on it, and three kisses underneath.

Nathalie took it and read the number out loud. She wanted to rip it into tiny pieces and burn the remains, but instead, she kept a straight face and handed it back to Lena.

"Are you going to call her?" she asked in a shaky voice.

"Maybe." Lena walked over to the kitchen counter. "Maybe not." She shrugged. "I'll see how I feel tomorrow. Coffee?"

22

Lena looked at the piece of paper on her nightstand, picked up her phone and started dialing Nora's number. She'd been distracted by the number all day while catching up on paperwork and wondered why the hell she hadn't dialed it yet. Her finger was hovering over the call button, just about to press it, when she decided to put the phone back down.

Damn you, Nathalie. What was the big deal? Nothing would happen between her and Nathalie, yet she couldn't bring herself to ask a gorgeous tourist out to dinner. A gorgeous tourist who had basically thrown herself at her feet. It couldn't be more perfect and uncomplicated. But Nathalie had somehow found a way into her system, and she wasn't able to stop thinking about her. She had locked herself up in the annex, trying to get her tax returns out of the way, and hadn't spoken to her all day. She picked up the book that Nathalie had returned after finishing it and smiled as she flicked through the pages, tracing the marks where they had been folded.

"There's definitely something there, Gumbo," she said to

the sleeping dog on the pillow next to her. Gumbo opened one eye at the sound of his name and went straight back to sleep. Nathalie had asked for another book in the same genre, and had Lena search for a good hour to find one. Nowadays, she didn't read much romance anymore. Picking someone up had almost become second nature to her, and that had consumed many of her nights ever since Selma had left. Until now, because now, she spent most of her nights with Nathalie. And even though there was no steamy sex involved, she enjoyed her company so much more than some meaningless encounter with a stranger, however good-looking. Nathalie was something else altogether. She was beautiful, smart, clumsy, adorable and far from the stiff businesswoman Lena had expected her to be. She admired Nathalie for being brave enough to let go of everything she had; everything that had shaped her into who she was. Lena turned on her knees and peered out of the window, the way she had many times that week. The candles on the terrace table were lit, faintly highlighting Nathalie's silhouette. She was reading a book with her feet up on another chair.

Don't go over there. She might want to be alone. That had been Lena's dilemma for days. She looked at the alarm clock on her nightstand. It was only nine o'clock and if she didn't go out there now, she'd be torturing herself with regret all night, unable to sleep. Why the hell had she shown her that piece of paper with Nora's number yesterday? Had it been provocation? It was out of character for her, rubbing a potential fling in someone's face. And why had Nathalie seemed upset about it? Lena got up, put on a t-shirt and grabbed a bottle of wine from her fridge on her way out.

"Hey." Lena held up the bottle as she walked towards

Nathalie. "Please be honest and tell me if you want to be alone." Nathalie looked up from her book with a big smile on her face.

"Not at all, I was hoping you'd come," she said, running a hand through her long, blonde hair. "In fact, I was thinking of knocking on your door, but I wasn't sure if you wanted to be alone either."

"I guess we're on the same page then." She nodded towards Nathalie's leg under the table. "How's the ankle?"

"It's okay. The ice really helped, I think. The worst swelling went down over night, and I can put my weight on it now, so it might have looked worse than it was."

"That's good." Lena shuffled in front of the table. "Just to make it clear, Nat, I have no intention of asking Nora out." She chuckled. "I don't know why I'm telling you this. I just wanted you to know."

Nathalie's eyes met Lena's. The flickering lights from the candles cast a warm glow over her face as she stood there, looking down at her, and she melted at the sight of. "Thank you for telling me, Lena. I appreciate it. Although I'm not sure why either." She shrugged, "I'm sorry if I acted weird today."

Lena waited for an explanation, but Nathalie didn't continue, so she opened the bottle, took Nathalie's glass and topped it up.

"Do you mind if I help myself to a glass in the kitchen?" she asked.

"Of course. I'm sorry, where are my manners? There are plenty in the top cupboard above the back worktop." Nathalie pointed towards the general direction of the wine glasses, when she saw Lena through the kitchen window, already walking back with a burgundy glass. "Oh, never mind. You know where they are."

Lena stalled in the doorway like a deer caught in headlights. "Yeah. I know where most things are." *Why don't you just tell her the truth?* She took a seat opposite Nathalie. "So, are you enjoying the new book?" she asked, changing the subject.

"I am." Nathalie folded the page she was reading and put the book on the table in between them. "You must think I'm weird. A newly divorced woman, fully engrossed in lesbian romance novels."

"I don't think it's weird at all," Lena said. "I think you're curious, sure. And maybe even a little bit more to one side of the scale than you'd like to admit, but there's nothing wrong with that. This is the time, if you want to explore other sides to yourself."

Nathalie laughed, rubbing her temple. She'd had half a bottle already and apart from being a little bit tipsy, she was feeling braver than usual. "Okay, Lena. I'm not going to lie, I am interested in this." She pointed at the book. "Maybe more than I'd like to admit, sure." There was a silence. "But I wouldn't have a clue how to figure it out for myself. I mean, hypothetically speaking, if I wanted to explore my horizons... how would I approach a woman? The thought of it freaks me out, and to be honest with you, at this point in my life, I wouldn't even know how to approach a man. It's been too long."

Lena couldn't help but smile. *I knew it.* "Well, hypothetically speaking," she said, "I could take you out with me one night and show you how easy it is. You'll be amazed." She put her feet up on the table and leaned back in her chair. "If that's what you're interested in, hypothetically speaking."

Nathalie shook her head and chuckled into her wineglass. "Oh, I don't know. It sounds like a reasonable idea now that I've had a couple of drinks, but I'm sure I will have changed my mind by tomorrow." She hesitated. "Where would you take me?"

Lena shrugged. "A beach bar in St. Tropez maybe? They're quite busy on Friday nights."

"A beach bar, huh? So not a gay bar?"

Lena laughed. "No need. But we could go to a gay bar, if you wanted to. Hypothetically speaking."

Nathalie shook her head. "No, a beach bar sounds good. Maybe some night just before I leave so I don't have to face you after I've made a fool of myself. If you don't mind?"

"I don't mind taking you," Lena said. "I'm just not sure how I'll feel when..." She took a sip of her wine, avoiding eye contact. "Never mind." *Damn it. I should have kept my mouth shut.*

"What?" Nathalie asked. "When what?"

"Let me ask you a question first," Lena said, leaning towards her. "Then I'll answer yours."

"Okay." Nathalie shifted in her chair and pulled her feet up on the seat, cupping her sore knee.

"This afternoon, when I showed you Nora's number... Were you jealous?" Lena watched Nathalie break out in cold sweat at her question. Her eyes shifted from Lena, up to the sky, into the garden and back. She was clearly nervous. "Well?"

"Maybe a little," Nathalie finally said.

Lena nodded. "That's okay. I think I'd feel the same if I saw you flirting with another woman. That's what I was trying to tell you."

"Oh." Nathalie blushed. There was a silence. "Does that mean you like me, as in..." she struggled to find the right words. She held her breath when her eyes met Lena's. They were darker than normal, almost black, and although she'd had a bit too much to drink already, she could have sworn she saw desire in them. For a moment, Nathalie forgot everything else around her.

"Yes, Nat. I'm attracted to you." Lena was surprised to feel her hands shaking under the table. She never had trouble speaking her mind, especially not when it came to women.

Nathalie bit her lip, lowering her gaze to Lena's mouth. "I think I'm attracted to you too," she whispered. "I don't know what it is, but you make me feel so aware of my own body. It's... it's the most physical thing I've ever felt." She sighed. "I can't believe I just said that." Her cheeks were bright red now.

Lena felt her insides flutter. She was tempted to grab Nathalie's hand, pull her in and kiss her, but it was too soon. She didn't want to scare her or do anything to ruin the honest conversation they'd just had, so she stood up, leaving her glass half full.

"I'm going back now. Not because I don't want to be here with you, but because I don't want you to do anything you'll regret tomorrow." Nathalie looked up at her, shook her head and opened her mouth to speak, then closed it again. She nodded.

"Okay. Goodnight, Lena."

"Goodnight, Nat."

23

"So, is there a pool at your place?" Brenda asked when they were cleaning up after another class. Nathalie finished blow-drying her still life and rolled it up carefully before pushing it into a tube. She'd felt inspired today and was happy with her work. It wasn't great, but it wasn't bad either, and the improvement in her technique was clearly noticeable. Perhaps her conversation with Lena had something to do with it. She couldn't stop thinking about her.

"Yes, there is." Nathalie turned to Brenda, who had been asking questions about *Villa Provence* all afternoon. Telling Brenda where she was staying had been like opening a can of worms. The woman couldn't seem to stop obsessing about it, after she and Samantha had driven past the gates on their way home one day.

"It looks big from the outside." Brenda sighed. "Oh, it must be lovely having so much space to yourself." Nathalie wished she would stop talking about it. It made her feel guilty about her wealth, and she didn't like to feel that way.

"Why don't you all come for dinner on Saturday?" she

heard herself say, immediately regretting ever opening her mouth. Inviting people over for dinner was possibly the most stupid thing she could ever do. She couldn't cook and had, in fact, never entertained anyone other than clients in restaurants, where all she'd had to do was ask her assistant to make a reservation. But Brenda was one of the kindest people she'd ever met, and there was no doubt that she'd been digging for an invitation. What else could she have done?

"Really? Are you sure? We would love that!" Brenda balled her hands into fists in excitement.

Samantha nodded. "A dinner party at your place? Of course, that would be amazing."

"Great," Nathalie said, turning to Graham. Cherie wasn't in class today, and the absence of her talent had made them all feel much better about their own work. "Graham, please bring your wife if you can make it, I'd love to meet her."

"Thank you, that sounds like a wonderful idea," Graham said.

"I would love to come," Marie-Louise shouted from the kitchen, where she was rooting through the freezer. She came out, carrying a bag of ice-cubes and a bottle of sparkling water. "I can't remember the last time I visited, it must have been six or seven years ago. I used to go to François and Robert's parties when they were both still alive." She shook her head. "So sad how time flies."

"So, you knew the old owners?" Nathalie asked.

Marie-Louise divided the water over five glasses. "Oh yes. They were a wonderful couple. Always made sure their guests were served the best food and cocktails. Their Sunday dinner parties used to be the highlight of my week." She handed Nathalie a glass. "I'd love to see what Lena's made of the place, I'm sure she's done her grandfather proud, bless his soul." She crossed herself and looked up at the sky.

Nathalie frowned. "Lena is the owner's granddaughter? You mean Lena, the caretaker?"

"Well, yes." Marie-Louise sat down on a stool and took a sip of her drink. "Lena's the owner now, her grandfather left it to her in his will." She hesitated. "Did you not know that?"

Nathalie shook her head. "No, I didn't. I mean, she told me about her grandfather, but it never clicked that he was the owner of the estate."

Marie-Louise shrugged. "Lena is very modest. Perhaps she didn't want to... what do you Americans say? Brag?" She laughed. "Anyway, I'm looking forward to your dinner, Nathalie. I'll bring a nice bottle and please let me know if you need anything else."

"Thank you, I will."

Nathalie left the gallery, puzzled and full of questions. *Why didn't she tell me she owned Villa Provence?*

24

The Porsche wasn't there when Nathalie returned to the villa. She looked down at the package in her hands, addressed to Lena. Alain had asked her to take it with her when she passed his café on her way home. She took a good look around the estate, trying to imagine Lena living there and having the whole place to herself. All the beautiful décor, the art collection, the colorful bedrooms, the impressive wine cellar... It was all Lena's doing. If Nathalie had been fascinated with Lena before, her new-found knowledge had only heightened that fascination. *Why didn't she tell me?* She walked into the house, put the package down on her kitchen counter, then changed her mind and took it over to the annex.

Nathalie knocked, although she knew it was pointless. The car wasn't there, which meant Lena wouldn't be there either. There was no barking, so Nathalie assumed Gumbo was gone too. Lena rarely left without him, anyway. She tried the handle; the door wasn't locked, and so she opened it carefully and peeked through the gap in the door, into the kitchen. *Don't go in. It's her house. You're breaking and entering, dumbass.* She shook her head and took a step back, then changed her mind again. Her curiosity had gotten the better of her, and before she knew it, the door was wide open. Nathalie sneaked inside and looked around the cottage. It looked nothing like a caretakers' cottage. It was warm and welcoming, but surprisingly luxurious too. She could tell the leather couches were of great quality, and that the open kitchen was equipped with the same professional appliances that she had in her kitchen. *No*, she corrected herself. *Lena's kitchen.* There was a pile of post on the kitchen table, next to a vase with orange roses. The artworks on the walls looked like they were painted by the same artist who had done the paintings in the main house, Nathalie guessed. She walked over to a drawing board in the living room. There was a technical drawing of a garden that looked like it was designed for a commercial project. Next to it, photographs of plants and different types of flowers were clipped onto the board, numbered, and representing the sections in the sketch. She leaned in closer to read the description. *Monaco Jardins Royaux, entrée est, prop.3, section 5*

"Busted." Nathalie jumped up at the sound of Lena's voice, dropping the package from her hands. She quickly picked it up, walked back to the kitchen and handed it to Lena.

"I'm so sorry, I hope there's nothing fragile in there. I... I was just..."

"Breaking in?" Lena leaned against the counter.

"I know it looks bad." Nathalie grimaced. "I had a package for you and I thought you were home. When I knocked, I realized the door was open. I'm so sorry, I didn't mean to..."

"It's okay," Lena said. "Don't worry about it." She put the package on the kitchen table and inspected it. Gumbo was at her feet, staring up in anticipation. "Yeah, I believe this is for you, Gumbo," she said, tearing open the box. She put it on the floor in front of him and laughed as he dove in, pulling out a Frisbee.

"He knows it's for him?" Nathalie took the Frisbee he put down in front of her, stepped into the doorway and threw it across the garden. They watched Gumbo sprint after it, jump up and catch it. Nathalie sighed, relieved that the dog had taken the attention away from her for a moment.

"I only order stuff online for him," Lena said, "so whenever there's a package, he knows it's his." She turned back to Nathalie and cocked her head, crossing her arms. "So, now you know what my home looks like."

"I'm so sorry for snooping," Nathalie stammered. "I saw the drawing board in the back and couldn't resist having a look." She nodded towards Lena's work. "I had no idea you did such big projects. What's this for, if you don't mind me asking?"

Lena walked over to the board and beckoned Nathalie to follow her. "It's my biggest project so far and the reason for my recent trip. I've designed a new side entrance for the Monaco Royal Gardens on the grounds surrounding the palace. The committee signed it off two weeks ago, we've already started some of the work." She pointed at a circle in the center of the drawing. "This is the water feature in the middle. The other elements and the road leading up to the entrance will be built around it. I'm going for marble edges and have recruited a French artist to design a statue to go in the middle." She traced the lines that marked where the driveway was. "There will be trees lining up to the entrance and big flowerbeds on the hill right here," she said, moving her finger, "showcasing the Royal Family's crest. We've got three months to get everything done, so we're on a tight schedule."

"I didn't realize you were such a big-shot," Nathalie said, glancing over the budget stated at the top left corner.

"I'm not. I simply love what I do, and my clients tend to appreciate that."

"Marie-Louise told me you were modest." Nathalie turned back to Lena. "She also told me something else about you."

Lena blushed, which was a rare occurrence. "I see," she said, looking down at her feet.

Nathalie held up a hand. "We weren't gossiping, I swear. But I invited my art group over for dinner and Marie-Louise mentioned your grandfather and how they used to be friends. Why didn't you just tell me that this is all yours?"

"I'm sorry," Lena said. "I should have told you, but the first people who stayed here gave me the feedback that they weren't happy with the fact that I lived on the premises because I was the owner, and that it felt more like a guesthouse due to my presence. Even though I hardly ever saw them." She shrugged. "The second couple told me the same, although it didn't bother them as much, so they still gave me a five-star rating. I talked to a rental agent who was of the opinion that most tenants prefer staff over the owner, so they don't have to feel like they're walking on eggshells. That's why I decided to try a different approach this time." She took Nathalie's hand. "I didn't like lying to you, but I never expected us to get close either. I was going to tell you, at some point."

Nathalie nodded. "Okay, I get that. But now *I* feel bad. This is your house, and you're staying in the pool house."

Lena laughed. "That's exactly the reaction I was worried about. But come on, it's not that bad Nat. I mean, look at this place. I'm pretty sure anyone would be delighted to move in here."

"But I invited people over for dinner on Saturday..." Nathalie bit her lip. "And now I know that this is your place, it feels wrong."

"Please Nat, let's not make a big deal about this," Lena said. She let go of Nathalie's hand. "Look, I apologize for not telling you, but I made that decision because I wanted you to feel at home here, and I wanted you to feel like it was *your* place for the duration of your stay. So, however many dinner parties you want to throw, please go ahead, because it would make me happy to see this house come to life again. And above all, it would make me happy to see you happy."

Nathalie watched Lena make two cups of coffee while she let her words sink in. "Thank you," she said, following Lena outside to the bench in front of the annex.

Lena gave her an apologetic smile before taking a sip from her coffee. "Now you know everything. Are you mad at me?"

Nathalie shook her head. "No. Are you mad at me for breaking in? Even though I didn't really break in," she hastily added. "I was just going to put the box in your kitchen and..."

"No, it's fine." Lena laughed, interrupting her.

"So, you own all this?" Nathalie gestured to the house and the garden. Then she glanced over at the Porche. "And that?"

"Yes." Lena grinned as she stared at her beloved car. "I inherited most of it, but the Porsche was just one of those things I couldn't resist."

Nathalie nodded slowly, processing the information once more. "I don't get it, Lena. Why do you rent the place out?"

"I don't need all of this," Lena said, gesturing to the property and the land surrounding it. "It's just Gumbo and me. Besides, keeping a place like this is expensive, and although I make a decent wage, I don't want to spend everything on maintenance. This way, the house pays for itself, and I only live in the annex five to six months a year. It's not exactly a sacrifice."

"Okay, that makes sense." Nathalie took a drink from her coffee. "So, is this where you lived when you came from New York?"

"Yeah. My grandfather had bought this place with François, his partner. They gave me the annex, so I would have my own space and as an unspoken rule, I took care of the garden in return. I only had the pleasure of living with François for a couple of years, he passed away when I was twenty. He was a funny man. Very camp in the way he dressed and spoke, and the complete opposite to my grandfather. My grandfather was devastated by his passing. I tried to support him as much as I could but eventually, I wanted to move in with Selma, in Nice. He was lucky to have a lot of good friends, and we still visited him twice a week for dinners or lunch." She sighed. "As you know, it didn't end well with Selma, so after we broke up, I moved back here, and I'm glad I did now, because my grandfather died of a heart attack a couple of months later. It was completely unexpected, but at least I got to spend some quality time with him. We had fun then, him and me, wallowing in our own misery, competing about who was the most messed up between the two of us. At least we could laugh about it."

Nathalie could see the pain in Lena's eyes when she talked about him. "Sounds like he was one hell of a guy,"

"Yeah. He was."

"Did you ever think about selling the place?" Nathalie asked.

Lena nodded. "I thought about it for a while, yes. It broke my heart to be here without him, at first. It was so quiet. He always had people over, and he had a very eclectic circle of friends, of which many were musicians. There was live music at lunch and dinner parties, and he even hosted a couple of weddings. In the end, I couldn't bring myself to sell it. I don't think he would have wanted that. That's when I decided to advertise the house for the summer months. So, I'm happy you're here, and I'm happy you've invited people over."

"I was hoping you'd come too," Nathalie said. "I've never had someone I could talk to the way I can talk to you." She shook her head. "I sound pathetic, don't I?"

Lena took her hand. "No, you don't. And after our conversation last night..." She paused, meeting for Nathalie's eyes. "I hope you know that I really like you too, so yes, I would love to come to your dinner party. Do you need help? I'm working in Monaco on Saturday, but I'm sure I'll be able to leave early."

"No, of course not," Nathalie said. Lena mentioning their conversation stirred something inside of her, making her go warm and weak. She squeezed Lena's hand, holding her breath at the contact. Everything was different now, as if each touch was intentional, and each look meant so much more than it had before. "I'll be fine. Just be here if you can."

"Okay." Lena looked at her, still holding her hand. "Do you mind if I invite Alain?"

Nathalie shook her head. "Absolutely not. I love Alain."

"Great. Again, I'm sorry I lied. Can I make it up to you?"

"No need." Nathalie smiled. "It's not like I'm a saint either. I've been putting your porcelain plates into the dishwasher, even though the instructions on them say not to." She shrugged. "I won't do it again now, knowing that they're yours."

"Okay then." Lena gave her an amused smirk. "Let's start over tomorrow. I'll take you out for lunch in Antibes to apologize, and I'm going to be completely open and honest with you from now on. Deal?"

Nathalie swung an arm around Lena's neck and placed a kiss on her cheek.

"Deal."

25

Nathalie lingered in front of the mirror. Was her dress too short? She wasn't used to wearing short, but the grey V-neck dress seemed decent enough to wear out for lunch. She'd pulled her hair back into a ponytail and wasn't sure if she was happy with how she looked. She sighed, removed her earrings and slammed them down on the edge of the basin. *Don't overdo it, Nat. Just be yourself.* She was nervous, and that was ridiculous. They were only going to Antibes for some food and a bit of sightseeing. It wasn't like it was a date. She heard Gumbo bark, an indication that Lena was ready to leave. Gumbo always got excited when he knew he was coming along. She walked over to the French doors and looked into the garden. Lena was wearing a pair of light blue jeans and a white and blue striped shirt. Around her neck was a simple silver necklace that glistened in the sun. Nathalie took in a quick breath from behind the curtain as she watched her walk up to the house. Her insides did that thing again, where she seemed to lose all control over her body. Lena looked... sexy, she thought. She had never thought of other women as being sexy, but there was simply no other way to describe her. Lena ran a hand through her dark hair, exposing part of her stomach when her shirt crept up. She tucked it back into her jeans and waved in the direction of Nathalie's bedroom. *Damn it, she saw me looking.* Nathalie rushed into the kitchen to open the door, undoing her hair in the process.

"Hey. Are you ready?" Lena asked.

"Yeah. I think so." Nathalie stepped outside and closed the door behind her.

Lena looked her up and down, nodding her approval with a smile. "You look nice," she said, unable to keep her eyes off Nathalie's cleavage.

"Thanks. You do too." Nathalie's heart was racing. Only Lena could do this to her. "You look like... I don't know." She pursed her lips, taking in Lena's tight jeans and crisp shirt. It turned her on. "You look really good."

Lena fiddled with her keys as they walked towards the drive, seemingly nervous. "Thanks, Nat. Mind if we take my car?"

AN IMMACULATELY DRESSED server greeted them after Lena handed her car keys to the valet.

"Welcome back, Lena." He gave Lena two kisses, seemingly familiar with her.

"Hi Philippe. I've booked a table outside," Lena said, putting an arm around Nathalie. "For two?"

"Of course, follow me." He led them through the noisy restaurant. It was full to the brim with people feasting on indulgent looking seafood platters, filled with lobsters, oysters, prawns and langoustines. "After you." He opened the door to the terrace, walked them to their table and pulled out their chairs on the concrete surface that was built into the rocks. Glass screens surrounding the terrace protected the tables from the waves that were splashing up on either side. Everything was white. The concrete platform, the tables, the chairs, the candles... even most of the diners were dressed in white, although there wasn't a dress code.

"Swanky place," Nathalie said. "I didn't take you for a fine-diner."

Lena laughed. "Aha. So, landscapers and nice restaurants don't go together. Is that what you're saying?"

"No, of course not." Nathalie shook her head, appalled by the stupid remark that had slipped off her tongue yet again. "That's not what I meant. But you look different today. The way you're dressed, so smart... and then this place." She nodded towards a group of middle-aged women and their Chihuahuas, cheering with their Champagne glasses. "It's so fancy. I didn't expect it, that's all."

"I happen to like great food and great service," Lena said. "Whether that's in a bistro, a food truck or a high-end restaurant, I don't care. But since I'm taking you out, I thought this might be a good way of introducing you to some fantastic local seafood. We're on the coast after all."

"Well I'm certainly impressed," Nathalie said, looking at the menu. "What should we get? This looks lush."

Lena poured them both a glass of water. "How about a seafood platter for two, some bread and homemade mayonnaise. And a bottle of crisp white wine. How does that sound?"

"Couldn't have come up with anything better myself," Nathalie said. She watched the waves crash up against the glass walls, creating a fountain of foam around them. She couldn't stop smiling. It was a perfect day, with clear skies, and she couldn't have wished for better company. Lena let

Gumbo off the lead, put a blanket down on the floor next to her and held her finger up before him.

"You're going to stay right next to me, Gumbo. Do you understand? No tearing around and no humping the ladies." Gumbo looked at Lena, then to another dog at a table behind them, and back. "Not happening, do you hear me?" Gumbo sniffed in protest before settling down on his blanket with his head between his front paws.

Nathalie pursed her lips. "He looks devastated."

"Yeah, well let's see how he feels when he has to pay alimony for a whole litter of Chihuahua puppies. He's extremely frisky this time of year and I don't want to risk it with these pedigrees. Smart female breeds are often intact and so is he." Lena laughed. "He can play with any dog on the beach or in town, but out here, I'm keeping a close eye on him."

Lena ordered, and Nathalie was surprised to find that she could understand most of her conversation with the server today. She'd started to pick up on familiar sentences and had practiced her French when doing her groceries. It was exciting to feel like she was becoming less of an outsider.

Lena turned her attention back to Nathalie. "This is going to be good. I used to come here with my grandfather and François when I was younger. It was a whole different world, compared to the conservative household I came from, and I loved it."

"What did you grandfather do for a living?" Nathalie asked.

"He was an architect, had his own firm. First, in New York and later, when he moved here, he worked from home. There are some amazing buildings in Nice that he designed, but he worked internationally too and managed to make quite a name for himself."

Nathalie thanked the server as he poured the wine. "Wow, I'd love to see some of his work. Maybe we could take a trip to Nice one day? If you're not too busy?"

"Sure, we could do that." Lena leaned in, resting her elbows on the table. "It's funny that he bought *Villa Provence*, considering he was a modernist. The estate shows no reference to his style whatsoever. I think that was François' influence on him. They bought it together after my grandfather moved to France."

"His partner?" Nathalie asked.

"Yeah. François was an artist. In fact, he painted most of the work in the house. My grandfather and I tracked down his family after his death. We thought they might want them, but they were simple farmers who had distanced themselves from him because he was gay. They had no desire to collect his explicit rubbish as they called it, so we kept them. It's their loss in the end. They're worth a lot of money now." She took a sip from her wine. "What about your parents? What do they do?"

"My parents are simple farmers," Nathalie said with a smirk on her face. "Very simple." She laughed at Lena's startled expression. "I know, you didn't expect that, did you?"

Lena shook her head. "I did not. And I didn't mean any offense by the simple reference. You know that, right?"

"No offense taken."

Lena gave her an apologetic smile. "Tell me about them."

"Well, they grow corn and potatoes amongst other crops, and they run a small chicken farm. For the eggs," she added. "My father loves his chickens more than life itself, and he could never kill them. Funny enough, his favorite food is fried chicken. I actually think he's in denial about the main ingredient of the dish. My mother makes it once a week and she buys it from one of the neighboring farms. They also have a shop where they sell farm food. You know, homemade bread, eggs, pies, vegetables, that kind of stuff. They get up at five every morning and they're in bed by eight. I used to feel sorry for them, but they love what they do, and they wouldn't want it any other way. Apart from that, they go to church every Sunday and play bingo in the community center twice a month."

"I suppose it's safe to say that you turned out quite the opposite of your parents," Lena said.

Nathalie laughed. "Yeah. I never had much interest in farming as a child. I always wanted to get away, live in a big city and do something totally different with my life. And I did, I suppose." She paused. "I have no regrets. In fact, I'm proud of what I've achieved. My perspective has changed over the years, though. I never understood how my parents could live like that, but I get them now. I get why they're happy. Their life is calm, predictable. They enjoy what they do, and the community supports them despite the big supermarkets that are taking over small retailers nowadays. They're proud people. I've offered to help them out financially a couple of times, so that they could enjoy an early retirement, but they still refuse to take my money."

"Good for them," Lena said. "And you? Are you still enjoying your simple life here?"

Nathalie laughed. "I am. I'm not sure I'd call it simple, since I'm staying in an eight-bedroom villa, but it sure is uncomplicated. I couldn't do it forever, though. I need to work eventually, otherwise I'd go crazy." She sighed. "I still haven't found any interesting vacancies and I'm not sure if I'm ready to go back to Chicago in six weeks. I love it here.

But then again, maybe some time at my parents' farm will do me good..."

"Or you could extend your stay in France?" Lena suggested. "I've got a new tenant coming, but it's only a three-week booking, so the house will be free again after that." She hesitated. "You're welcome to stay in the annex with me for those weeks."

Nathalie met Lena's gaze, her eyes darkening. "You mean, you wouldn't mind me living in the annex with you?" She pursed her lips. "But you only have one bed, right?"

"Right." Lena gave her a broad smile, causing Nathalie's heart rate to accelerate at the sight of her dimples. "It's a king size bed, and I can keep my hands to myself, if that's what you're worried about. Or one of us could sleep on the couch? It's comfortable enough."

"No, I'm not worried," Nathalie stammered. *On the contrary.* "It's just very generous of you to offer. You haven't known me that long."

"Maybe I don't want you to leave so soon either." Lena's reply was direct and honest, and now, the unapologetic desire in her eyes was impossible to ignore.

Nathalie blushed, but she didn't shy away. "Okay. I'll think about it," she whispered.

26

"Would you like to go for a walk before we head back?" Lena asked. "Antibes is beautiful." She took the two takeaway coffees from the server and thanked him for his service, discreetly handing him a generous tip.

"I think someone is keen," Nathalie looked down at Gumbo. He started wagging his tail when he realized they weren't going back in the car and sprinted ahead of them, following the narrow footpath along the sea.

They wandered through the old town of Antibes, browsing the covered farmers' market, pretty boutiques, galleries and second-hand bookshops. The charming jumble of old buildings built up against the hill along the coastline drew Nathalie to take pictures each time they turned a corner. The smell of fresh bread and Camembert made her mouth water when they strolled along the market, and she bought enough cheese to get her through the rest of the month.

"That's the Picasso museum," Lena said, pointing at a

tower that rose above the town. "He used to live around here. Some old restaurants still have his original paintings. He used to trade them for meals when he was out of money."

"Wow. There does seem to be an exciting art scene here. There are galleries everywhere."

"Yeah." Lena stopped in front of a gallery window. "It's a great town for young artists to start their career." She took Nathalie's hand and led them inside the space that was shared by four graduates, as advertised on the door. Inside, she retracted her hand, but in a reflex, Nathalie tightened her hold. *Shit. I didn't mean to do that.* Lena looked down at their hands and smiled, leaning in against Nathalie's ear.

"Whatever makes you happy, Nat," she whispered.

Nathalie tried to stay calm as they walked past the paintings and sculptures, but her heart was almost beating out of her chest at the feeling of Lena's hand wrapped around hers. She hardly noticed the work on the walls or on the floor in front of her, consumed by the joy of being so close to Lena.

"Which one's your favorite?" she asked, trying to sound like she was genuinely interested in the exhibition. She wanted to be interested, and she would have been, on any other day, in any other company. But now, her mind was consumed by Lena, and she was unable to focus on the work.

"I like this one," Lena said, pointing at an abstract bronze statue. "I think it will look nice in the garden, next to the roses." She reached into her back pocket and handed her card to the gallery manager. "Could you ask the artist to contact me please? I love that statue, but I'm thinking two might look better than one. Perhaps he could do me another one? It doesn't have to be the same, of course. Whatever he thinks works with this one will be fine."

"Sure. I'll let him know." The woman smiled at them and held open the door as they left. Nathalie waited for Lena to let go of her hand, but she didn't. Instead, they walked down towards the beach together, following Gumbo through the old streets in a comfortable silence.

THE SMALL DOG-FRIENDLY beach was busy, and Gumbo couldn't believe his luck when he spotted one of his best friends by the shore. Nathalie and Lena sat down on a bench, watching him chase his friend through the water.

"You have a great life, Lena." Nathalie said. "You live close to the beach, you do whatever the hell you like, and you love your job." Lena put an arm behind Nathalie, resting it on the bench.

"I'm pretty happy," she said. "I know I've been lucky. My life could have turned out a whole lot different if I'd stayed in New York." Her hand reached for Nathalie's hair and she twirled a blonde lock around her finger. Nathalie shivered and closed her eyes for a brief moment. The light touch felt heavenly, and the warm sensation that spread down to her core made her crave more. Lena moved her hand down to Nathalie's shoulder and pulled her closer against her. "But you don't have much to complain about either, Nat."

"That's because I don't have much in general," Nathalie said in a shaky voice. "No job, no relationship, no children, no home." Lena's body felt warm and soothing. She sighed. "Apart from money. I have money, so that's a start."

"Look at it from the positive side." Lena turned to Nathalie and met her eyes. "You've got a blank canvas and you can paint it any way you like. It's a fresh start, a whole new beginning and you've got no one to answer for but yourself. If you try something and you don't like it, you can paint over it, no big deal. Sometimes you have to try different things to find out what it is you really want."

Nathalie couldn't help but wonder if Lena was referring to her job search or her sexuality. "You're right," she said. "I haven't thought of it like that." She hesitated, looking down at Lena's mouth. "I suppose I should open myself up to new experiences." There was a silence, and for a moment, Nathalie forgot everything around her. The beach, the people, the noise... it all blended into one big blur as she focused on the beautiful woman beside her and her lips. And God, did she long for those lips. *Kiss me, damn it! I need to know how it feels.* At that moment, Gumbo jumped up against her legs with a stick in his mouth. She bent over and took the stick that was now in the sand in front of her, releasing herself from Lena's grip.

"Here you go, boy." She stood up and threw it as far as she could, but Gumbo wasn't impressed. He sat down next to the stick, waiting for her to run over and throw it again.

"Go and play with your friend, Gumbo," Lena shouted. "Leave us in peace for a minute." They laughed at his wide eyes and his tongue that was dangling out of his mouth, pulled up into an insane smile. Reluctantly, she stood up too, and walked over to him for a game of fetch.

27

Let the beef simmer on a low heat for about ninety minutes. Nathalie lifted the lid on the heavy cast-iron pan as she read the recipe. So far, cooking had been a lot harder than she had anticipated, and she'd been doubting herself every step of the way. Apart from that, the mess that came with trying to do anything food related was simply astonishing. During a bout of panic in the middle of the day, she had tried to order pre-made food to be delivered, but all the local restaurants were fully booked with orders. Apparently, she wasn't the only one in a food panic. She took the bread dough out of the fridge, removed the plastic wrap and poked it. She had no idea whether it was ready to go into the oven or not. Why did they always make it so complicated in recipes? What did 'slight bounce' even mean? Why not just say; 'The dough should feel like an older woman's saggy tits', or 'The dough should feel like your thigh after a night of heavy drinking'? At least she would know if she was on the right track. She tried to arrange the dough into a round shape, put it in the oven and said a prayer for a successful outcome. *Why did I think cooking would be a good idea? This is going to be a disaster.* She looked around the kitchen, not sure if it was too early to start on the salad. Maybe laying the table would be a better call. Instant results always made her feel better. Nathalie covered the wooden table on the patio with a white cloth and laid it with plates, cutlery and glasses. Then she unpacked the flowers she'd bought at the market and divided them over three vases which she spaced evenly on the table. In between, she placed salt and pepper grinders and small bowls of olives. At least she'd been smart enough to buy them. *If only I'd bought the bread too, or everything for that matter.* Nathalie hadn't been able to concentrate on anything all day. Her flirtatious conversations with Lena were all she could think about. Why hadn't Lena kissed her yet? She wanted to, Nathalie was sure of that. She could feel the tension between them growing, the more time they spent together. Was Lena waiting for her to make the first move? She took a step back and inspected the table setting. It looked respectable, but she'd forgotten to buy more candles, after using up the ones in the house. She searched the cupboards in the hallway and the living room but didn't manage to find any. There was a funny smell coming from the pan on the stove. Perhaps that was the caramelization they mentioned in the recipe, she thought, although technically, that should have happened in the early stages, when she browned the onions. She read through the recipe one more time. *Leave the lid on and let the beef simmer on a low heat for about ninety minutes.*

Does that mean I can't take the lid off to check? Just in case, she left it on and searched for her salad ingredients, wondering why the hell she was able to close multi-million-dollar deals, but wasn't capable of cooking a simple meal.

28

Lena wiped her muddy hands on her overalls and sat down on the edge of the fountain in the Royal Gardens of Monaco. She calculated their progress against the day's schedule, which entailed re-scaping the flower beds. It had taken her longer to design the layout of the garden than it would to create it, with three rejects on the first drafts. But that was nothing new. Her clients always had a certain picture in their minds, and if she wanted to convince them it would be better otherwise, it was a long process of towing and throwing, especially with clients as big as the princely family. But all the hard work had been worth it, and now they were in the exciting phase of bringing it all to life. Lena was loving every minute of it. Despite their setback of overnight rainfall - there had been a lot of that lately - it was coming along nicely. The driveway was down, the base of the fountain on the small roundabout, which would be the focal point of the garden, was laid, and the trees were planted. There was still a lot to do, but she could already imagine how it would look on the day of the grand opening. It was sunny, and despite the sea breeze in Monaco, she'd been sweating all afternoon. Lena had twenty people on site today, only the best of the best. It hadn't been hard, finding good landscapers. Besides the fact that it paid well, anyone would jump at the chance to put the Royal Gardens on their CV. Technically, she was only supposed to oversee the work, but she could never resist getting stuck in herself. There was something about soil on her hands that made her feel great, but it also seemed to earn her respect from her employees. Yard work was still perceived to be a male occupation, even in a country as liberal as France, and she didn't want them to think she was some stuck-up designer who never got her hands dirty.

"Water, guys?" she yelled. She walked over to her car and pulled a cooler from her trunk.

"Thanks Lena." Oscar, one of her loyal freelancers, walked over to her and grabbed a bottle. He drank half and poured the other half over his head, shaking the water out of his hair. Then he burped as he threw the empty bottle back in the trunk. "Are you leaving early today? That's the second time this week. Something special going on?" he asked when Lena pulled a packet of wet wipes out of her front compartment. Due to the lack of showers in most venues, she always used them to remove the worst dirt before getting in her car at the end of the day.

"Yeah. Nathalie, my tenant, is having a dinner party tonight. She invited me. Do you mind keeping an eye on things and sign off the hours at the end of the shift?"

"Sure, no problem." Oscar took the pile of timesheets she handed him, laid them on the edge of the fountain and weighed them down with a brick. "So, let me get this straight," he said with a puzzled look. "Your tenant is hosting in your house and you're invited?"

"Something like that." Lena grimaced. "I only just

admitted it was my house. She found out through someone in the village. Before that, she thought I was the caretaker."

Oscar howled. "Why on earth would you tell her that? And where the hell are you sleeping? In a tent?"

Lena shrugged. "I'm in the annex. I did it up last year, so it's got all the comforts of the main house. It's just a bit smaller. My previous tenants told me they weren't comfortable with me living on the premises, so I decided to tell the next tenant I was the caretaker." She paused, chewing on her lip. "But I didn't expect us to get close. Anyway, we've had a good talk, and we're fine now."

"So, you're close, huh? Is she hot?" Oscar asked, wiggling his eyebrows.

Lena pulled a couple of wet wipes out of the packaging and cleaned her hands.

"She's my tenant, Rob. It doesn't matter if she's hot."

Oscar grinned. "Yeah, you just keep telling yourself that."

29

"Hey, you're early!" Nathalie looked Lena up and down when she stepped out of the car. The vehicle didn't seem to match her outfit today, but there was something very attractive about that. "You... you look..."

"Dirty?" Lena said.

Nathalie shook her head. "No, I didn't mean that. I mean, I like it. You look good." She put her hands on her hips and let her eyes wander over Lena's toned arms and torso, only covered by a stained, white tank top. Her overall was pulled down, and the sleeves were tied around her waist, securing it low on her hips.

Lena arched an eyebrow, locking her eyes with Nathalie's.

"Thanks," she said, brushing off her mud-stained overall. "You have eclectic taste, apparently."

Nathalie watched her wipe her face, leaving a dirt mark under her left eye. In a reflex, she licked her thumb, took a step forward and cleaned it off.

Lena's eyes darkened at the contact. When Nathalie

retracted her hand, she looked over at the annex as if searching for an escape. "I need a shower. I'll be quick. Do you need help with the food?"

"No, I think I'm good." Nathalie said, still staring at her. "I forgot to buy candles, though. Do you have any?"

"Yeah. Just give me twenty minutes and I'll get you as many candles as you want. I've got plenty."

"Jesus, what happened in here?" Lena looked around the kitchen, wide-eyed. There was a big pile of washing up in the sink, flour all over the kitchen counter, and on the floor. A trail of white footprints showed where Nathalie had spilled water and walked through it, up and down to the fridge. Besides that, something was seriously burning on the stove. She ran over to the pan and lifted the lid. Thick, dark smoke came out, filling the kitchen.

"Holy shit, it's on fire!" Nathalie yelled, jumping back when a flame shot out.

"What did you expect?" Lena took the pan off the hob, placed it on a chopping board and covered the burnt food with a wet towel. She opened the door and the windows. "It smells burnt, and by the looks of it, it's been crisping away for a while now." She turned to Nathalie, who looked like she was about to cry.

"Oh God. I messed up and they'll be here in two hours." Nathalie looked at her watch. "Should I cancel?" Lena shook her head. She felt sorry for Nathalie, standing there with a hand over her mouth, defeat written all over her face.

"Of course not. We'll figure something out." She gestured to the pan. "What were you trying to cook?"

"Boeuf bourguignon," Nathalie said in a thin voice. "The

recipe told me to cook it until it went dark in color. I thought it was supposed to look like that."

"Okay." Lena couldn't help but laugh. "Have you ever cooked before?"

Nathalie thought about the question, before slowly shaking her head. "Not in a while, no. I cooked pasta occasionally, when I was in University. And I know how to make an omelet. But apart from that, I haven't bothered, mostly because I didn't have the time. And it's not unheard of to never cook when you live in Chicago. There are decent restaurants and takeout places on every street corner." She sighed. "I think I might have overestimated my cooking abilities."

"Don't beat yourself up," Lena said, opening the oven. She took out the bread that Nathalie had made and placed it onto another chopping board. She poked it, broke a piece off and smiled. "Your bread, on the other hand, is absolutely perfect. Do you have any idea how hard it is to make good bread?" She laughed. "Okay, the shape might resemble a penis, so it doesn't necessarily look appetizing to me, but it tastes great." She winked at Nathalie, who seemed to appreciate the compliment.

"You're right. It does look like a penis." Nathalie joined Lena at the kitchen counter. She bent over the bread and frowned. "How the hell did that happen? I'm pretty sure it was round when I put it in. I made it round... Oh well, at least it smells and tastes like bread," she said, taking a bite. "I'll just cut it up." She looked up at Lena. "So, what do we do now?"

Lena opened the fridge and inspected the vegetable drawers. They were empty. Nathalie nodded towards the bowl of salad she had made.

To Lena, it looked like a five-year-old had chopped the

ingredients, but she didn't comment on it. It would be fine as a side-dish. "Have you ever lit a barbeque before?" she asked.

Nathalie shook her head. "No, I haven't."

"Okay... I'll do it then. Do you know how to use that?" Lena pointed to the blender on the corner of the kitchen counter.

Nathalie shook her head again and sighed. "Just tell me what to do and I'll give it my best."

"Okay, wait here. Don't touch anything." Lena ran outside and came back five minutes later with garlic, parsley, basil, thyme and fennel. She also had a bag of potatoes under her arm and a larger-than-life zucchini, shaped like a horse-shoe. "Fresh from the garden," she said, handing everything to Nathalie. "Rinse the potatoes and wrap them in aluminum foil. Then, put these herbs in the blender with olive oil and a bit of sea salt until it's a semi-smooth mixture. Not too smooth," she added. "We want to see what the ingredients are, okay? Just keep your finger on the red button until it all blends. You can't go wrong. After that, you can cut up the zucchini in bite-sized chunks, sprinkle them in salt and let the moisture drain out. I'll go and get some fish from my freezer."

"Thank you. I think I can do that." Nathalie smiled, relieved that Lena had taken charge. She turned on the tap and started rinsing the potatoes.

AN HOUR LATER, the potatoes were on the barbeque, alongside a couple of herb-stuffed red breams and zucchini kebabs. Lena had added crystal glasses, a wine cooler on a marble stand and lots of tall candles on crystal chandeliers to the table.

"Are you sure it's okay if I use all this stuff?" Nathalie asked.

"Absolutely. That's what it's here for." Lena nudged her. "I think we did a pretty good job together, don't you?" To her surprise, Nathalie flew around her neck.

"Thank you, thank you, thank you," she said, squeezing her tight. "You're a life-saver."

Lena closed her eyes at the close contact. Nathalie's face in her neck felt like angels were breathing on her skin, and she shivered when Nathalie's fingers grazed her back.

"You're welcome." She forced herself to take a step back before she lost all self-control. "Do you need to get ready?"

Nathalie looked down at her flour-covered summer dress and grimaced. There was herb pesto on her neck and there was still dough under her fingernails.

"Yeah. I think that might be a good idea." She took off her apron and threw it over the edge of the chair. "Would you mind letting them in when they arrive?"

30

Nathalie rushed out at the sound of someone screaming, but relaxed when she realized it was Brenda, expressing her delight with the garden and the table setting.

"Hey Brenda, hi Samantha." She gave them both two kisses on the cheek. "Thanks for coming." She gestured to Lena. "You guys remember Lena from last week, right?"

"We sure do." Samantha accepted the glass of chilled white wine Lena handed to her and took Brenda's glass too. "Mum? Your wine." She tried to get her mother's attention, but Brenda had wandered off towards the pool.

"This is amazing," she yelled, looking over the garden and the pool. "You must be so proud, Lena."

"Thank you, I appreciate that," Lena said. "It's a lot of work though, keeping a place like this."

"I don't doubt that for a second." Brenda was panting when she returned to the terrace. "Do you mind if I have a peek inside?" She ignored her daughter, who was nudging her to calm down, and waltzed into the kitchen. Nathalie glanced at Lena and shot her an apologetic look.

"I'm sorry," she whispered. "Do you mind if I show them around?"

"Of course not," Lena said. "Go ahead, I'll wait for the others. And Nat?"

"Yes?"

"You look stunning in that dress." Nathalie smiled, blushing at the compliment.

"Thank you," she said. "You look great too." She was still smiling when she led Brenda and Samantha into the living room. Lena made her feel sensual in a way she'd never known, and she loved to feel Lena's eyes on her just as much as she loved looking at her in return. She'd bought a new dress for tonight, after carefully weighing off each outfit in the dressing room, wondering what Lena would think of them. The loose, peach colored dress was both sexy and bohemian, and she felt attractive wearing it.

"Nathalie?" Samantha's voice finally managed to penetrate Nathalie's conscience. She shook her head in apology.

"I'm sorry, I was lost in myself for a moment. What did you say?"

"I was just wondering who painted all those lovely pieces," Samantha said.

"Those are François'. He was Lena's grandfather's life partner." Nathalie looked up at the landscape above the fireplace that only consisted of horizontal streaks of color; green for the fields, and blue for the sky. Despite its simplicity, there was something very complex about the depth in the hues that drew her in each time she looked at it.

"They're beautiful," Brenda said. "Oh, look at this, Samantha! Isn't this vase gorgeous?" Brenda was milling around like a puppy on a protein kick, touching every piece of furniture and art in the house.

"Mum, we're not in a museum," Samantha said,

lowering her voice. "This is Lena's home, have some respect."

"It's fine, don't worry." Nathalie turned when she heard voices behind her.

"Hello folks!" Graham and Sally, his wife, were in the doorway, waving.

"Hi guys. I'm so glad you made it." Nathalie greeted Graham and introduced herself to Sally before leading everyone back out to the terrace, where Marie-Louise had just arrived too. She was talking to Lena, admiring the garden.

The night was pleasant, with lots of laughter and interesting stories. Lena looked after the food, while Nathalie assisted her and refilled their glasses. They worked together seamlessly, and Nathalie thoroughly enjoyed herself. Everything felt so natural with Lena, even hosting a dinner together.

Alain arrived later, after having closed up his café. He handed Nathalie the Champagne and chocolate mousse he'd brought and immediately stole a seat next to Samantha.

"Ah! If it isn't the English rose who was sitting on my terrace." He kissed her hand. "I'm glad we meet again." Alain was on a roll, clearly trying to charm the hell out of Samantha. He leaned in closer, ignoring Lena's warning looks.

"So, tell me about yourself, Samantha. You seem smart, but you're also gorgeous. Those bright green eyes with that strawberry blonde hair, that's a powerful combination." He paused for dramatic effect. "I'm intrigued." He leaned in closer, brilliantly faking genuine interest while trying not to stare at her ample cleavage.

Samantha rolled her eyes. "I've been warned about you,"

she said. "And you're quite the charmer indeed. But you have no way of knowing I'm smart as we've never exchanged so much as a word." She turned back to her food, a small smile playing around her mouth.

"I'm only curious," Alain said, crossing a hand over his chest, producing his most enigmatic grin. "How can I not be? I mean, look at you. You're stunning."

"Somebody stop him," Lena mumbled against Nathalie's ear.

Nathalie giggled and took Lena's hand under the table. "Samantha doesn't seem to mind," she whispered back. "Look at her, she's beaming."

After a couple of drinks, someone finally worked up the courage to ask Marie-Louise about the parakeets in her hair. She had three in her top-knot tonight; a yellow one and two green ones, matching her green dress and sheer yellow wrap. She had attached vine leaves around the birds, giving the impression they were sitting in a tree.

"What's the story with the birds?" Samantha inquired, pointing at her head. "Are they real? They look real…"

Marie-Louise raised a hand to her head, stroked one of them and crossed herself. "They were my pets," she said, looking up as if expecting them to suddenly fly out of her hair. "My friends. The yellow one was Dillon. He was my first. I had him in a cage in my bedroom for a year, he was a present from my cousin in Lyon. But I felt sorry for him and decided to set him free. He didn't leave though, like birds normally would. He just stayed in the garden and became even tamer than he was before. I hand-fed him every morning and every night." Marie-Louise smiled, taking a sip from her wine. "I was worried he was lonely, so I got him two female friends." She pointed to her head again. "Dorine and Jaqueline left for a couple of weeks, but they both came back. It was like a miracle, these birds living in my garden, choosing to be there. I painted them for many years, especially Dillon. He would sit on the same branch for hours, chattering away as if he was talking to me." She sighed. "I was heartbroken when he died. I wanted to keep his memory alive, so I took a taxidermy course and tried to stuff him, but I didn't have the talent that my teacher had, and so I lost one of his eyes." She bent over for everyone to see Dillon's scruffy one-eyed face. Nathalie looked at Samantha, who was trying her hardest not to laugh.

"It's okay to laugh," Marie-Louise said with a smile. "I know it looks funny. Who wouldn't? Anyway, after Dillon, I stuffed all my birds when they died, and I got better at it." She looked around the table. "So, in case you were wondering if I kill them for hair pieces, no I don't. I have twenty-two stuffed parakeets and I loved every single one of them. I wear them on top of my head, so I feel close to them." She spread her arms to the group. "You must all think I'm crazy, but I don't care."

"We don't think you're crazy," Brenda shook her head. "A little bit eccentric, maybe. But certainly not crazy."

"I think it's sweet," Lena said. She looked over at Gumbo. "God knows, I might do the same if he…" She shook her head. "Never mind, I don't even want to think about that."

Sally looked startled. Her high-combed peroxide blonde coupe wiggled as she stared up at the parakeets.

"So, Sally, are you enjoying your time in France?" Nathalie asked in an attempt to make her feel more comfortable.

"Very much," Sally said, still a little taken aback by the taxidermy story. "I'm thinking about joining a tennis club for a couple of months, as Graham is doing his art class twice a week. I haven't played in fifteen years, but I'm willing to give it a try again." She looked at Graham and arched an eyebrow. "Graham says he wants me to meet new people but I've got the feeling he's trying to distract me from shopping."

Brenda laughed. "Yes, Graham's told us you love the shops in Cannes. Is there a sale on? I wouldn't mind taking a trip either."

That remark seemed to draw Sally's attention. "Oh yes. There's always a sale corner somewhere." Sally's eyes lit up as she lifted a purse from underneath her chair. "In fact, I bought a new bag this morning." She leaned over the table and lowered her voice. "Fifty percent off, Brenda. Grab your chance now or these will be gone."

Graham took the bag from her and examined it. It was made of pink crocodile leather and had a pink fur trim around the edges. "And how much did you pay for this monstrosity of a corpse after the fifty percent discount, Sally?" Graham's left eye was twitching, Nathalie noticed.

"Why don't you ask me how much I saved instead," she retorted with a proud smile.

Graham looked from his wife to the group, clearly regretting getting himself into a public discussion with his wife. He cleared his throat and turned to Sally.

"Alright, Sally. How much money did you save today?"

"Four-hundred Euros." Sally beamed. "It's a bargain, right? Imagine if I'd paid the full price?" She winked. "But I didn't, so basically, I saved us four-hundred Euros, Graham. We could rent a boat for that money." Brenda and Samantha stared at Sally in disbelief.

Graham was silent for a moment, clearly trying to compose himself.

"Let's talk about this when we get home," he said, letting the topic slide.

Sally rolled her eyes at him and turned her attention to

Nathalie and Lena, who were sitting opposite her. "So, how long have you guys been together?" she asked.

Nathalie and Lena chuckled, both a little bit tipsy from the wine.

"We're not a couple," Nathalie said. "I'm renting the house. Lena is the owner."

"Ah!" Sally looked puzzled. "I apologize, I thought you two were..."

"It's fine," Lena jumped in. "I can imagine what it looks like when you're invited to a dinner that two women are hosting together." She paused. "But no, Nathalie and I are just friends. Actually, it's her dinner but she made quite a mess of it so I decided to chip in." She gave Nathalie a teasing look and squeezed her hand under the table. "You should have seen her when I came home, she was covered in flour and the beef was on fire."

Nathalie nudged her.

"Easy tiger. You forgot to mention that I managed to make my own bread with no cooking experience at all. I think I should at least get some points for that." She blushed when Lena put an arm around her.

"Credit where credit's due. Your bread is great." Lena took a demonstrative bite of the bread next to her plate and laughed.

Marie-Louise observed them silently, smiling with a twinkle in her eye. "Well, you guys might not be a couple," she said, "but this house happens to have a history of gay couples. Lena's grandfather bought it from another male couple, before he moved in with his lover François, who was also one of my best friends." She held up her glass for Lena to refill it. "I remember it like it was yesterday, sitting here in this very same chair, alongside ten others, including your grandfather, François and yourself." She looked at Lena.

"You had just arrived here, and you were terribly shy, didn't speak a word of French. We all tried very hard to make you feel welcome."

Nathalie felt a sting of pity for Lena. She could picture her as she'd just arrived in a place where she didn't know the people or the language. Without thinking, her hand reached out to Lena's thigh under the table, and she squeezed it. Lena folded her hand over hers and held it there.

"It was the most surreal night of my life," Lena said, looking around the table. "Everyone thought I was shy, but really, I was simply trying to process the scene I'd been thrown into. There was my grandfather, openly holding hands with his partner. Then there was you, Marie-Louise. You were wearing some sort of vampire cape and your hair was pinned up into the shape of a unicorn horn." Lena held up a hand. "No offense, you looked amazing, but back then, I'd never seen anything like it. There was also a man wearing a white kaftan and a turban, if I remember correctly. I think he was a White Sikh, and there was a younger couple who had brought five poodles along. It was chaos." She laughed. "Add to that the fact that everyone was smoking weed and drinking absinthe after dinner, and that I came from an extremely strict and protected household where any sort of fun was sinful, well, let's just say that I needed some time to adjust."

"You adjusted fast though," Marie-Louise said. She turned to Nathalie. "After a couple of weeks, she was having basic French conversations with all of us and even flirting with the neighbor's nannies."

Nathalie laughed. "I don't doubt that for a second," she said, moving her hand further up Lena's thigh. She was feeling braver with each glass of wine, and simply couldn't resist touching her.

"Hey, I wasn't that bad," Lena said in defense. "I was just experimenting, trying to find my way in a new world of endless possibilities."

"What's it like for you living here now?" Graham asked.

Lena took a long drink from her wine and paused for a moment to think. "It's nice," she said. "Very different, but nice. I'm not my grandfather. I don't need an abundance of people in my life." She looked at Nathalie. "But it's been amazing having Nathalie here, and it feels great to have people around this table again." She looked up at the stars. "I wouldn't be surprised if my grandfather is looking down at us tonight, smiling in approval."

"Amen," Graham said, holding up his wineglass. "To you both, ladies. Thank you so much for your hospitality."

31

"That was fun," Nathalie said after everyone had left. "Thank you so much for everything, Lena. There wouldn't have been a dinner without your help."

"No problem, I had fun too," Lena said, piling up the plates. "Your friends are lovely, and it was great to have some quality time with Marie-Louise again. It's a shame we lost touch over the years." She carried the plates into the kitchen and put them next to the rest of the dishes that had been sitting there all night. "Why don't we forget about this for now, huh?" She gestured to the mess. "Let's have a nightcap by the pool instead, I'll help you clean up tomorrow."

"Sure." Nathalie folded up the tablecloth and put it on the kitchen counter. "I would love that." She was nervous but tried not to let it show. The wine had gone to her head and she felt like a teenager on her first date. There was no point denying the tension that had been hanging between them all night, and Nathalie was far beyond her breaking point now. If Lena kissed her tonight, she would kiss her back. And if she didn't kiss her, well, she'd probably be lying awake all night again, fantasizing about it.

"Pastis?" Lena asked, holding up a bottle with yellow liquid.

Nathalie studied the label. "I've never had it, but I'll try anything once."

"Anything?" Lena poured two tumblers with a smirk on her face.

Nathalie didn't answer. She took the glass from Lena, who held on to it for a fraction of a second too long.

"Come on," she said, beckoning Nathalie to follow her to the poolside.

They sat down on the edge of the pool and lowered their feet into the water. Nathalie felt a warm sensation in her throat, spreading all the way down to her toes as she drank her Pastis. It was strong but pleasant.

"It's good," she said. "Aniseed?"

Lena nodded. The light from the pool cast a glow on her face. It brought out her dark eyes, and when she smiled, Nathalie felt herself going weak. There was only so much she could take.

"I'm really glad you're here, Nat."

"Me too," Nathalie whispered. *Kiss me. Please kiss me.*

"Do you want to go for a swim?" Lena asked.

Nathalie looked at the dimly lit pool in the now dark garden, then fixed her gaze back on Lena. There was something in Lena's eyes that made her shiver with anticipation. Lena was hungry for her, and she knew it.

"Yeah." She hesitated. "I'll go and put on my bikini. I'll be right back."

Lena took her by her wrist when she was about to get up. "You don't have to." She smiled, biting her lip. "We could go skinny dipping? It's not like anyone's going to see us here."

"Oh... Okay." Nathalie nodded slowly. She tried to stay calm, but her body was doing its own thing. Lena's proposal filled her mind with thoughts she wasn't sure she could handle.

They stood up in silence, both far too aware of what the other was thinking. Lena pulled her shirt over her head and took off her shorts and boxers. She threw them onto one of the sun loungers and dove in. Nathalie's jaw dropped as she watched her reappear, stunned at the sight of Lena's small but full breasts, shimmering in the faint light. Naked, in the pool, she looked more beautiful than Nathalie could have ever imagined.

"Come on in, it's nice!" Lena waved from the far, shallow end of the pool.

Nathalie decided not to overthink it. She took off her dress and unclipped her bra at the back. She felt Lena's eyes on her as she let it drop to the ground. Then she removed her panties and dove in too. When she came up, Lena was right in front of her. There was a silence that seemed to last forever, but Nathalie didn't mind. She needed the time to process what was happening, and to deal with all the feelings that were jumbled up inside of her.

"You're perfect," Lena finally said. Her eyes stared deep into Nathalie's. There wasn't even a hint of a smile on her face, and Nathalie realized she'd never seen her this serious before. She watched Lena's chest heaving up and down, leaving ripples on the surface of the water. Her hair was slicked back, the water dripping down her face, and the light of the pool made her look like she was shimmering.

"You're perfect," Nathalie whispered in return. There was no wind, no noise, and Nathalie could hear Lena's heavy breathing, knowing that she was longing for her.

Lena took a step forward, bringing her face close to Nathalie's. "Then let's not waste any more time." She carefully pushed Nathalie into the corner. Nathalie took in a deep breath when she felt Lena's naked body pressed against hers, and a thigh between her legs. Lena put her arms around her, holding on to the edge. She pulled herself closer.

"Oh God," Nathalie whispered, her mouth close to Lena's. "I'm not sure if I can handle this." Lena tilted her head and brushed her lips against Nathalie's. She held them there, teasing her. Nathalie closed her eyes and moaned quietly, savoring the moment. She could feel Lena's breasts, tight against hers. Her heart was beating dangerously fast and Nathalie was hungry, every cell in her body craving for Lena, begging for her touch. She parted her lips and felt a jolt of pure delight shoot through her core when Lena's mouth took hers in a possessive kiss, her tongue dancing around Nathalie's. Nathalie closed her eyes and felt herself getting wet. If there was any reservation left in her, it melted at the sound of Lena's moaning. Her body convulsed, and she lowered her hands into the water, exploring Lena's shoulders, and her back. Holding on tight, she wrapped her legs around Lena's waist, kissing her like she'd never kissed anyone before. It was the most sensational thing. Arousal and excitement were racing through her veins, breathing life into her. Lena pulled out of the kiss and stared at her with a bewildered look on her face.

"Wow," she said, unable to keep her eyes off Nathalie's mouth.

"Yeah." Nathalie whispered. She still had her arms and legs wrapped around Lena and had no intention of letting go. "Do that again, please. Kiss me like you just kissed me."

"Are you sure?" Lena asked, her voice trembling. "Because as much as I'd love to take you in ways you can't even imagine..." She paused. "I don't want you to regret anything in the morning."

Nathalie shook her head. "No regrets. I promise."

A small smile formed around Lena's mouth, as she closed the distance between them and kissed Nathalie again, this time, without holding back. Her hands moved from the pool's edge to Nathalie's hair, combing it with her fingers while she deepened the kiss. She traced Nathalie's face and her jawline, down to the side of her neck and her shoulders until Nathalie moaned louder, grinding her center against Lena's stomach. Lena moved her hands down to Nathalie's waist and around her back towards her bottom. She cupped her behind with both hands and lifted her up higher, exposing her small breasts above the surface of the water. Nathalie steadied herself on the edge of the pool, leaning back on her elbows.

"God, you taste good," Lena whispered, pulling out of the kiss. She lowered her head to take an erect nipple into her mouth. Biting it softly, she drew a cry from Nathalie's mouth. Nathalie had surrendered. She was helpless, way past the point of no return, and she was ready to give herself to Lena with every fiber of her being. She threw her head back when Lena took her other nipple into her mouth, twirling her tongue around it.

"You have no idea what you're doing to me," Nathalie panted. "I want you, Lena." The rough surface of the limestone behind her was scratching her skin, but she didn't feel any pain, distracted by the throbbing between her legs. Nathalie held her breath when Lena took one hand off her behind and traced the inside of her thigh, still caressing her breasts with her tongue. She felt Lena's fingers move up higher, hesitating before touching her lightly between her legs.

Nathalie cried out, surprised by the impact Lena's touch had on her. "Oh God, yes."

Lena bit her lip and smiled, exploring Nathalie's center. Softly at first, then with firmer strokes as she brought her mouth against Nathalie's again, dampening her moans with her kiss. Nathalie pushed herself against Lena's hand when she entered her. She pulled out of the kiss and buried her face in Lena's neck, clinging on to her while her body tensed. She inhaled deeply, taking in Lena's scent and moaned as she exhaled. Lena pushed deeper and faster, taking her in a possessive hold. Nathalie let go of all restraints and moaned louder when she felt a warm, delicious feeling spread through her core. She gave herself over to Lena, let her take her, devour her breasts, her neck and finally her mouth, where she kissed her with such conviction that Nathalie forgot to breathe. There was nothing she could do but close her eyes and give in to the waves of ecstasy that shot through her like fireworks. She trembled all over while she dug her nails into Lena's back and pulled her in.

Lena held her tight and kissed her while Nathalie rode out her orgasm, finally relaxing in her grip.

Nathalie opened her eyes and sighed in amazement at the sight of the woman who she'd just had the best sex with in her life.

Lena was smiling, and she stared at her with such intensity, that Nathalie immediately felt another stir of arousal. "Would you like to see my bedroom?" She whispered, stroking Nathalie's cheek.

"Yes." Nathalie shivered at the touch. "I would love to see your bedroom." She took Lena's hand and followed her to the steps where they got out and shared a towel. They didn't speak as they slowly dried each other off, kissing and exploring in the process. Nathalie finally allowed herself to trace Lena's breasts, down to her waist and her stomach, marveling at the feeling of Lena's soft skin and hard nipples under her fingertips. She kissed her neck, felt the curves of Lena's hips, and the muscular tightness of her core as she let her hands wander over her body with a curiosity she could barely fathom. It was feminine, strong and smooth. And it felt so right.

Lena released herself from Nathalie's grip, her chest heaving up and down as she looked at her, aroused and bewildered. "Come on," she said.

Her bedroom in the annex was practical and simple, decorated with a white washed wooden wardrobe, a king size bed made up with white bedlinen, and a nightstand on each side. In the corner was a chesterfield chair with a pile of clothes on top. There was a large painting of a landscape above her bed, the predominant blue in it matching the curtains. Lena searched for a lighter and lit the candles on the nightstands. Her hair was wet and brushed back. Nathalie was captivated by the sight of her naked body when she walked over to her.

"Are you sure you're okay?" Lena asked.

Nathalie nodded. "Never been better."

"Good." Lena pulled off the towel that Nathalie had wrapped around her and threw it on the floor. "Because I'm not done with you yet." She gestured towards the bed. Nathalie let herself fall on top of the bedsheets and sank her head back into the pillows. She was shaking with anticipation when Lena crawled onto the bed and lowered herself on top of her with a thigh between her legs.

Nathalie gasped at the contact. "You feel so good," she whispered. "I want to..."

Lena kissed her again, hard and deep, silencing her while she hooked her arm under Nathalie's leg and spread her open. Nathalie moaned and closed her eyes when Lena pushed into her. She felt Lena's wetness against her own. It felt amazing, liberating. The warm sensation between her legs made her ache for more, and she spread her legs further and thrust into Lena, following her rhythm. Nathalie had never imagined that another woman would be able to take her like this, to own her and to send her to heights entirely new to her. Lena was sexy and confident. She took control and she took what she wanted, moving faster as she pulled out of the kiss, looking down at Nathalie. Nathalie could tell she was close by the way her breathing had accelerated. Her pupils were dilated, and her lips parted. She moaned quietly.

"Don't stop, Lena," Nathalie pleaded, begging her with her eyes. Lena was so intuitive, as if she knew exactly what Nathalie wanted. She felt another orgasm growing, building up inside of her until she couldn't hold it back any longer. Lena thrust into her hard rubbing their cores together as they both climaxed. Nathalie closed her eyes and let go when her body exploded into a million tiny sparkles of heavenly bliss. They lay still, breathing fast. Nathalie stared up at the ceiling, her eyes wide.

"Are you okay?" Lena asked. She wiped the hair from Nathalie's forehead and pressed a soft kiss between her eyebrows. Nathalie nodded, still clinging on to her. Their legs and arms were entangled, and to Nathalie, it felt like their souls were too. As if everything had fallen into place, and every decision she'd made in her life, good or bad, was just right, because it had led her here, to this moment, with Lena. How could she feel so close to someone she'd only known for a couple of weeks? And how could she feel like nothing else mattered, like lying here with Lena was everything and more?

"Do you have to ask?" She pulled Lena's face down and gave her a lingering kiss. "Why didn't we do this sooner?"

"Because you were straight," Lena said, smiling. "Maybe not as straight as you thought you were, but still..."

"I guess that's a fair statement."

They rolled on to their sides, facing each other. Nathalie felt relaxed, and she was tired for the first time in weeks. She snuggled closer against Lena with an arm and a leg draped over her. When Lena took her in her arms, something broke inside of her. The tenderness that Lena held her with. The emotions, the connection and the passion. It was something she hadn't felt in a long time, in fact, never, to this extent, and it suddenly hit her how much she'd missed intimate contact, how lonely she'd been. She tried to stop herself from crying, but it was too late. A tear trickled down her cheek, landing on Lena's wrist.

"Hey, don't cry," Lena said, stroking her face. "Did I say something wrong?"

Nathalie shook her head. "No, I'm sorry, I didn't mean to cry." She sniffed and wiped her eyes. "I'm just happy, I guess. God, you must think I'm an idiot."

"No." Lena smiled and kissed her forehead. "I think you're amazing." Nathalie buried her face in Lena's neck. She could feel her heart pumping in a steady beat. It was comforting, and it made her sleepy. The sound of the raindrops that had started to fall on the roof became louder and more frequent, until it poured. Nathalie had always hated rain, but tonight, the sound of it was soothing.

"Lena?" she mumbled.

"Yeah?"

"Can I stay here tonight?"

32

"Gumbo, stop licking my face," Lena mumbled, still half asleep. Gumbo stopped for a second, then decided he wasn't going to be told what he could or couldn't do. "Seriously Gumbo, stop it. You're going to wake her up." She opened her eyes and gave Gumbo a warning look. Nathalie was sleeping on top of her. It felt good, and she didn't want her to go. It had been years since Lena had woken up with someone she wanted to be with, and she'd almost forgotten how great it was. Nathalie's weight on top of her seemed to have some kind of calming effect, like she was drugged with oxytocin and quite possibly hooked. Lena felt blissfully happy and she didn't want to get up, not even for a coffee. Lying there with Nathalie was too good to give up just yet. She pushed Gumbo away and sighed as she put her arms around the sleeping woman on top of her. Nathalie stirred and moved her hand through Lena's hair, burying her face in her neck like she had so many times the previous night.

"Shhh... it's okay, go back to sleep," Lena whispered.

Nathalie giggled underneath the cover. "I was only

pretending to be sleeping," she said in a hoarse voice. I've been awake for a while but if you want me to move, I'll move." She yawned. "But it feels so nice."

Lena smiled and took her into a tighter hold. "No, I don't want you to move."

Gumbo, however, had other plans. As soon as he realized Nathalie was awake, he jumped on top of her and started licking her face too.

Nathalie laughed. "Oh my God, is this how you wake up every morning?" She turned her head to face him and before she knew it, his tongue was making its way up her nostrils. "Stop it, you silly dog!" She moved off Lena and sat up next to her in bed, trying to fence off the overexcited terrier. "I think he wants to go out in the garden. Can I let him out?"

"Sure." Lena said. "As long as you come back." She watched Nathalie jump out of bed and walk into the kitchen to open the door for Gumbo. She was still naked, and she looked even more stunning in the light of day. Her sleepy face, the way she moved her hips when she walked, the sound of her laughter coming from the kitchen... *I'm in over my head. How the hell did this happen?*

"Do you want a coffee?" Nathalie shouted from the doorway.

"Sure. Do you need help?" Lena heard cupboards open and close.

"No, I'm fine, I think I can manage."

A LITTLE LATER, Nathalie came back with two cappuccinos. "So, you took the good coffee maker and left the old one in the main house, huh?"

Lena grinned. "You mean I took *my* good coffee maker?"

"Okay, fair enough." Nathalie handed her a cup and got back into bed. "So…" she said. "Here we are."

Lena nodded and shot her an amused look. "Yep. Here we are. And that's what people say when they're uncomfortable."

"I'm not uncomfortable," Nathalie leaned back into the pillows and took a sip from her coffee. "In fact, I was the most comfortable I've ever been until Gumbo started sticking his tongue in places it doesn't belong."

Lena laughed. "I'm glad to hear that," she said. "Because I was the most comfortable I've ever been too." She hesitated. "So, no regrets?"

Nathalie shook her head. "No regrets, but I already told you that last night, before you did all those amazing things to me." She smiled, put her coffee cup on the bedside table and buried her head in her hands. "Oh God, I can't stop smiling. I don't even recognize myself."

"You don't need to stop smiling. Your smile is gorgeous," Lena lowered her voice. "I'll let you in on a little secret. I can't stop smiling either."

Nathalie draped herself back over Lena and looked up at her. "Yeah. I've noticed. And I like your dimples. They've been making me doubt my place on the spectrum ever since I first saw you."

Lena chuckled. "Oh yeah?" She put an arm around Nathalie and pulled her closer. "Have you figured out where you are on the spectrum yet?"

"I'm pretty sure I'm on your side now," Nathalie said. She pressed her lips against Lena's and everything she had felt the night before came straight back, making her ache for Lena all over again. Lena deepened the kiss, tracing her fingers across Nathalie's back and down to her bottom.

Nathalie hesitated when she finally pulled out of the

kiss and stared into Lena's dark eyes. "I want you to teach me how to touch you," she said, her cheeks turning rosy. She'd been awake for hours, wondering how she would bring up the subject.

"You're blushing," Lena teased her.

"Of course, I'm blushing. This isn't easy for me." Nathalie gave her a playful nudge. "But I want to know. So, show me, please."

"Okay." Lena's face turned more serious. "If you insist. But I can assure you, that any way you touch me will send me right over the edge." She took Nathalie's hand and pulled it in between them, before slowly bringing it down to the strip of hair between her legs.

Nathalie let her fingers run through the soft curls, her hand trembling. When Lena directed her hand lower, she took in a quick breath at the wetness she felt between Lena's legs. It felt silky and warm as she ran a careful finger down and back up, tracing her center. *She wants me. Oh God, she wants me.* Lena gasped when Nathalie's fingers touched her most sensitive spot, and she pushed down her hand, moving it in circular motions. Nathalie watched Lena sigh in pleasure when she removed her hand, leaving only Nathalie's fingers there. Nathalie couldn't keep her eyes away from Lena's face as she continued the circling motions, slow and steady. The way Lena moved underneath her, threw her head back, closed her eyes and licked her lips... It was a beautiful sight.

"Yeah, like that," Lena moaned, arching her back. Nathalie lowered herself on top of her hand in between them and kissed her softly. When Lena moaned louder, she deepened the kiss, suddenly overcome by a sense of power. Pleasuring Lena was an amazing sensation, and one that sent her into whole new heights. Lena was breathing fast now, lifting her hips as Nathalie lowered her fingers. She hesitated, unsure of what she wanted her to do.

Lena turned her head and placed her mouth against Nathalie's ear. "Fuck me, Nathalie," she whispered.

Nathalie's lips parted, and she closed her eyes at the words, a quiet moan passing her lips. She felt Lena's wet warmth around her fingers when she entered her. She moved into her, deep, slow and steady, losing herself as she listened to the sounds that made her go weak in every limb. Paying close attention to Lena's reaction, she cupped her center with the palm of her hand and pushed down on her clit as she moved in and out of her.

Lena pulled her in and wrapped her legs around Nathalie's waist, begging for more.

"Oh God, yes. That's so..." Lena took in a quick breath and held it as she climaxed. Nathalie could feel her orgasm as she kept her fingers inside her, marveling at the eye-opening sensation of pleasuring another woman. She smiled when Lena opened her eyes and let out a deep sigh.

"Was that okay?" She asked, before pressing a kiss to Lena's mouth.

Lena looked up at her and chuckled. "Are you seriously asking me that?" She turned them around, so she was on top, and traced Nathalie's jawline with a huge grin on her face. "You, Nathalie Kingston, are very, very talented."

33

Nathalie bent over the car door and gave Lena another long kiss. Lena had been trying to get to work all morning but each time they started kissing, they were unable to stop themselves from taking it further.

She pouted as she started the engine. "I don't want to leave right now, but it's best if I'm on site while they do the planting," she said. "It's a crucial stage and I don't want anyone to make mistakes."

"Of course." Nathalie stepped back, allowing Lena to reverse. "I'll see you in a couple of days." She blew her a kiss and waved, reminding herself to keep her mouth shut, so she wouldn't let anything corny slip.

Lena waited for the gates to open and looked over her shoulder at Nathalie.

"Hey Nat?"

"Yes?"

"Can I take you out for lunch when I'm back?"

Nathalie's face broke into a huge smile while she shielded her eyes from the sun. "I would love that."

"Great. I can't wait." Lena beeped the car horn before she drove off with Gumbo on her lap.

Nathalie stayed in the driveway until the gates had closed, missing her already. Her head was spinning from the all-consuming lovemaking the previous night and that morning. Her legs were still shaky, and her restless core kept reminding her that everything was different now. It was only early afternoon, but the overload of entirely new feelings forced her to open a bottle of wine to calm herself down. She poured herself a glass of Chablis and walked over to the pool where she sat down on the edge with her feet in the water. Nathalie had no idea what to do with herself. Drive into town? Read? Paint? She didn't really feel like doing anything and was quite happy to just sit there, reliving her steamy encounter with Lena in the pool. Their first kiss had been mind-blowing, just like every other kiss after that. Lena's touch had been electrifying, her voice soothing and sexy. Nathalie closed her eyes and shivered at the thought of Lena's naked body pressed against hers in the pool. She took a long drink from her wine, stood up and removed her clothes. It felt sensual, standing there with the soft breeze caressing her skin. She turned to the south, allowing the sun to warm her naked body and stretched out before diving into the pool.

LATER THAT DAY, Nathalie's phone rang for the first time in weeks. She reluctantly reached over, rummaging through her purse. She hesitated when she saw the name on the screen, but knew that Jack would keep on ringing. He wasn't one to let things linger.

"Jack?"

"Hey Nathalie." There was a pause. "How are you doing?"

"I'm good." Nathalie swallowed hard at the sound of his voice. It wasn't that she missed him or regretted the divorce. It was the reminder of all the years she'd wasted that was hard. She'd invested her time, energy and love into something that would be reduced to nothing more than the batch of money they were about to discuss, and that was a sad thought. *Trade in your marriage and your life's work and get cash in return.* By the end of the day, she'd have a lot of it.

"Are you calling to discuss the transfer of the buy-out?" Jack was quiet, but Nathalie knew he was nodding on the other side of the line.

"Yeah. It's all done. The money should be in your account at the end of the day." He chuckled. "You'll be a multi-millionaire by five o'clock."

"Right." Nathalie said. The thought of that didn't even excite her very much. "Will the company be okay?" She knew she didn't have to ask. Greentech would be okay, she'd spent weeks slaving over forecasts and potential scenarios to make sure all shareholders were comfortable with the arrangement.

"Yeah. I think so," Jack mumbled. "Everyone misses you here. I'm about to hire a new CFO. The board is worried he might be a softie." He chuckled. "But he seems right for the job."

"And Darla?" Nathalie still felt sick, saying his new girlfriend's name out loud. "Are you guys still together?"

"We are. We're good." Jack paused. "Listen, Nathalie. I'm sorry about everything. I messed up and I still wake up every day with guilt weighing heavily on my gut, knowing how much I hurt you."

Nathalie closed her eyes, appreciating one of the rare

apologies he'd ever given her. But that was only because he rarely messed up. Jack was one of the kindest men she'd ever known and, despite the fact that he had ruined their marriage, she still liked him as a person.

"But you're happy, right?" she asked.

"Yes. I am."

"Well, then you didn't mess up. You did the right thing." She cleared her throat. "Any more news on the apartment?"

"We've got a bid," Jack said. "That's another reason I'm calling you. I sent you an email, but I wasn't sure if you were checking it daily, with you being in France and all." Nathalie heard the rustling of paperwork on the other side of the line. "One point two million. That's their final bid." Jack waited for a reply, but knew Nathalie needed time to think. They knew each other so well. "I know it's not the one point three," he continued, "but it's more than we expected to get at such short notice."

"Fine. Take it, I'm in." Nathalie said.

"Are you sure?" Jack sounded surprised.

"Yes. I'm sure. Take it, I trust you to deal with it." There was an awkward silence.

"How is France?" Jack finally asked. "What are you doing out there? Interviews?"

"No. I'm renting a place in the south, near Cannes. I spend most of my time reading and painting. I'm doing a watercolor course. It's relaxing."

Jack laughed. "You? Reading and painting? What's the next thing? Are you thinking of joining the surfing community? What have you done to my wife?"

Nathalie shook her head, rolling her eyes at his remark. "I'm not your wife anymore, Jack." She paused, trembling at the thought of what she was about to say out loud. "I've also spent some time making love to a beautiful woman." She waited for a reply, but Jack was silent. It was a dig, sure. But she wanted him to know that she'd moved on too, that she wasn't just sitting around being miserable, missing him. "Jack, are you there?"

"I'm here," Jack said in a thin voice. "Are you serious, Nathalie?"

"Uhuh." Nathalie got great joy out of trying to sound casual, even though she was trembling on the phone. It was the first time she'd said it out loud. Admitted that she was into women, or at least into Lena. And the person she'd just admitted it to, was no other than her ex-husband. She couldn't help but smile because it felt so good.

"What are you telling me, Nathalie? That you've suddenly turned gay overnight too? Are you having some kind of breakdown?" Jack paused. "Should I be worried?"

"No, Jack. I'm fine. In fact, I'm better than ever." Nathalie decided it was time to end the call. She would leave him hanging with tons of unanswered questions to brood over. Not because she wanted revenge, but she couldn't deny that his infidelity had hurt her confidence, and there was no harm in surrounding herself with a bit of mystery. "I have to go now," she said. "Give me a call if there are any more developments on the apartment, will you? Bye now." She'd hung up before he had the chance to get another word in.

34

"Let's set up here, guys." Marie-Louise parked her vintage Volkswagen van along the side of the road, next to a violet field just outside Tourrettes-sur-Loup. The van looked like an old hippie bus, with flowers painted all over the sides, surrounding the logo of *Galerie Valbonne*. "I hope you didn't forget to bring your blue paint."

"This feels like a school trip," Brenda said as she jumped out of the van with bags full of utensils. "But much more fun."

Nathalie followed her course mates into the blue field. It was early morning, and although most of them had complained about the ungodly hour, it had all been worth the drive. They had packed a picnic too, prepared for a long day ahead. Marie-Louise had told them to bring sunscreen and caps or hats to protect them from the sun in the open fields. Brenda and Samantha had taken the dress code to a whole new level, with big floppy summer hats, decorated with leaves and fresh flowers. They looked great together, walking towards the rising sun. Nathalie had seen a shift in both of them as the weeks had passed. They had started to dress differently. Perhaps bohemian was a good way to describe their new-found look, Nathalie thought. The floaty floral summer dresses were for sale in every boutique in the area, and they had embraced the style, flaunting their tans and their new bangs after a recent visit to the hairdresser. Graham wore an LA Lakers cap and a matching purple t-shirt. His arms were white from the thick layer of sunscreen he had applied in the van. Cherie was quiet as always, casually dressed in a black cap and a grey tracksuit.

Although the group couldn't have been more different from her, Nathalie had enjoyed getting to know them better. Cherie still didn't say very much, but she was always sweet and helpful during class.

The low sun skimmed the violet flower roof, creating the perfect scene for a painting. Nathalie took a deep breath, looking out over the fields that seemed to stretch out in an endless sea of purple and blue.

"Toilet paper is in the van," Marie-Louise yelled, breaking the magic moment for everyone who stood there, focused on the scene in front of them. "If you need to go, run over to the woods." She pointed in the direction of the forest that was at least a ten-minute walk from where they stood.

They set up in a semi-circle, the same way they always did in the gallery garden. Marie-Louise stood in the middle, slightly more to the front, so they could see her demonstrations.

"Today we are at one with nature," she said, spreading her arms. "There's no better place to paint than in the French fields, non?" She had put on a blue dress for the occasion, blending in with the landscape. Her hair was pinned up in a thick braid, this time topped off with two blue parakeets; Adele and Fleur. Adele had died of old age,

Marie-Louise told them, and that much was clear. Graham speculated Fleur's death had been more violent, as she had numerous stitches across her chest, but no one asked.

Nathalie mixed French Ultramarine and Chroma Blue with water on a paper picnic plate, dipped her brush into it and put her first blobs of color on the paper. Not only had her technique improved, her confidence had grown too. She found herself relaxing into the painting now, rather than getting frustrated with her mistakes, and she was able to correct things she didn't like, instead of starting over again.

"Isn't it a lovely day for painting in the fields," she said. "I've got the feeling this is going to be a great session."

"Someone's chirpy today," Graham remarked, looking over at Nathalie.

She turned to him, unsure of what he meant, when she suddenly realized she had a big grin on her face. *Oh God, I must have been carrying this cheesy smile the whole morning.*

"I'm just happy," she said. "The sun is shining and we're in this beautiful field... what else could anyone want?"

The group eyed her in suspicion.

"Are you sure it's just that?" Brenda asked. "Graham's right. You do look happy. You're glowing, as they say." She cocked her head. "Have you met someone?"

Nathalie couldn't help but giggle. Brenda was the most intrusive person she knew but it always came from a good place. "No. Why would you think that? Can't I just be in a good mood?" She stepped closer to her easel, trying to hide her blush.

"Look at that face," Graham teased. "You *have* met someone." Everyone laughed, including Cherie, who was curiously staring her way.

"Lena?" she asked.

Nathalie's eyes widened at Cherie's remark. She hadn't

said much in the weeks they'd been painting together. Still as a mouse, she came, did her thing and left with a polite wave. And now this? How could she possibly know?

Cherie said something to Marie-Louise for her to translate. It made her laugh. "She knows Lena through her father, Bernie," Marie-Louise explained. "He works for her. Cherie says she wouldn't be surprised if Lena managed to seduce you. She has her ways, apparently."

That brought another wave of laughter from the group. Nathalie felt drops of sweat trickling down her back. *Is it that obvious?* It wasn't that she was ashamed of what she'd done. On the contrary. She'd been thinking of Lena and the night they'd spent together every second since Lena had left for Monaco. Visions of her gorgeous smile and toned body were permanently on her mind, and she loved to indulge in them. But Nathalie had never been with a woman before, and it still felt strange to admit it, to say it out loud to people she didn't know that well. Besides, she had no idea what their fling had meant to Lena. Perhaps it was just a one-time thing to her, and there was a chance that it would never be any more than it was. Nathalie wasn't ready for all the questions she wouldn't have the answers to. She straightened her back and shook her head.

"I'm sorry to disappoint you all," she said, shifting her focus back to her painting. "As I said, I'm just in a good mood."

Marie-Louise gave her an amused look over the brim of her glasses and smiled when their eyes met.

35

Lena sat down to sample one of the marble benches that had just been delivered and stared at her phone. She hadn't heard anything from Nathalie for the past two days, but then she hadn't contacted Nathalie either. Ever since she'd arrived in Monaco, she'd been worrying about Nathalie, wondering if she regretted their night, now that she'd had time to think about it. Gumbo was barking at her from the little garden that Lena had set up for him with a folding fence, an umbrella that provided shade, and a blanket to lie on. Nathalie had offered to look after him, but she was still her tenant, and Lena didn't like to rely on anyone when it came to favors.

"What's up, boy?" she shouted at him. Gumbo gave her a heart-wrenching look from underneath the umbrella. "I know," Lena said, giving him a smile. "You want to go home, don't you?" *Me too, Gumbo, me too.* If everything went to schedule, and she assumed it would by the looks of it, they could have an early start in the morning and she would be back by midday. The trees were lined up perfectly along the driveway, all equally spaced and cut down to the same height. It was starting to look good, and Lena felt proud of the work they'd accomplished in such a short amount of time. Her crew was in a good mood, and that was all down to her meticulous planning. There wasn't a single gardener she'd ever employed who didn't appreciate an early finish without losing out on the money. She unlocked her phone again and looked up Nathalie's number. This wasn't the way it was supposed to go. The mind-blowing night, and the passionate morning after.... She hadn't planned any of it. Or had she? Lena wasn't sure of anything anymore, apart from one thing; she missed Nathalie, and she needed to be near her. It was the first time since Selma had broken up with her that she'd even thought of another woman this way. Casual sex was one thing, but this wasn't just casual anymore. It was too late for that, because Lena was crushing on Nathalie like a twelve-year-old. She started typing, still deciding whether to send the message or not.

Hey Nat. I had a really great time the other night. Are you still up for lunch? I'd like to take you to Italy. I'll be back tomorrow around noon to pick you up if you're available. Let me know. X Lena.

Lena read it over three times before she pressed send and buried the phone deep in her pocket. Then she walked over to one of the flowerbeds, where three of her men were securing rope over the fluffy earth, marking the middle and the side points of the crest they were going to recreate with flowers.

36

Nathalie jumped up when she saw the message come in. *Lena.* With shaking hands, she picked up her phone and read it, smiling from ear to ear. She hadn't sent anything herself. Lena was working on her biggest project yet, and Nathalie had assumed she'd be too busy. Still, she'd secretly been hoping for a message. She thought for a while and typed a message back.

Hey Lena. I had a great time too and I can't seem to stop thinking about you. Hope it's all going well. I'd love to go to Italy with you, and I can't wait to see you again. XXX Nat

She sent it before she had time to overthink her response, then turned back to her laptop on the terrace table. In front of her was an email from a head-hunter, enquiring about Nathalie's interest in a vacancy. The job was in Singapore. She hadn't really considered Singapore before, but the role seemed challenging and interesting. She sent a short reply, agreeing to an initial interview. There was no harm in talking, right? Then she switched to another tab that was open and browsed all available offices for rent in Monaco. The third one down caught her attention. It was small, but in a premium building that housed other financial corporations. Nathalie had no intention of building a company from scratch again, but the thought of being a consultant had crossed her mind on a few occasions. The concept seemed perfect. She could work from anywhere, as long as she had someone minding the office. An exclusive postcode was important when dealing with multinationals or big brands, so she would need a place to receive her clients for meetings. But other than that, no one would care if she was there or not. *Don't be silly.* She closed her laptop and got up from the table, frustrated with herself for getting carried away. *Think, Nathalie. You only spent one night with Lena and now you want to move here? That's ridiculous.* Yes, it was ridiculous. Lena liked her, she was sure of that. But the fact that she was a tourist and therefore long-term unavailable probably played a role in that too. And even if Lena was genuine, could she really spend the rest of her life with a woman? What would she tell her parents? They would never understand. And what if it didn't work out, just like her marriage? She would throw away a steady career for what? A crush? No, she couldn't do that. *Think about yourself now. Just get on with it and find a decent job. Stick to the plan.*

The wind had picked up, blowing her paperwork off the table. Nathalie rushed over to gather the pages of the sales agreement she'd printed out. Jack had been thorough. She'd read it over and didn't see any reason not to sell their apartment. The buyer's only condition was that he wanted to move in within two months. Very soon, she would have no financial obligations whatsoever and nothing to tie her down.

37

"So, is this a date? Or do you make a habit of doing your shopping in Italy?" Nathalie asked, looking at Lena over the brim of her shades. She pulled the lever on her seat and pushed back, making herself comfortable with Gumbo on her lap. They were driving along the coast on the scenic route, passing through Monaco. The view of the French Riviera in Èze and Villefranche-Sur-Mer had been stunning, and now, it was the extravagance of Monte Carlo that took her by surprise as they passed yachts in the harbor and outrageously over-the-top villas that lined the coastal road to Italy.

"I do tend to go once or twice a month," Lena said. "But today is definitely a date." She gave Nathalie a flirty look as she stepped on the gas, speeding through a tunnel.

"You're such a show off." Nathalie laughed. She couldn't have been happier, with the coastline to her right, and the most stunning woman in the world to her left. Lena was wearing a crisp white shirt, jeans and suede navy loafers. She looked like she'd stepped right out of a yacht club with her dark shades and swanky silver watch that completed her outfit. Nathalie hadn't been able to eat for two days. Her stomach did funny things whenever Lena was around, and even when she wasn't there, Nathalie thought of her constantly, reliving their passionate night over, and over again. She still felt a bit funny about being on a date with a woman. It was probably something she had to get used to. But the delight of Lena's presence, her touch, and her company made such thoughts fade into the background as fast as they came. She didn't want to think about the fact that time was flying by, and that she would have to go back home soon. Because when Lena had pulled into the driveway that afternoon, Nathalie felt a happiness she couldn't quite comprehend.

As they neared Italy, the landscape shifted significantly. The palm trees that lined the roadside were replaced by cacti, roses and carnations. The stone houses were smaller, with fruit orchards and gazebos, where the homeowners sold fruits from their own front yard. Even the traffic changed after they'd passed the Italian border. As opposed to France, where the back roads were reasonably quiet, the Italian roads were busy and chaotic, especially near the coast. Nathalie winced at the sound of beeping horns when they entered the city center of San Remo. Lena was a good driver, and she seemed to naturally adjust to the traffic around her as she scooted into an alleyway and parked the car in a tight space between two other cars.

"Are you hungry?" she asked after she'd turned off the engine.

"I am now," Nathalie said, looking for Gumbo's lead between her feet on the floor. "I haven't been able to eat much." She smiled. "Let's just say I've been distracted, but my body is finally screaming out for food."

"Distracted, huh?" Lena looked at her, arching an eyebrow. She reached for the door handle to step out of the car, then changed her mind, grabbed Nathalie's arm and pulled her towards her. She ran her other hand through Nathalie's hair as she kissed her hard, deepening the kiss even more when Nathalie moaned softly. Nathalie's head started spinning as she sank into Lena's arms, desire shooting through her like lightning. She felt like a teenager, making out in the car in a dark alleyway, but she didn't care.

Lena finally pulled out of the kiss, licked her lips and smiled. "I've been wanting to do that for days."

"I was hoping you would." Nathalie melted when she looked into Lena's eyes. They were so full of longing and promise of more to come.

Lena held her gaze, then chuckled and shook her head. "I'm going to step out of the car now, before I try to ravage you on the front seat." She got out and opened the door for Nathalie and Gumbo. He was pulling on the leash, desperate to get to the nearest peeing spot.

Nathalie was blushing, still recovering from the amazing kiss they'd just shared as she let him drag her along with him. "I'm not used to people opening doors for me, driving me around and taking me on dates, Lena." She waited for Gumbo to empty his bladder.

"Did Jack not do that for you?" Lena put an arm around her as they walked towards the city square.

"It wasn't like that. I didn't want it, I suppose. I've always liked to be in charge, to make the decisions."

Lena gave her an amused look. "Would you like to drive? I'll let you open doors for me if that makes you happy."

Nathalie laughed. "No, it's nice. I like it. I feel like a woman when I'm with you, and I get all giddy when you do these things for me." She rested her head on Lena's shoulder. "It's strange how much I've started to doubt who I was all those years, who I am now. Not in a bad way," she added. "It's just that the past weeks have been very insightful, that's all." Lena pulled her closer and placed a kiss on her temple.

"Any insights in specific?" she asked. Nathalie gathered her thoughts as they walked up a hill towards a network of narrow cobbled streets. There was no traffic, so she let Gumbo off the leash.

"I guess my place on the spectrum would be the biggest one." She grinned. "But you already figured that one out. The control thing is another. I've had nothing to manage here apart from my own time, so I've just focused on the here and now, not planning too much ahead. And I have to admit, it's been liberating."

"You look liberated," Lena remarked. "You look different from when you first arrived. It's like you've got more energy and you smile a lot more." She chuckled, pointing at Nathalie's permanent grin. "In fact, you smile all the time now."

"I think you might have something to do with that," Nathalie said, squeezing Lena's arm. "And this..." She looked around as the street disappeared into a passageway. "This is an exceptionally romantic choice of location for a date. I'm impressed, Lena." The old buildings and narrow tunnels reminded her of Arabic architecture. The network of steps and alleyways was like a maze, spiraling up the hill.

"Yeah, it's nice, isn't it?" Lena took a right turn half way up the hill. "Sorry about the climb though, but it will be worth it."

Two young men passed them, both staring at their entwined hands. One of them yelled something in Italian and blew Nathalie a kiss.

"Don't mind them," Lena said. "Italian men tend to get a bit worked up when they see two women holding hands." She turned to Nathalie, whose cheeks had turned bright pink. "You don't have to hold my hand if you feel uncomfortable, you know. I'm not going to be offended."

Nathalie squeezed her hand and took a tighter hold. "No, it's fine. I don't care what anyone thinks of me. It just never occurred to me that…"

"That people might notice?"

"Yeah." Nathalie bit her lip, looking up at Lena. "Do you get this a lot?"

Lena shrugged. "Not really. But then I don't normally hold hands with women either."

"Oh. You don't? Ever?"

"Never. I don't go on dates, and Selma didn't like to hold hands in public, so we might have to get used to this together." Lena raised their entwined hands and planted a kiss on Nathalie's knuckles. "But as I said, if you're uncomfortable, we can…"

"No," Nathalie interrupted her. "I feel flattered." She smiled. "I'm not uncomfortable, Lena. I'm happy."

They entered a quaint little courtyard. It was cool, shaded by buildings on either side. The shutters on the residential apartments were painted red, enhancing the bright flowers that hung down from the window sills of the brick facades. Half of the courtyard was taken up by the restaurant's terrace, marking its space with a cast-iron fence that surrounded the tables and chairs.

"How on earth did you find this place?" Nathalie asked. "I feel like I've stepped back in time."

"It was by accident," Lena said. "I was doing some shopping on the lower streets one day and Gumbo decided to chase another dog up the hill. I followed him all the way up here to find him getting it on with his new girlfriend." She laughed and looked over at Gumbo, who was sniffing around the fence. A server greeted them and showed them to their table. Without checking, he placed a jug of red wine and a bottle of water in between them before handing them the menus.

Lena thanked him and said something Nathalie didn't understand.

"Do you speak Italian?" Nathalie asked.

"A little bit." Lena poured them both a glass of wine. "I've been buying trees from some of the farmers around here and most of them don't speak a word of English or French, so I had to learn the basics."

"Well, whatever you just said to him, it sounded pretty damn sexy." Nathalie hid her blush behind her menu. She didn't seem to have a filter when it came to Lena. Things just kept on escaping from her mouth.

"Oh yeah?" Lena slipped out of her shoe and traced the inside of Nathalie's calf with her foot. "I'll talk Italian to you if it turns you on."

Nathalie cast her a flirtatious glance. The courtyard, the wine, Lena's foot against her skin... If Lena was trying to charm her, she certainly succeeded. "You are one smooth talker, you are," she said. "Has anyone ever told you that?"

Lena laughed. "Not in those words, no." She cocked her head. "I don't want you to think I'm like this with everyone, Nat. Because I'm not."

"Yeah right." Nathalie rolled her eyes. "I bet you say that to all the girls."

"No, really. I mean it." Lena seemed taken aback by

Nathalie's comment. She reached over the table and covered Nathalie's hand with her own. "It's different with you. I'm..." She paused. *Don't tell her you're head over heels with her. You're going to freak her out.* "I really like you."

"I really like you too." Nathalie took a sip of her wine and looked at her intently. "You have no idea, Lena..." There was so much more she wanted to say but she couldn't. She would be leaving soon, and there was no point telling Lena how she felt, and that she was starting to fall in love with her. Because that would sound completely crazy. Besides that, she needed time to process the fact that she had feelings for a woman. It was all so new, yet it was also so much better than anything she'd ever experienced. She opened her mouth to continue but decided against it when the server came over to take their orders.

"Signore." He looked from Lena to Nathalie and back, as if he could sense the tension between the two women. Nathalie glanced down at her menu and realized it was in Italian.

"Would you order for me, Lena?" she giggled helplessly.

"Sure. What do you feel like?" Lena's dark eyes stared right into hers and Nathalie immediately forgot the question. Flashes of their night together entered her mind. Lena kissing her in the pool, Lena on top of her in bed...

"Nat?" Lena asked again.

"Sorry. Oh yes, the food..." Nathalie shook her head and smiled. "Anything you want. I'm happy to share."

Lena talked to the server, who suggested what sounded like a ten-course meal. He laughed, waved his hands around as he spoke, refilled their glasses and disappeared back inside.

"Are you okay?" Lena asked when they were alone again.

"Yeah. I'm okay." Nathalie shifted in her chair. "I'm

sorry if I'm being weird, but how do you expect me to concentrate on anything when you're sitting there, looking the way you do? It's you, Lena." She sighed in frustration, still smiling. "You confuse the hell out of me. When you look at me I lose my train of thought, all sense of direction, not to mention my ability to form a decent sentence. Haven't you noticed?"

"Okay..." Lena looked amused. "Well, just so you know, you confuse the hell out of me too."

"I do?"

"Yeah. I might be better at hiding it than you, but I can't even begin to describe the turmoil inside that fogs my brain when I'm with you. I didn't expect this to be so... I don't know." She paused, fiddling with her napkin. "Everything changed after we spent the night together. Everything's different now. To me, at least."

Nathalie nodded. "Yeah. I know what you mean." There was a silence.

Lena picked a red olive from the bowl between them, put it back and took a black one instead. "I'm not sure where this is heading," she finally said, "but we can't let ourselves get dragged in too deep. I mean, you're looking for a new job and..." Her eyes met Nathalie's. "How's the job hunt going anyway?"

Nathalie shrugged. "It's going. I found some vacancies."

"Anything interesting?" Lena asked.

"There's one in Singapore that seems perfect, and they're keen to have an interview with me." *Don't mention the office.*

"That's great." Lena tried her best to sound cheerful, ignoring the stab she felt at the thought of Nathalie being so far away. "So, are you going to do it? The interview, I mean."

"I think so." Nathalie didn't want to talk about it. It only reminded her of the little time they had left. "I don't know, we'll see. I guess I have to take the opportunities as they come, and this is a big one."

"Have you been to Singapore before?" Lena asked.

"No, I haven't. But as I said, I've never felt attached to a place, and I doubt I ever will, so it doesn't matter to me where I live as long as I've got a job I enjoy."

"Really? That's sad." Lena moved back, allowing the server to put down the antipasti starters. "So, there's not a single place you like to call home? Or even just somewhere you feel good, and at ease?"

"Not really." Nathalie picked at a piece of marinated mozzarella. "I have to admit, I feel good here. I love France, but I'm on holiday, and that's always better than real life, right? The sun, the atmosphere, the food..." She looked up at Lena. "You."

"Maybe." Lena scooped some grilled vegetables onto her plate. *You'll never know if you don't try, Nat.* "Have you thought about staying longer? In the annex, with me?"

"I have." Nathalie hesitated. "Of course, I've thought about it, and I'd love to take you up on your offer, but it's so damn hard to plan ahead right now. I don't know where I'm heading. If I get through to the final interviews for this job, they're not going to take place here, and eventually, I'll have to pack up my stuff in Chicago too because the sale of our apartment's gone through a hell of a lot faster than we thought it would. The buyers want to exchange in two months' time."

"Sure." Lena managed to hide her disappointment. "You need to do what you need to do. I get that."

"It's not that I don't want to, it's..."

"You don't have to explain yourself, Nat." Lena's said. "We both knew this wasn't going to last forever. And I'm fine with that, so please don't feel like you have to apologize."

She painted on a cheerful face. "Hey, let's not worry about any of that right now, okay? It's only our first date after all."

"Okay." Nathalie squeezed Lena's hand. "I suppose when you put it like that…" She smiled and let out a sigh. "And what a great first date it is."

38

"Do you mind if we stop by a tree farm on the way home?" Lena asked. "There's this place someone told me about. I've never bought from them before, but I spoke to the owner on the phone yesterday and it seems like they do a pretty good deal on olive trees. I need to order a couple for a private customer."

"Sure, I'd love to." Nathalie was busying herself with her phone, taking pictures as they drove back. "Anything new is exciting, and besides that, I don't know much about what you do. I'm kind of intrigued."

"Okay, well don't get too excited." Lena laughed. "It's just a farm." She turned onto the coastal road and followed it back in the direction of the French border, until they entered the very last strip of rural Italy. The boot of the car was stuffed with fresh Italian produce and a couple of souvenirs Nathalie had bought after lunch. They had explored the shops and the markets, strolled through parks and quiet residential neighborhoods, talked and laughed, holding hands as if they'd known each other forever. Nathalie was surprised by how easy it was between them.

Lena had pulled her into a quiet alleyway and kissed her possessively until she almost burst with the need to rip her clothes off. That same desire was still stirring inside of her, with no sign of subsiding any time soon. Nathalie hadn't felt this before. Not even close. Her body seemed to scream out for Lena's touch, for her attention, and just one look was enough to make her heart jump. Lena pulled into the muddy driveway along the farm and checked her notebook for the name of the man she'd spoken to.

"I'M JUST GOING to ask if I can use the bathroom," Nathalie said as she got out of the car. She crossed the carpark, along rows of trucks and containers full of compost. A man was on the phone behind the counter when she entered the office.

"Could I use your toilet please?" she asked, waving to get his attention. She pointed at the lavatory door. The man nodded, rooted under the counter while he continued his conversation in broken English and threw her the key dangling from an enormous olive branch hanger.

"Thanks," Nathalie said, wincing as she scratched her hand when she caught it. She locked the door behind her, washed her hands and studied her reflection in the mirror. It was unusual for her to check herself out during the day, but since she'd met Lena, she did a lot of things she didn't normally do. Nathalie ran a hand through her hair, and established she was happy with how she looked. Her face and neck had taken on a great tan, and the tiredness around her eyes was completely gone. She looked healthy and fresh-faced, perhaps even a bit younger than when she arrived. She'd gotten rid of the serious hair bun she'd always worn, and now her blonde locks were hanging loosely around her shoulders, still messy from the drive.

BACK OUTSIDE, Lena was looking at the trees in the orchard.

"Do you know anything about olive trees?" she asked, when Nathalie joined her.

Nathalie laughed and shook her head. "I'd never even seen one up close until I got to France, so no."

"Of course. You don't get them in Chicago, do you?" Lena pulled down a branch and inspected the flowers. "Want me to bore you with some facts?"

Nathalie took a step closer, leaning into her. "You couldn't bore me if you tried."

"Okay... well, these yellow flowers are the male ones. They produce pollen. You know what pollen is, right?"

"I think so." Nathalie didn't sound too sure of herself. "Isn't that the yellow powder that bees drag around? They carry it from tree to tree or from flower to flower, so they get pregnant and grow fruits?"

Lena laughed. "Didn't you tell me you grew up on a farm, or did I imagine that?"

Nathalie held up a hand in defense. "Hey, I was never that interested in farming when I was a kid, so the information never stuck."

"Okay." Lena pulled down a branch. "Well you weren't wrong. It's close enough anyway." She pointed to the smaller greenish flowers. "These are the hermaphrodite flowers. They have both male and female parts, and these are the ones that develop into fruits." She gestured to the different types of trees in the orchard. Some of them were already growing olives. "Olives are wind-pollinated, and to get the best out of your olive trees, you need to have a variety of them for cross-pollination with compatible trees." She looked over at the man who exited the office, making his way towards them.

"These trees," Lena continued, "will be a perfect match to a batch that I already bought from a farm outside Marseille, so I think I'm going to order them." She shook the man's hand. "Barto?" she asked.

Barto nodded.

"Lena." Nathalie listened to Lena's Italian introduction, while she pointed to the trees. The man glanced at the Porsche next to his office, then at Lena's watch, and held up five fingers.

"Cinquanta Euros," he said with a steely expression.

"Fifty Euros?" Lena frowned, held up two fingers and barked something back at him in Italian. She took her phone out of her pocket, opened the website to his farm and pointed at the price of a tree, advertised on the first page. The conversation got heated, with Barto throwing his hands around as he kept repeating himself, although Nathalie had no idea what he was saying.

Finally, Lena shook her head. "Let's go, Nat. I'm not going to let him ruin my mood."

"Wait, what's going on?" Nathalie asked, before Lena got the chance to walk away.

"Just leave it, Nat. He's trying to charge me over twice the price I should be paying." She sighed. "I think I'll just stick to my regular suppliers in future."

Nathalie looked from Lena to Barto and back, suddenly overcome by rage.

"Hey!" she shouted at Barto, who had already turned his back to them. "Come back, you bald little olive dude. Listen, my friend here called you earlier and you made a verbal agreement. You know what a verbal agreement is, right?" Barto stared at her blankly. "And now that she shows up in a fancy car, you suddenly decide to double the price? What kind of sales strategy is that? Huh?" Nathalie didn't wait for an answer. Her eyes were angry as she pointed right at him. "I know you speak English, and I know you understand me perfectly well because I heard you speak on the phone in your office earlier. Now I suggest you give my friend the batch of trees at the agreed price, or we'll take our business elsewhere. I'm sure there are lots of other tree farmers who would love to be able to claim they've sold their trees to the Grimaldi's garden architect." Nathalie fixed her stare on him, straightened her back and crossed her arms. Barto was stunned. He blinked in silence, processing the latest information Nathalie had thrown at him. Nathalie arched an eyebrow. "Well? I'm giving you ten seconds to think about it. Ten, nine, eight…"

"Okay, okay," the man said in a thin voice. "She can have them for…"

"Excellent," Nathalie interrupted him, a small smile forming around her mouth. She took the phone from Lena and scrolled through the website. "We'll expect them to be delivered for free, as your website states." She read the last sentence out loud, pointing at it. "Free of charge. Now go get the paperwork if there's any involved."

"You go, girl. What was that?" Lena turned to Nathalie when they were back in the car. "If I didn't know you better, I'd be terrified."

Nathalie shook her head and held up a hand in apology. "I'm sorry, I shouldn't have interfered, but people like him infuriate me. It's the worst way of doing business."

"Right…" Lena paused. "Well, thank you. It was certainly

helpful." She laughed. "I thought he was going to pee his pants back there. I didn't know you had it in you."

Nathalie sat back and put her seatbelt on. "Yeah, well, he deserved it."

Lena waited for Gumbo to hop in before starting the engine. "So, is that what you're like at work?" she asked, maneuvering the car out of the parking space.

"What do you mean?" Nathalie frowned.

"What do I mean?" Lena repeated. "Isn't it clear what I mean? You just turned into a completely different person back there."

"Oh right, that." Nathalie shrugged. "I know how to deal with sneaky scumbags, that's all. Anyway, I thought I was pretty mild on him." She giggled at seeing Lena's perplexed expression. "Hey, you don't get to grow a global company by being nice to people all the time. Besides, it doesn't make me a monster. Work me isn't the same as private me."

"Of course, I get that," Lena said. "I'm just surprised that the two can be so blatantly different, that's all." She tried to concentrate on her driving, still brooding over Nathalie's sudden personality shift. "But I have to admit, it's very sexy."

39

"Thank you for today," Nathalie said when they were back home. "I had a great time." She sat on the kitchen counter in the annex while Lena made them both a coffee. She couldn't keep her eyes off Lena, not even for a second. All she wanted was to kiss her and rip her clothes off, but she wasn't sure if Lena wanted the same. It had been so long since she'd last dated. In fact, she couldn't even remember her first date with Jack. They had been friends long before he asked her out for the first time, and she had never felt those memorable nerves with him. Nothing close to what she felt now.

"I'm glad you had a nice day." Lena handed her the coffee. She stared at Nathalie a little longer before adding foam to her own cup. Then she walked over to her and nestled her hips in between Nathalie's legs. "For some reason, I'm not sure how to behave around you anymore, Nat... And I don't normally have that problem." She gazed into Nathalie's eyes. "In case you're doubting whether I want to jump your bones or not, I can assure you that I do." A smile played around her mouth. "But the ball is in your court now. I can imagine this is all very new and maybe even a bit strange to you..."

Nathalie shook her head slowly, indulging in the dark depths of Lena's eyes.

"I think you know what I want, Lena." She put her coffee mug aside, took Lena's wrist and pulled her closer.

Lena leaned in and brushed her lips over Nathalie's. "I do now," she said, lowering her voice. Her hand slipped underneath Nathalie's dress and squeezed her thigh while their mouths crashed into one another. Lena's kiss was so persistent, so intense, that Nathalie felt herself getting wet within seconds. Lena cupped her neck with her other hand and pulled her in even closer. Nathalie let out a sigh when Lena's hand moved up towards her hipbone and curled around her back, hiking up her dress.

"I want you," she whispered, breaking away from the kiss. "God damn it, Lena. I want you so badly."

Lena's hungry gaze traveled down to her mouth and back up, where she fixed her eyes on Nathalie's while unbuttoning her dress at the front. It was a painfully slow process, but Lena seemed to enjoy the teasing, time-consuming action. Nathalie shivered when Lena opened the front of her dress, her eyes darkening when she saw that she wasn't wearing a bra. She could hardly believe that she was sitting on a kitchen counter in France, being undressed by a beautiful woman whom she was about to make love to. Lena smiled as she looked Nathalie up and down. She brought her lips to her breasts, taking a nipple into her mouth. Nathalie cried out in pleasure when she bit down softly and circled it with her tongue. Lena dug her nails into Nathalie's back and pulled her closer towards her as her mouth explored Nathalie's other breast, before placing a trail of kisses down to her belly.

"These will need to come off," Lena said in a teasing voice, tugging at the lace panties. Nathalie shifted on the counter so that Lena could pull them down. She felt exposed, being naked in broad daylight, but there was something incredibly exciting about that too. Lena tossed her panties on the floor and kissed her hard while her hand slipped between Nathalie's legs. She slowly traced a finger over Nathalie's center, causing her to moan into the kiss. She loved teasing Nathalie, loved making her wait. She could feel her longing and knowing how much Nathalie wanted her turned her on like nothing else. Lena pulled out of the kiss and watched Nathalie's expression turn into one of sheer delight as she circled her clit with her fingertip. She was beautiful, with her hair tousled, her eyes closed, and her lips parted.

"You're so wet," she whispered in Nathalie's ear. "I want you to give yourself to me. Don't hold back." She cupped Nathalie's center and spread her open, entering her with two fingers.

"Oh God!" Nathalie steadied herself on her hands behind her, threw her head back and moved forward, pushing herself against Lena's hand between her thighs in a slow rhythm. Each time she moved forward, she felt Lena's fingers deeper inside of her, filling her up. It was sexy, and raw, and thrilling to be taken by a woman who knew exactly what to do. She didn't think she could take much more, until Lena pulled out and kissed her way down her breasts and her stomach again, taking her time to make sure she didn't miss a single inch of Nathalie's skin before kneeling down in front of her with her face between her legs. Lena pulled them over her shoulders and spread them wider. Her hands slipped underneath the back of Nathalie's dress, holding her in a tight grip while her tongue traced Nathalie's folds, up and down, applying more and more pressure each time until Nathalie started grinding into her, begging for release. Nathalie gasped. She felt her body convulse as Lena entered her with her tongue. The warm glow that spread throughout her core went straight to her head, forcing her to close her eyes at the intensity of her orgasm. She shook and cried out, tightening her legs around Lena's shoulders. When Nathalie finally came to her senses, Lena was still between her legs with her mouth against her center, licking her slowly.

"Jesus, Lena," Nathalie panted. Lena looked up at her with a cocky grin as she got back on her feet, facing her again. She took Nathalie's bottom lip between her teeth and bit it softly before she parted her lips and sank into Nathalie's mouth. Nathalie tasted herself as they kissed and was overcome by a need to taste Lena too. "Can we go to your bedroom?" she whispered.

"Bed sounds good." Lena's voice was low and hoarse, and Nathalie could hear the longing in it as she spoke. She lowered herself down from the kitchen counter and took Lena's hand as she followed her to the bedroom. Nathalie shed herself from her dress that was still hanging open, turned to Lena and pulled her shirt over her head. Lena unclasped her bra at the back and let the straps slide off her shoulders.

Nathalie sighed. Lena was even more beautiful in the light of day and seeing the hard nipples on her small breasts made her wet and ready all over again. She unbuttoned Lena's jeans and pulled them down along with her boxer shorts, allowing her to step out of them. Her hand moved down Lena's side, tracing the small curve from her waist to her hips. She had tan lines on her thighs, from the hem of her shorts, and on her shoulders, from the tank tops she wore at work. Nathalie took a step forward and pressed herself against Lena as she kissed her. She sighed in delight at the soft warmth of her skin. Lena moaned into the kiss when Nathalie tightened their embrace. The sound of it made her knees go weak. She couldn't wait any longer and directed Lena towards the bed, surprising herself by taking charge as she crawled on top of her. The arousal in Lena's eyes alone was enough to send her over the edge. Nathalie lowered herself on top of Lena and gasped at the skin on skin contact as she sank into the soft body underneath her. She pushed her thigh between Lena's legs as she kissed her, wallowing in the sounds of pleasure that escaped her lover's mouth. She felt Lena's wetness when she spread her legs apart. A spark of joy shot through her, knowing that she was the cause of Lena's arousal. Nathalie kissed her way down to Lena's belly. She took her time to explore her, to appreciate her skin against her lips. When she reached the strip of dark hair between Lena's legs, there was no hesitation, and no doubt. She wanted to taste her, needed to taste her. She placed a soft kiss on the dark hair and moved further down until her lips found Lena's wet center. She kissed it, then opened her mouth to explore her, slowly tracing her length with her tongue. Lena buckled and let out a loud moan, sending waves of pleasure through Nathalie's core. Her hands were clasped around Lena's hips and she pulled her closer, while she licked her in teasingly slow motions. She felt Lena's hands in her hair while she listened to her ragged breathing. Nathalie was overcome by desire at the sweet taste of her, and the sounds she was making. She continued teasing her, listening to the quiet moans that became louder when she moved up, towards her clit.

"Don't stop," Lena begged. "You're amazing, Nat." Then she took in a deep breath. "Right there."

Nathalie circled the spot with her tongue, applying more pressure, until Lena started to shake underneath her. She took a tighter grip of Nathalie's hair, pushed herself against her mouth and lifted her hips off the mattress as she climaxed. Nathalie smiled at the sound of Lena's release. It gave her a satisfaction she couldn't even begin to describe. It was all so new and strange and wonderful.

"Wow, I could do this all day." Nathalie whispered, as she pushed herself back up towards the bed head and buried her face in Lena's neck.

Lena chuckled and put an arm around her. "Don't mind if you do."

40

"Look, Gumbo, there's your friend!" Lena pointed at Bouche, a Doberman, who was at least six times the size of Gumbo. Gumbo sprinted over as soon as he spotted the larger-than-life dog that came tearing down the steps towards the beach. Bouche saw Gumbo too and galloped through the sand to greet him before rolling him through the sand. Lena waved at his owner, who took a seat next to her on the wooden bench.

"Hey Lena. It's been a while." The woman kissed Lena on both cheeks, produced a pack of cigarettes out of her pocket and lit one.

"Delphine. Always a pleasure." Lena shook her head when Delphine offered her a cigarette. She rarely smoked, apart from the few times she'd ended up in bed with the woman who was now sitting next to her. Delphine was a lawyer from Nice, who was a regular at the same dog beach that Lena visited twice a week with Gumbo. Lena wouldn't call her a friend. They rarely saw each other outside the beach, apart from a few summer nights last year when they'd had a couple of drinks after their dog walk and ended up in bed together. They'd been attracted to each other and the sex had been good, but there was never the spark that made either of them want to pick up the phone to set a date. Besides, they were too similar, especially when it came to women. They both liked the chase too much.

"How have you been?" Delphine asked. Lena watched her take a deep drag from her cigarette, exhaling towards the sky. Delphine had gained a bit of weight, she noticed, from the way her face had filled out, and it suited her. She was dressed in running tights and a sweater, and her blonde bob was tied up in a messy knot on top of her head. Lena always wondered what Delphine looked like in the courtroom, because she'd never seen her in anything other than her casual dog walking attire.

"Can't complain." Lena smiled as she watched the Doberman chase Gumbo over the beach, trying to keep up with him. "The business is doing well. I've been renting out the house. Other than that, there's not much to tell." She turned to Delphine and propped a foot on the bench. "What about you? You look good."

"Thanks," Delphine grinned, rolling her eyes. "I've met someone. Her name is Alice. We've been together for three months now." Her cheeks turned pink. "She owns a bakery in Nice. I bet you can tell I have a newfound passion for pastry." She laughed and slapped a hand on her thigh. "But I'm happy. She makes me happy."

"That's great. So, someone finally managed to tame you, huh?"

Delphine gave her a playful nudge. "Come on, I wasn't that bad, was I." She cocked her head. "What about you? Still single?"

Lena shrugged. "Yeah. I think so." She shook her head. "I mean, yes. I'm single." There was no need to tell her former fling about her infatuation with her tenant who would be leaving soon anyway. "But it suits me just fine."

"Of course it suits you. I've never known you any other way." Delphine hesitated. "But if you're ever thinking about going on a serious date, Alice has a couple of nice single friends. I'm sure she'd be happy to introduce you to them." She grinned. "Turns out being in a committed relationship isn't so bad after all. Even you might like it."

Lena laughed and shook her head. "Dog Beach Delphine is in love. Who would have thought? But as great as you are at selling this relationship stuff, I think I'm good. Thank you, though, it's nice of you to offer."

"Dog Beach Delphine? Is that how you referred to me when you discussed me with your friends?"

"I never discussed you, Delphine. What happened between us was private."

Delphine gave her a mocking look. "Yeah right. Nicknames don't just appear out of nowhere."

Lena held up a hand. "Okay, okay. I might have called you Dog Beach Delphine once or twice over a drink. But I can assure you that I never had a bad word to say about you." She stared ahead and frowned. "Wait... did you have a nickname for me too?"

Delphine shot her an amused look. "Of course I had a nickname for you, silly. We all need a bit of bragging material for our friends on a Friday night, right? Besides, without nicknames it would get terribly confusing because as you know, you weren't the only woman I messed around with at the time." She laughed. "So, I used to refer to you as 'The Gardener'."

Lena's eyes widened. "'The Gardener'? You couldn't come up with anything more original? Come on, Delphine, I deserve better than that. I recently found out that my staff call me 'Magic Lena' behind my back. I mean, I'm not happy with it, but at least it sounds a little bit more intriguing than 'The Gardener'."

"Oh, and I don't deserve anything better than 'Dog Beach Delphine'?" They both laughed. "So where did the 'Magic' come from?" Delphine asked, still chuckling. "Is it because you do that thing with your tongue when you..."

"No," Lena interrupted her, shaking her head with an amused smile. "God, no. It's a little bit more complicated than that and I'd rather not talk about it." She scratched Bouche behind his ears and threw the big stick he'd just dropped in front of her. The Doberman sprinted off in an attempt to beat Gumbo to it, leaving a trail of sand in Lena's lap. Gumbo caught it just before him and ran a little victory lap, trying to keep his head up while clenching the heavy stick between his teeth. "That's my boy. Well done, you won, Gumbo!"

"Come on, that's not fair," Delphine protested. "Bouche's legs get all tangled up when he tries to run. You have to give him a headstart."

"No excuses, Delphine. Gumbo is the fetch-champion today." Lena gave Delphine a playful wink. "Anyway, all nicknames aside, I'm glad to hear you're happy with your new lady friend. I'm sure she'll have a couple of nicknames lined up for you too." She suddenly realized it was much more relaxed talking to Delphine now they both knew they wouldn't end up in bed together. In fact, she genuinely enjoyed seeing her again. Lena was just about to invite her for a coffee, when Delphine looked at her watch and stood up.

"I'd better get going. I was on my way to Antibes when I saw your car parked up there and I figured Bouche would love to say hello to his friend." She put two fingers in her mouth and whistled hard, upon which Bouche came running towards her. "I'm sorry it was so short, I'm in a rush. Maybe a drink next time?" She flicked the cigarette stub into the sand and buried it with her foot. "Catch up properly?"

"Sure, that would be nice. You know where I live. Stop by anytime with Bouche if you're around and feel free to bring Alice too." Delphine beamed at the sound of her new girlfriend's name.

"Really? You wouldn't mind?"

"Of course not. I'd love to meet her." Lena winked. "As long as she brings pastries."

Lena stayed for a while, waiting for Gumbo to exhaust himself with two other dogs who had just arrived. She wished she'd asked Nathalie to come with her, but she wanted to be careful not to come across as too needy. Because the truth was, she did feel a little bit needy. She loved having Nathalie around, and she was already dreading the day she would leave. Nathalie was something else altogether. She was special, different to all the other women Lena had ever engaged with. Lena had taken a liking to her from the moment they'd met, and now, with each day they spent together, she was getting to know her on so many levels. Despite that fact that Nathalie had just been through a divorce and given up her life's work, she was beautiful, funny, clever, sharp, and didn't shy away from a bit of self-deprecation. Watching Nathalie argue with the olive tree farmer the other day had shown a whole different side to her. Nathalie didn't need protection. She didn't need Lena to help her heal or find her way. She was strong and independent, and Lena admired her for that. But it also made her realize that Nathalie would find a new job in no time and leave her without looking back. She'd have to look after herself and be careful not to get too attached, because Nathalie was someone who could quite possibly make her world crumble all over again. And that was something she wouldn't be able to handle. Not this time. Not with Nathalie.

41

"Nat?" Lena let herself into the kitchen.

"I'm here!" Nathalie yelled from the bedroom. "I'm just getting changed, I'll be right there."

Lena looked at the laptop on the table. She told herself it wasn't snooping. Nat knew she was here, after all. The open page advertised a Head of Finance vacancy in New York. The top tabs showed more job titles, all with headhunting agencies and all in the US or South-East Asia. She felt a knot tighten in the pit of her stomach. *What did you expect? That she'd be hanging around here with you doing nothing forever?*

"Hey you." Nathalie waltzed into the kitchen and flew around Lena's neck.

"Hey, gorgeous." Lena inhaled the scent of her freshly washed hair and placed a trail of kisses from her forehead down to her lips. "How was your day?"

Nathalie smiled and closed her eyes as she slid a hand under Lena's t-shirt, tracing her back.

"Uneventful. Just looking at some vacancies."

"And?"

"To be honest with you, I'm in a good place. There are quite a few options to consider. I had no idea so many companies would take an interest in me." Nathalie scrolled through the list of vacancies she had saved on her laptop and sighed before closing it down. "I'm not sure if I want to do anything in the corporate sector, but I don't think I have the energy to start my own company again either. Frankly, I'm dreading going back to work. Any type of work, really." She shrugged. "But hey, I'll need to dive back into it at some point, or my CV will be as dated as those bananas." She pointed to the fruit bowl that she'd filled the week before with the intention of embarking on a healthier diet.

"Really? Is that how it works?" Lena picked up one of the blackened bananas, squeezed it and threw it in the bin. "I thought taking a sabbatical year was all the rage nowadays."

"Not in my world." Nathalie sat down at the table. "If I'm applying for a director's role, they'll get suspicious when they see a gap, especially when that gap is longer than six or seven months. They might assume I've had a burn-out and that I won't be able to handle another leading position."

"But you can explain it," Lena said. "You've been bought out, and you've been through a divorce. Surely people deserve some time off after a divorce."

"I know." Nathalie looked up at Lena, patting the seat of the chair next to her. "Still, it's best if I show interest and apply now, while there are lots of opportunities. Who knows what the job market will be like next year?"

Lena sat down. "Sure. But is that what you want?"

"I don't know." Nathalie shook her head. "Can we please talk about this some other time? I'm not in the mood for it, and I'd love to take you out for dinner."

There it was. Nathalie had put on her director's tone, steering the conversation away from herself and her plans. It made Lena feel uneasy, reminding her that Nathalie had another side to her that she rarely saw. That she'd always have another side to her and that she needed more from life than a simple existence in a small village in France. She decided to let it go. It wasn't worth having a fight over.

"Alright, boss. We'll take it offline."

42

"How's everything with your hot new lady friend?" Alain asked, wiggling his eyebrows.

"She's looking for a job," Lena said, leaning back in her chair. "She's considering taking on some high-powered job with a manufacturer in Singapore. It's ridiculous." Alain looked at her as if he had no idea where she was coming from.

"Why ridiculous? It's what she does. And you always knew she was going to leave, right? She's on holiday. It was always going to be like that."

"I know." Lena stared into her beer. "You're right. I know that, and it's fine."

"Then what's the problem? You're not in love with her, are you?" He sighed, narrowing his eyes at the sight of Lena's flushed face. "Oh my God, you are. Jesus, Lena. You've managed to stay as far away as possible from anything serious for the past three years and now you decide to fall for your American tenant?"

"I didn't decide anything," Lena said in defense. "It just happened. I thought I had it under control."

"When is she leaving?" Alain's voice took on a softer tone when he finally sensed Lena's desperation.

"In three weeks." Lena sighed. "Maybe it's best if I go away for a while, hire another caretaker for the time being. It feels like Selma all over again. No," she corrected herself. "It's worse."

"Whatever you do, you can't blame her, Lena." Alain leaned in and lowered his voice to make sure his male colleagues didn't hear their un-manly conversation. "She didn't trick you into this. In fact, I'd be willing to bet a hundred Euros that you were the instigator of this mess. Have you asked her how she feels about leaving?"

Lena shook her head. "Every time I bring it up, she cuts me off and changes the subject. I already offered her to stay in the annex with me if she wants to extend her holiday, but she can't commit to anything right now. Or maybe that's just an excuse. Maybe I really am just a holiday fling to her."

Alain rolled his eyes. "You women. Always beating around the bush and mulling things over in your heads until you get so confused that you start making things up. Why don't you just tell each other what's on your mind?"

"Isn't that supposed to be the deal with men?" Lena asked in a sarcastic tone. "Aren't they the ones who never express their feelings?"

"That's what women think. But in fact, we don't have much going on up here so there's not much to worry about," Alain said, pointing at his head. He chuckled. "Our priorities are different. Women, on the other hand, overthink things. Imagine two of you!"

"It's not that simple, Alain. No matter how much we talk, nothing's going to change the fact that she'll be leaving at the end of the month and if I don't keep my distance now, I'm going to be a mess again. Hell, I'm a mess already."

"You're not a mess." Alain patted her on the shoulder. "You're strong and attractive and a real catch. Everybody loves you, Lena. You'll have distraction from Nathalie in no time and within a year, you won't even remember her name."

"I don't know. Maybe you're right, maybe not." Lena managed a smile. "Anyway, let's talk about you. What's happening with my favorite sleazebag?"

"I've got a date tonight." Alain looked pleased with himself as he downed his beer in record time.

"You always have dates," Lena said. "What's so special about this one? And anyway, shouldn't you take it easy on the alcohol if you're planning on having a civilized conversation over drinks tonight? Or do you skip that step entirely nowadays?"

"I'll be fine." Alain pushed his glass away. "And no, I'm not going to skip getting to know her. I'm taking my date out for dinner because this one is special. But you're probably right, I'll stop drinking now."

"So, who's the lucky lady?" Lena grimaced. "Although I'm not sure if lucky is the right..."

"Samantha," Alain interrupted her. "The woman from Nathalie's art class."

Lena's eyes widened. "Tell me that's not true, Alain. Please, you promised me you'd keep it in your pants around people I know."

"Come on, Lena. Technically, she's not *your* friend, she's Nathalie's friend. So, I don't think that counts as breaking the deal." He grinned. "I've always had a thing for redheads."

"Well, you'd better be a gentleman. She's a nice person." Lena gestured for the check and put some money on the table before getting up. "Be a good boy, Alain." She turned as she walked off. "Oh, and don't forget to have a shower. I can smell you from here."

43

"Nathalie, we need to talk," Lena started when they sat down to have dinner together. She had chosen the busy location on Valbonne Square, so their conversation wouldn't feel too loaded. They were opposite Alain's café, at an Italian restaurant. It was crowded with people, mostly groups of women with heaps of shopping bags under their tables.

Nathalie frowned. "Talk?" She held up a hand for the server and ordered a bottle of white wine in French, pleased with how her basic conversational skills were developing.

"Yes, talk." Lena was starting to feel mildly irritated by how Nathalie kept ignoring the elephant in the room. "You know, the thing where one person speaks their mind and another one reacts to it and vice versa."

Nathalie flinched, taken aback by Lena's sudden change of mood. She knew their talk was long overdue, but she was terrified of ruining what they had by analyzing things they wouldn't be able to change.

"Okay, I suppose you're right." She sighed. "I was going to stick my head in the sand and go with the flow until my time here was up, and that was selfish of me. I'm sorry. I know there are two of us in this situation but I'm so happy, Lena. I don't want anything to change between us."

"Don't be sorry," Lena said, her expression softening. "I've been trying to do the same thing, but I'm not sure if that's still an option anymore."

"What changed?" Nathalie played with the stem of her empty wineglass, twirling it in her hand.

Lena shrugged. "I can't do this anymore, Nat." Her eyes met Nathalie's worried stare. "I'm in it too deep. I... I have feelings for you. It was never supposed to go this way, I don't know what I was thinking. With you being you and all..."

NATHALIE PUT the glass down and waited for the server to pour the wine. Unable to hide her surprise at Lena's confession, she leaned back and stared at her for what seemed like an eternity.

"Please say something," Lena said. "It took a lot for me to tell you this."

"You have feelings for me?" was all Nathalie could manage to say.

Lena nodded. "Yeah." She said it with such ease and certainty, as if she was talking about the weather.

Nathalie opened her menu, realizing how ridiculous that was in the middle of their conversation, so she closed it again and put it aside. *Oh God. She does have feelings for me.* She looked down at her hands on the table, searching for words.

"I guess that makes two of us, then," she finally said. "I have feelings for you too." Her eyes met Lena's in a nervous stare. "I'm not very good at talking about my feelings. It's not something I'm used to doing."

Lena seemed relieved by Nathalie's confession. She gave her a soft smile. "I wasn't sure if you did. I thought that maybe you were just looking for a distraction from your divorce, or that you needed me to feed you curiosity. And that was fine by me. But now... I get this feeling of dread each time I think about the fact that you're leaving, and I need to protect myself, Nat. I can't have a Selma situation all over again. It's taken me three years to finally open up to someone. Sometimes I just wish it wasn't you."

"Don't say that." Nathalie propped her elbows on the table and leaned in, lowering her voice. "I'm glad it was me. And I'm glad it was you, who made me realize that there is such a thing as passion. That it's possible to want someone so much, that everything else seems insignificant. No one but you could have taught me that." She sighed. "I can't believe I'm saying this, but I need you, Lena."

"I need you too," Lena said. "I want you and I need you and that's why we have to end this. It's going to be a big mess if we don't." She skimmed the top of Nathalie's hand with her fingertips. "I'm thinking of staying somewhere else for a while. I'll still come in to do the garden and to clean the pool, or maybe I'll hire someone. But I think it's best if I don't sleep in the annex anymore."

"No! You can't do this to me, Lena." Nathalie raised her voice. "I want to spend as much time with you as I possibly can before I leave. I love being with you." She blinked away a tear. "I've never felt this happy before."

"But what good is that when it's all going to end anyway? Huh?" Lena retracted her hand. "Have you ever thought about that? That we'll have to say goodbye and that we won't see each other again? Ever? Saying goodbye is only going to get harder if we keep on doing what we're doing, Nat."

"It doesn't have to be over." Nathalie blushed. She couldn't believe she was sitting here, begging Lena to stay. But it was the truth. She didn't want it to be over. It was simply not an option. "We could still see each other. It's not like we're short of funds. I could fly here, you could visit me, wherever I'll be by that time. We can do this, Lena. I know we can."

Lena shook her head. "I've tried that before and it doesn't work. You'll have forgotten about me in no time once you start a new job and a new life somewhere else; I know how these things work. Been there, done that. Besides, don't forget that this is different for you. It's all new, and it's exciting because I'm your first woman."

"That has nothing to do with it." Nathalie took on a defensive tone. "Who do you think you are to seduce me, make me fall head over heels in love with you and then drop a bomb on me like this?"

"You're right." Lena nodded slowly. "I shouldn't have flirted with you and I shouldn't have kissed you that night in the pool. And I certainly shouldn't have taken it any further. It's all my fault and you have every right to be angry with me."

"It's not your fault," Nathalie said. "It takes two to do what we did. I'm in love with you, Lena." *There, you said it.* "It's not some crush or some stupid infatuation. I'm not a teenager. You may be the first woman I've been with, but I like to think that I'm at a point in my life where I know what I want, and what I want is to be with you."

Lena drank from her wine, silently processing Nathalie's confession. Her mind was full of conflicting thoughts. *She's in love with me. It won't work. It might work. I can't do this again. Maybe this time it will be different...*

"I feel the same," she said. "I'm in love with you too, and

that's the whole problem." She paused. "It's going to hurt too much."

The server came over to take their orders.

"Do you still want to eat?" Lena looked like she was ready to leave, pulling her wallet out of her back pocket.

"Of course, I want to eat." Nathalie opened her menu again. "In fact, I'm feeling particularly hungry now. I think I'll have six courses." She looked at Lena over the leather binder. "If that gives me more time to convince you not to move out." Lena couldn't help but smile when Nathalie started pointing out lots of random dishes to the server, clumsily explaining in French that she didn't want them all at once, but with half an hour in between each course. He gave her a puzzled look, then shrugged and turned to Lena, who sighed and rolled her eyes.

"I'll have the same."

44

"Okay, I'm still here. You got what you wanted," Lena said as they waited for the gate to open. They'd both had far too much to drink while working through the restaurant's entire menu and were lucky to hitch a ride home with one of the neighbors who had been dining at the same place.

"I only want this if you want it too." Nathalie took her hand as they walked towards the house. "But I know you do, I can see it when you look at me." She turned to face Lena. "Don't be afraid, Lena. Let's do this and see where it takes us." Lena was silent as she followed Nathalie into her bedroom, wondering how the hell she'd gotten herself into the same situation once again. Nathalie was a damn good negotiator with convincing arguments. Each time Lena had come up with excuses, she'd talked her right under the table. Whether she brought up the distance, different time zones, the fact that Nathalie would have to work around the clock in her new job... Nathalie had a solution for everything. Of course, the wine also had something to do with Lena giving in at the end. The fact that Nathalie looked stunning as always, didn't help either. Her hair was pulled back into a casual ponytail and she was wearing a flowy blue summer dress that made her breasts look exquisite. And so, before she knew it, Lena was undressed lying on Nathalie's bed, kissing her.

"Make love to me," Nathalie whispered as she pulled the covers over them. Lena smiled, tracing her cheek. There was something about the way she said it that made everything seem different now. But maybe everything was different, now that they both knew there were feelings involved. Big feelings. She looked into Nathalie's blue eyes and was suddenly overcome with something so much more than just lust. She kissed her again, slowly, and felt a spark run through her body at the touch of Nathalie's lips. Nathalie's soft moans were like the sweetest song, and her skin felt like velvet under her fingers as she traced her neck and her shoulders. Her eyelashes fluttered at every touch, no matter how light.

"Make love to me, Lena," she whispered again.

45

"Why are we here?" Marie-Louise asked, turning to her students.

"To paint?" Graham chuckled at his own joke.

Marie-Louise rolled her eyes. "Yes of course we're here to paint, Graham. This is a painting course after all. But I mean why here, on this busy beach? Why not on a quiet one where we have all the space in the world?" Nathalie looked over the Croisette, the main promenade in Cannes. As fitting as Marie-Louise's van seemed in the fields, right here, it was definitely out of place. The whole area oozed money, with flashy cars zooming past, big yachts anchored not far from shore, and wealthy women flaunting their oversized shades and designer purses on the two-kilometer stretch of beach, lined with tall palm trees, expensive hotels, shops and restaurants. But Cannes was also clearly an artistic town, with many galleries and street artists, who were selling their work along the promenade or painting portraits of tourists. They had set up behind the promenade wall, facing the beach, which was starting to get busy despite the early hour.

"Are we going to paint people?" Nathalie asked.

"Exactement!" Marie-Louise raised her voice and made a theatrical gesture, as if Nathalie had just qualified for the next round of a quiz show. "Many famous beach scenes have been painted throughout history. Renoir, Picasso, Van Gogh, Dali, Monet... Are you all familiar with Henri Matisse?"

The group nodded.

"Well, let me tell you that no one painted people like Matisse. You see, when you look at most of his beach paintings from a reasonable distance, you can see people engaged in activities. Whether they're fishermen, swimmers, or children playing, they're clearly there. But when you get close up, you realize that they're just mere blobs of color. I mean, they're brilliant blobs of color, no offense to Matisse." She held up a print out of one of his paintings, named *The Red Beach*, as an example, and next to it, a close up of the same work. "See? They're not realistic in the sense that they resemble the exact human form, but our imagination finishes the job *for* him." She put the sheets back in her bag and gave a demonstration, painting a group of people below them on the beach. Nathalie watched her jot down a beach scene in less than three minutes. *God, she's talented.* The demonstration had attracted heaps of tourists, who were admiring her skills. Marie-Louise stepped back from her easel and smiled at them before turning back to her students.

"What I'm trying to say is, don't overthink it. Don't be intimidated by the fact that you'll have people in your work this time. Treat them the same way as you treat trees or flowers, or even water. Just color, form and light. That's all there is to it."

As the group went to work, the beach got more crowded. It was a lot harder to paint a moving scene than it was to paint a field, Nathalie thought, but she tried to steer away from details and capture the essence of the bigger picture. Graham told them about all the great restaurants he and his wife had visited and pointed out a network of streets behind them that he referred to as *Satanville*, his wife's favorite shopping area.

"I'm telling you, that woman is working her way through her savings and her pension and soon she'll start chipping into mine," he said.

Marie-Louise, who was also very familiar with Cannes, gave them tips on great places to paint in case they wanted to practice. Everyone was in a good mood, but Samantha was especially chirpy. She hummed along to the music coming from one of the beach cafés, looking stunning in a green dress that complemented her red hair.

"Samantha didn't come home last night," Brenda announced to the group with a wink.

"Jesus, Mum. That's private." Samantha shot her mother a fierce look.

"I wasn't worried though, she sent me a text, so I knew she was safe," Brenda continued, ignoring her daughter. "She was on a date with your handsome friend," she said, turning to Nathalie.

"My handsome friend?" Nathalie frowned and looked from Brenda to Samantha and back until it finally clicked. "Alain?"

Samantha tried to keep a straight face but was unable to suppress a smile as she nodded. "Yeah. Alain." She said his name in a whisper.

"And how was the date?" Nathalie asked. "I assume you had a good time, since you didn't come home?" She wasn't going to ruin everything by telling Samantha that Alain was a lothario. It wasn't her place, so Samantha would have to figure that one out for herself, if she hadn't already.

"It was great, actually." Samantha smiled broadly now. "I wasn't that keen, at first. I know his type, but he kept on begging me to go out with him until I finally gave in. He took me out for dinner at a fancy restaurant and ordered Champagne. No one's ever done that for me before. We're meeting again, tonight."

"Wow, that's... great." Nathalie glanced over at Cherie, who was quietly giggling behind her masterpiece. *She understands a lot more than she lets on.*

"I love it when my students fall in love." Marie-Louise sighed. "There's nothing more inspiring in life than art and French romance." She gave Nathalie a sideways look as she mixed the colors on her palette.

Nathalie laughed, finally giving into Marie-Louise's prying.

"So true," she said.

46

"So, who's your next tenant?" Nathalie asked in a teasing tone. "Is she pretty? Should I be jealous?" They were strolling down the promenade in Nice with Gumbo on a tight leash. He'd had two warnings in his first half hour of freedom already, yet he couldn't seem to stop himself from chasing the skateboarders that were zooming past them.

Lena laughed and shook her head. "Do you think I make a habit of sleeping with my tenants or ask for a photograph before I accept their booking? And why do you even assume it's a *she*?" She gave Nathalie a flirty smile.

"Come on, just tell me." Nathalie winced. "I don't want to know, yet I need to know." She covered her face with her hands. "Oh God, I think I'm jealous already. This is ridiculous."

"Okay, okay," Lena said, chuckling in amusement. "*His* name is Marcus Obermeier. He's a real estate developer from Austria and he's currently building offices in Monaco. That's about all the information I have on him, but he paid up front, so who cares?"

"Thank the good Lord." Nathalie threw her hands in the air. "For Marcus Obermeier. I'm not sure if I could have handled some other woman staying in my bed because it feels like my bed now. Is it weird that I say that?"

Lena laughed. "Maybe a little. But I kind of like your jealous streak. It's cute." She bit her lip, staring at Nathalie in adoration. "You look beautiful today."

"Thank you." Nathalie smiled. "You do too. I mean, you always look gorgeous." She looked down at their entwined hands. It felt so natural now, holding Lena's hand in public, and she was proud to be by her side. "My parents would have a heart attack if they saw me like this, holding hands with a woman."

"Yeah, well, so would mine." Lena let out a sigh. "Do you think you'd ever tell them? That you're into women?"

"I don't know." Nathalie pondered over the question. "I'm not sure if it's worth ruining their peace of mind over. Not anytime soon, anyway. It would only hurt them, and I don't think I'd have anything to gain from it. We don't really talk much when we're together. Not about things that matter."

"So what *do* you talk about with your parents?" Lena's voice wasn't accusing, just simply curious.

"Nothing in particular. The chickens, the weather, the neighbors, the new families that have moved into town, church..." She looked up at Lena. "I've got the feeling you know what I mean."

"I do. We never talked about anything significant either."

"You haven't mentioned your family much," Nathalie said. "Do you have any siblings?"

"No. I was an only child, like you. Apart from their twisted point of view on sexuality and about a million other things, my parents weren't bad parents. But they were strict as hell and it was hard growing up like that, because I didn't have anyone to rebel with or talk to at home."

"Did you have any friends you could talk to?" Nathalie asked. "About your sexuality?"

"Not really. I was the weird kid, the daughter of a pastor and a born-again Christian mother. I suppose being in New York made it worse, somehow. In a city that's so liberal, coming from an extremely conservative family doesn't exactly help you with your popularity factor in school. We had no TV, and I wasn't allowed to listen to popular music. While my classmates hung out in the mall or at the skate park, I spent every free afternoon in a bible study group. I hated dresses, as you can probably imagine, but my mother still picked out my clothes for me when I was sixteen. I looked so out of place, you'd laugh if you saw the pictures."

"That's quite extreme," Nathalie said. "It must have been hard for you."

Lena put an arm around Nathalie. "Don't feel sorry for me. I came out of my shell when I moved here and made up for my lack of fun in my childhood in tenfold within no time."

"What made you decide to tell your parents?" Nathalie took her hand and pulled it further down over her shoulder.

"I saw a flyer one day, for a Christian LGBT social club. It was pinned on to the community notice board in the local pool where I used to go swimming. I couldn't stop looking at it, and finally, after a couple of weeks, I managed to work up the courage to go. It was eye-opening. People spoke about coming out in a Christian family and there were a lot of positive stories. It gave me strength, and I made friends who were like me and accepted me for who I was. Within no time, I had a crush on a girl I met there. Her name was

Delilah. I was so smitten with her, that I decided to tell my parents."

"And that didn't go the way you hoped it would go." Nathalie rested her head on Lena's shoulder as they walked.

"No, it didn't. But in a way, I'm glad things happened the way they did. I wouldn't have been here otherwise."

They had reached the end of the pier and crossed the road into town, passing museums, art deco cinemas and traditional ice cream parlors. Lena led them across the busy main road and into a side street, where she looked up at a big, white building that resembled the shape of an egg. It was smooth, only broken up by five long, curved windows that stretched over the front on each floor.

"That's one of my grandfather's creations," she said. "One of his proudest pieces, in fact. The windows were a nightmare, it took him several attempts to get them right."

"Wow, I've never seen anything like it." Nathalie studied the post-modern building, which now housed a handful of design agencies. "It's unconventional, but it's not out of place either." The building was the only freestanding one in the street, surrounded by a white wall with rounded corners that looked like it was there to protect the egg from rolling over. She traced the smooth surface of the wall and squeezed Lena's hand.

"You must be proud to be his granddaughter. But then again, he would have been so proud of you too, for everything you've achieved. I bet you inherited your creative talent from him."

Lena shook her head and laughed. "I wouldn't compare myself to him. Not ever. What I do doesn't even come close to his work, but it does inspire me." She turned to Nathalie. "It's a shame you won't be able to come to the opening of my project in Monaco. I'd love for you to see it."

"Yeah." A sad smile crept across Nathalie's lips. "I'm sorry I can't make any promises. But I might be able to come. It just depends how things work out." She bit her lip. "It's not going to be over, Lena. Things will just be a little different."

47

"Marcus Obermeier." Nathalie said his name out loud as she typed it into the search engine. She had no idea why she was looking him up, although the words *offices* and *Monaco* seemed to have stuck with her, somehow. She got a match straight away, including a picture of him. He was a stern looking man, with cold, grey eyes and blonde hair that was combed into a side-parting and held in place with generous amounts of gel. His suit looked expensive and so did his watch, she noticed as she clicked on his PR photo. She found the link to his company and clicked on the Monaco branch. Rendered images of the yet unfinished offices popped up, showcasing luxurious interiors and magnificent views. *Nice one, Marcus.* Nathalie scrolled through the pictures, intrigued by the small, but extremely stylish, rental spaces that were still available. The lease was crazy expensive but, considering the location, that could be forgiven. She clicked on one of the corner offices and stared at the pictures, in awe of how perfect it looked. There was a corner window, looking out over the ocean, and a small balcony with sliding doors, facing the South. Each office contained two desk areas, a meeting corner that seated six, a modern kitchen, and a restroom. The advert stated that the office also came with basic appliances such as a printer, a Smart TV and high-speed internet. There was a gym on the top floor and an IT department in the basement, serving all offices free of charge. Marcus certainly knew how to get people excited.

Without thinking, Nathalie clicked on the link to contact one of the representatives. *What are you doing? This is crazy.* A message came up, informing her that the waiting lists were full, but that she was welcome to give their office a call if she wanted information on future developments. *You see? It's not for you. Just do the sensible thing.* She sighed, scrolled through her calendar and clicked on the meeting invite for the Skype interview she'd been pondering over all afternoon. She had accepted it, and everything was set up. Lena was in Monaco, so she decided to have an early night. Tomorrow was going to be a big day.

48

A seagull landed on Lena's picnic blanket. It hopped closer and picked up a breadcrumb. Lena glanced over at Gumbo to make sure he was asleep, tore a corner off her sandwich and threw it in the bird's direction. Gumbo looked up when the large bird jumped towards them and picked up his lunch. He did a quick risk analysis before deciding that the bird was too big, and that the danger of being humiliated by it, outweighed the potential rewards. He propped his head back between his front paws, pretending not to care about the intruder. Lena had stopped on her way back from Monaco, tired of the traffic jams, and had found a great spot along one of the smaller roads facing the coast. The sun was setting, and the tide was high, leaving only a small strip of beach on the outskirts of Juan-les-Pins; a sweet, touristy town along the French Riviera. She couldn't wait to get back to Nathalie but being stuck in a car for hours wasn't her idea of fun either. The invitation to the opening of the new garden, and side entrance of the Princely Palace she'd been working on for months now, was in front of her. It was five weeks from now, and it looked like it was going to be quite an affair. There was a plus one option, waiting to be filled in and sent back to the organizer. If everything went to plan, she'd soon have people lining up to work with her. She could do commercial projects or museum gardens, work with famous artists or established botanists, not to mention the celebrities who would be willing to pay a hefty sum for her to design their gardens. That was an exciting thought, yet she wasn't over the moon. *Nathalie will be gone by then.* They hadn't spoken any more about extending her vacation and Lena wasn't going to bring it up. For now, she treasured every moment with Nathalie, and every day she opened her eyes to find her in her arms felt like a blessing. For now, they also lived together as if it was the most natural thing in the world. They just fit, somehow. They talked about everything and anything, laughed and socialized together. The house had come back to life, and it was all because of her. It was going to be tough when Nathalie left, but maybe it was worth the pain.

49

Nathalie closed her laptop and let out a sigh of relief. She looked at her watch; it was four pm. She'd been answering questions and selling herself for the past two hours. The Skype interview had gone better than expected. The hypothetical cases the HR and finance representatives had put forward weren't rocket science, and she'd been sharp and to the point with her problem-solving scenarios. At the end, they'd indicated that they were interested in her as a candidate, but said they'd have to discuss her with the CEO before confirming a second interview. She was on a bit of a high, after using her brain again, and felt like celebrating. Her interview outfit was unconventional, and she laughed when she saw her reflection in the mirror as she stood up from the desk in the living room. From the waist up, she was immaculately dressed in a crisp white shirt, topped off with a pearl necklace. Below that, she was only wearing bikini bottoms and a cheap pair of sliders. She removed her red lipstick and undid her hair, shaking it out until it fell over her shoulders. Lena was still in Monaco, so she swapped the shirt for a crochet top and a pair of shorts and decided to walk into town for some food and a celebratory glass of Champagne by herself.

The sun was still high when Nathalie finally arrived at Valbonne Square. She sat down at her usual spot and waved at Alain, who was in the process of taking an order from one of the neighboring tables.

"Nathalie!" He shouted as he walked towards her. "My favorite American."

Nathalie rolled her eyes at his standard joke. "Hi Alain. How are you?"

"I can't complain." He grinned. "Love is sweet, life is good, and the days are long."

"Wow, you're poetic today." She laughed. "What happened? Is it Samantha?" She said her name in a teasing tone.

"It might be." Alain searched for a pen in his pocket. "But a gentleman never kisses and tells." He tried to wipe the grin off his face, but his attempt was unsuccessful. "What can I do for you, Nathalie?"

"Could I have a goat's cheese salad and a glass of Champagne please?"

"Champagne?" He frowned. "But you're by yourself. You should never drink Champagne by yourself. Where's Lena?"

"She's in Monaco, working. She'll be back tomorrow."

A man at the table next to her turned at the mention of Lena's name. He was with a woman, and by the looks of it, they'd had quite a bit to drink already.

"You're Nathalie?" He asked. "Magic Lena's Nathalie?"

Alain shot him a nervous glance. "Yes, this is Lena's

tenant, Nathalie. Nathalie, meet Bernie and his wife Gladys. Bernie works for Lena."

Nathalie smiled at them. "Very nice to meet you both." She frowned when something suddenly clicked. "Does that mean you're Cherie's parents?"

"We are," Gladys said. "You take the same class as her, right?"

"Yeah." Nathalie paused. "But I don't understand... you're both English."

Bernie laughed. "Yes, but we moved here when Cherie was five, so she's more French than English, really. She goes to school here, and all her friends are French." He shook his head. "We've always encouraged her to hold on to her English roots but she's as stubborn as a mule, that girl. Refuses to speak a word of English, even with us."

Nathalie laughed. "Well, whatever she lacks in English, she certainly makes up for in artistic talent. We're all in awe of her skills." She nodded towards their empty bottle of Champagne. "Are you guys celebrating?"

"It's our anniversary," Gladys said in a Northern English accent. "Twenty-five years now. Can you believe it?"

"Wow. Twenty-five years!" Nathalie turned back to Alain. "In that case, could I have a bottle instead, please? And give these lovely people a glass too." She grinned. "See? Now I'm not drinking alone, so you don't have to worry."

Alain shrugged. "Very well. I'll get you a bottle instead." He gave Bernie a warning look, but Bernie was too tipsy to notice anything other than the empty glass in front of him.

"And another bottle for us too, please," he yelled.

Nathalie was surprised at her sudden flare up of sociability. *Offering drinks to strangers? Small talk?* Maybe she was starting to resemble a normal human being after all. She crossed her legs and turned sideways, facing Bernie and his wife.

"Don't worry," she said. "I'm not going to bother you guys on your anniversary. But I am curious about one thing. Why do you call her Magic Lena?"

50

"Lena, can I talk to you?" Lena looked up from the rose bush she was cutting and wiped her forehead. A grim feeling started to spread throughout her belly. A talk was never good news in her experience.

"Sure," she said, trying to sound calm. She straightened her back, put down her garden scissors and turned to Nathalie.

"Not here." Nathalie pointed to the terrace. "Could we sit down, please?" Lena nodded. *Definitely not good news.*

"What's up, Nat?" She asked as she sat down in front of the pot of coffee Nathalie had made them earlier.

"I've been offered a second job interview," Nathalie said. "With that firm in Singapore. I had my first interview yesterday over Skype and it went well. They just called to inform me that I got through and to tell me that the CEO is in New York at the moment. He wants to see me." She paused and took a deep breath. "So, I'm thinking about getting a flight out there tomorrow. It will be a lot easier if I can do the interview there, and then go to Chicago straight after to pack up my things and wrap up the sale of the apartment. I figured I might as well kill two birds with one stone." Her eyes were searching for Lena's, but she avoided her gaze.

Lena had imagined this moment many times, but living it was so much worse. The agonizing brick that suddenly weighed on her stomach made her feel sick as she swallowed down the lump in her throat. She tried to calm herself, but was unable to suppress the anger that welled up inside of her.

"Don't say you're *thinking* about going, Nat. You don't need my approval for anything, it's your life. Just tell me you'll be gone tomorrow, there's no point beating around the bush." Her expression was cold, her hands balled into fists under the table. She always knew the day would come soon, but she never expected it to be tomorrow. It stung in more ways than she'd anticipated. *It's over.*

"But I'll come back," Nathalie said in a defensive tone. "We talked about this, didn't we? Even if they offer me the job right there and then, which is highly unlikely by the way, I doubt they'll expect me to move there straight away. There's always a lot of paperwork involved in relocation. I'd have at least another four weeks here before I'd have to move."

"And then what?" Lena finally looked up and shot her a fierce look. "Then you'd be off again, and I'll be here picking myself back up. It doesn't work like that, Nat. I'm not just here for your convenience."

Nathalie blinked and stared at her in surprise. "I don't understand. I thought we talked this through. I mean, I know I wasn't supposed to leave for another three weeks, but what's three weeks in the grand scheme of things? I know we can make this work, Lena."

Lena shook her head. Who had she been kidding? This

was never going to work. Nathalie hadn't even left yet, and the familiar stab of loss was already starting to spread out from her gut. She recognized the pain because she'd been through this before, and she knew there was no point in trying. Sure, she was happy with Nathalie, perhaps happier than she'd ever been. But she'd also been happy with Selma and look where that got her. Three years of her life wasted on trying to get over her.

"You're right," she said. "We did talk this through but talking and reality are two different things." She stood up. "I can't do this."

"No!" Nathalie slammed her hand on the table. "You can't just walk away, Lena. You have to try at least. I'm willing to try."

"How do I know you're not going to fuck me over and run off with someone else? That you won't meet someone who's more suited to you?" Lena looked at Nathalie as if she was already guilty of doing just that.

"I'm not Selma, Lena." Nathalie tried to stay calm but it was hard when Lena was accusing her of cheating when she hadn't even left yet.

"No, you're not. But the situation is the same. Before you know it, our contact will be reduced to one lousy phone call a week and you'll be snuggling up to one of your new colleagues, wondering how the hell you're going to let me down easy."

Nathalie arched an eyebrow. "Me? How do I know you're not going to dive into bed with your next client? Isn't that your expertise?" She crossed her arms. "Magic Lena."

"Who told you that?" Lena shot her a fierce look.

"It doesn't matter who told me. It's true, isn't it? That you sleep around with all your clients? Break their hearts? Is that what you're doing here? Breaking up with me so you can move on to your next conquest?"

"I'm not moving on," Lena said. "You are. You're the one who's leaving, not me."

Nathalie raised her voice. "What did you expect? That I would stay here, go to my watercolor course twice a week and join the local knitting club? Huh? Forget about my life and my ambitions?"

"Your life?" Lena turned and walked back to the rose bush, picking up the garden scissors on her way. "You know what?" she shouted. "That's a great idea. Why don't you just go back to your life, because it sounded fucking amazing. And please leave me out of it."

51

A tear fell on to Nathalie's silk navy top. The stain spread out, creating a shapeless blob on the fabric. She stared down at it, then folded it up and put it in her suitcase. Her black suit was draped over the back of a chair, ready to be worn on her way back. She sniffed and wiped her eyes, before turning to the next pile of garments. She'd hardly worn any of the clothes she'd brought with her, and she didn't have enough space in her luggage to take everything she'd bought in the village. The concept of wearing a blazer again seemed alien to her now. Unable to choose what to take, she blindly picked up a pile and stuffed it in her suitcase, giving up on the coordinated packing she'd been so obsessed with, ever since she went on her first trip. She peeked out of the window to check if Lena was back, but there was still no sign of her. Lena had left early that morning, and they hadn't spoken since the fight. Not being able to see her before she went back was hard, but perhaps easier than having to face the anger and hurt in Lena's eyes. Nathalie felt sick when she thought of their fight. She knew that Lena was going to be upset by her sudden departure, but she hadn't expected her to dismiss everything they had and take off without saying goodbye. Nathalie had been tossing and turning all night, unable to sleep after Lena's fierce reaction. *She's been through this before. What did you expect?* Nathalie walked into the bathroom to check if she hadn't forgotten anything important. There was a piece of lavender soap on the edge of the basin that Lena had bought for her. She carefully wrapped it up in toilet paper and put it in the front compartment of her suitcase.

NATHALIE HAD A LONG SHOWER, put on her suit and stared at her reflection in the mirror, hardly recognizing the woman she saw. She felt like an empty shell, a doll, dressed up to play a part in whatever role she'd been assigned. She buttoned up her shirt and tucked it into her pants, then unbuttoned the top three buttons again, pulling the collar away from her neck. She felt like she couldn't breathe. It didn't feel right. *Don't be silly Nathalie. This is who you are. Now go back and make sure you get that job.* It still didn't feel right.

AFTER SHE'D LOADED her luggage into the car, Nathalie walked around the estate one more time. Bare foot, and with her heels in her hand, she let her gaze wander over the rose bushes, the lush garden and the pool where she'd had the most beautiful and memorable moments of her life. She walked past the annex, where she'd woken up in Lena's arms, blissfully happy. She smiled at the memory while she walked back up to the terrace where she'd spent her mornings drinking coffee while Lena worked in the garden, and so many nights reading and talking to her. Her cigarettes were still on the terrace table, next to the ashtray. She sat down and lit one, looking out over the place that had changed her life, and changed who she was forever. Nathalie loved it here, and she knew she would miss it every single day. But now, without Lena here, everything seemed like a dream, like it had never happened. She didn't have time to say goodbye to Alain, Marie-Louise, or the friends she'd made during her art course. It had all happened so fast. She would have to call them when she was back in Chicago, maybe send them a postcard, or an email. How was it possible, she thought, that she had arrived feeling optimistic, despite her divorce, and now she was leaving with a heavy heart and empty dreams. Lena was still not back, and it was time to leave. *She doesn't want to say goodbye. It's over.* Nathalie missed her so much that it hurt. She wasn't familiar with this kind of pain, the kind that almost choked her each time she thought of Lena, and the fact that she might never see her again. *If only I could feel her arms around me one more time.* Nathalie cried in silence, only woken up from her thoughts when the ash from her cigarette fell onto her lap. She brushed it off, stood up and walked to the car without looking back.

THE DRIVE to the airport went by quickly. Valbonne was quiet in the mornings, especially on a Monday. Nathalie stopped off at the town square to see if Alain was there, but his café was still closed, just like the shops and the gallery. She drove as slow as she could, savoring each view one last time. The sun rising over the mountains, the green valleys, the coastline in the distance, the medieval villages with their sweet little shops, antique markets and flowerbeds... It was gone before she knew it, and then, all that was left was the motorway and the airport, the check-in desk and finally, the plane that would take her away forever.

52

"She's gone?" Alain frowned as he put the espresso on the bar in front of Lena. "But I thought she had another couple of weeks left?"

"Job interview," Lena said. She felt hollow and full of regret. It was unlike her to behave in such an emotional manner and she was angry with herself for doing so. She always knew she was going to be hurt, she'd seen it coming from miles away. And still, she'd opened up her heart to Nathalie, let her in. But that wasn't Nathalie's fault, and she didn't deserve to be treated the way Lena had treated her. "I've been so stupid," she said, knocking back her expresso. "I should have said goodbye. I don't know why I walked away. I guess I felt hurt and I thought it would be easier that way." Alain gestured for one of his servers to take over, walked around the bar and sat down next to her.

"And she's not coming back?"

"What difference does it make?" Lena scraped her spoon over the bottom of the empty cup. "If she gets the job, she'll be moving to Singapore. And if she doesn't get it, she'll go somewhere else. Either way, it's not going to be here, is it?"

She sighed. "So it's best if we don't see each other again. I don't know what I was thinking."

"She really got to you, didn't she?"

Lena kept her gaze fixed on her empty cup. "Yeah, she did." She turned to Alain, resting her elbow on the bar. "Go on, say it. I got exactly what I deserved for messing with all those other women. Isn't that what you're dying to tell me?" There was a silence.

"No." Alain shook his head. "I don't think you deserve it. Nobody does." He sighed. "Samantha is leaving next week, so I know how you feel."

"Samantha?" Lena studied Alain's face, but nothing indicated that he was joking. "You're serious, aren't you?"

"We've been on a couple of dates since that first one I told you about," Alain said, with an awkward smile. "She's nice and funny, and she doesn't let me get away with any crap. She's one of those women who says what she thinks, all the time. Do you have any idea how great that is? There's no ambiguity, no guessing with her. And she's so beautiful."

"Wow." Lena cocked her head. "Who are you and what have you done to my womanizing friend?"

"I could ask you the same," Alain bounced back at her. "Magic Lena got tricked." Lena gave him a sad smile. "No, I didn't get tricked. It was real, all right."

Alain nudged her as he got off his stool. "Then why did you let her go?"

53

Packing up her life was a tedious chore. Although Nathalie had a team of seven professionals helping her, she still had to go through each item and decide if she wanted to keep it or not. Jack had already gone through his stuff, leaving the apartment half-empty. He hadn't taken any of their expensive furniture, apart from his favorite designer chair and the art he'd collected over the years that they'd lived there. Nathalie had no idea what to do with everything, so she'd hired a storage unit for three months, until she figured out whether to sell it or relocate it. It was sad, seeing the remnants of a life she'd lived not even that long ago, when she was still unaware of Jack's infidelity and her own desires that were buried deep down. *Wasted time. So much wasted time.*

"What do we do with all of this?" one of the movers asked her, pointing to the pots and pans cupboard.

Nathalie shrugged. "I only need a couple." She randomly picked three pans and put them aside. "The rest can go in the charity section. Or keep them for yourself if there's anything you need. Most of them have never been used." She watched him pile all the brand-new kitchen utensils into a box. She doubted if she'd ever cook again. Her cooking at Lena's house hadn't exactly been a success, although she had thoroughly enjoyed the evening. She shook her head, trying to rid herself of the memory of that beautiful night, where she'd felt part of something bigger than herself. The laughter, the company, the conversations and Lena by her side. It hurt too much to think about it.

"How about these?" the same man shouted again, this time referring to her cutlery. "You'll need knives, won't you?"

"Sure, you can pack those," Nathalie said, looking at the drawer with very little interest. "Take the bottles of olive oil home if you want them, they're amazing quality." The Italian mover inspected the bottles and smiled.

"Thank you, Mrs Kingston. I think the family will appreciate it."

"Just Nathalie is fine," Nathalie said with a sad smile. "I'm not Mrs anymore."

He nodded understandingly. "All right, Nathalie." He gave her a pile of red and green stickers. "Why don't you mark everything you want to keep with green and everything that can go with red? Then I won't have to bug you." He hesitated. "I'm sure you've got enough on your mind."

"Okay." Nathalie took the labels from him, wondering why she hadn't thought of it herself. Between the preparation for her move, flying to New York for her interview and returning to Chicago to empty the apartment, she hadn't even considered a system. But despite the stress, the interview had gone better than expected and they had offered her the role of CFO two days later. The expat package was generous, and the free accommodation nothing short of spectacular, yet she had still to experience the excitement that was supposed to come with a new challenge as big as this one. So why didn't she feel anything? No, wait. That wasn't entirely true. She felt sadness. Deep, dark sadness that haunted her day and night. Still, she had accepted the offer, of course. Jobs like this one didn't come up very often.

The movers stacked the kitchen boxes on to two trolleys, rolled them out and came back for more. *So much stuff. Why? Did it ever make me happy?* Nathalie's thoughts went back to Lena again, wondering what she would have thought of the abundance of unused things, most of them brand-new. Although Lena was wealthy herself, she wasn't someone who needed a lot. Sure, she had a nice house and an amazing car. But Nathalie was pretty certain she could do without all that, and as long as she had her job, a good coffee maker and Gumbo by her side, she'd be just as happy. Just like Nathalie, success hadn't come to her overnight, she'd worked hard for it. But the difference between them was that Lena didn't take herself very seriously when it came to her career. It came from her heart, not from blind ambition, and she'd gotten where she was by simply doing what she loved. *What about this new job, Nat? Is it what you really want?*

Lost in thought, Nathalie walked into the bedroom with the stickers in her hand, where she opened her bag and shoe closet. There was no end to the copious amounts of purses she had collected over the years, each and every single one of them by an exclusive designer label. Jack had gifted them to her on her birthdays, and for Christmas. She never cared that much for purses, but she'd never told him, and so he had kept on buying them for her. Some of them were still in the original packaging, the paper stuffing still inside. *What a shame.* Nathalie had always bought cuff links for Jack, but thinking back now, she couldn't remember him ever wearing them either.

"Hey, guys!" She waved at the movers as she walked back into the living room, trying to catch their attention. They looked up from what they were doing. "Does any of you have a wife or a girlfriend who likes purses?"

LATER THAT NIGHT, Nathalie found herself in an empty apartment. In one day, she had managed to shed herself from years of memories and now, there was nothing left but a hollow carcass. Even the fitted blinds were gone. The light from the city cast a faint shimmer over the now eerie living room that was only dimly lit by a lightbulb, hanging down from the ceiling where the dining table had been. The spotless white walls Nathalie used to love didn't seem so appealing anymore. Instead, the apartment reminded her of a clinic, or the reception area in a private hospital. It echoed when she walked around on her high heels. She hadn't even considered the fact that she wouldn't have a bed for the night. All that was left were her suitcases from France that she'd dragged with her to New York and then back to Chicago, lacking time to re-pack. A feeling of fatigue took over and she slumped down on the floor with her phone, searching for a hotel.

54

"Nathalie?" Nathalie's mother sounded surprised to hear her daughter's voice. "How are you? Why are you calling so late at night? Are you alright?" Nathalie looked at her watch. It was only eight. She'd spent the day in her hotel room, watching bad movies. After each movie, she told herself she was going to call her parents, yet each time, she put it off and searched for another mediocre romantic comedy. Not a single one of the options in the long list on her pay-per-view channel portrayed two women, she noticed.

"No, everything's fine," she lied. "Did I wake you up? I can call you back tomorrow?"

"No, not at all. Your father and I were just getting ready for the night." Her mother sighed. "It's so good to hear your voice, Nat-Nat." Nathalie smiled.

"It's good to hear your voice too, Mom." Nathalie picked up the piece of paper on her lap with her rehearsed speech. "As you know, Jack and I have just finalized our divorce. We sold the apartment and I cleared it out today."

"Oh yes, the divorce." There was a silence. "So, you went through with that?"

Nathalie rolled her eyes, crumpled up the speech and threw it across the room. The five scenarios she'd written out were useless now. She should have known her mother would come up with a reply as ridiculous as this one. "Yes, I went through with it, Mom. He was sleeping with his assistant. Besides, I don't think it would have worked out anyway." She opened her mouth to elaborate but decided against it.

"But honey, everyone goes through difficult patches. Your father and I haven't always been happy together, but we married each other in front of God, and we wouldn't dream of having a divorce. Life is long, if you're lucky. And it's not always great, but having someone to share it with is a blessing from the Lord. It's sacred."

"I know." Nathalie decided not to argue her mother's pre-historic view on marriage. There was no point. "But as I said, it was not going to work out, ever." She took a deep breath. "Anyway, I wanted to let you know that I've accepted a job offer in Singapore." She waited for a reply. "Mom, are you there?"

"Yes, I'm here, honey. Singapore? Where is that?"

Nathalie managed to suppress a chuckle. "It's in Southeast Asia." Her mother never failed to surprise her with her lack of geographical knowledge.

"But that's the other side of the world." There was a silence. "Isn't it? And we'll never see you any more if you move there."

"We only see each other once a year anyway," Nathalie said. "Okay, it's been a bit longer this time around but that won't happen again. I promise I'll still visit you every year. Besides, for as long as I've lived in Chicago, you and Dad haven't visited me once. So why does it matter if I'm somewhere a bit further away?"

"But Nathalie, you know we can't just pack up and leave," her mother said in a defensive tone. "Your father and I have a responsibility for the chickens and..."

"I'm sure that in all those years..." Nathalie paused, too tired to find the right words, "...you could have found someone to feed the chickens for a couple of days. I even offered to hire someone for you." She closed her eyes, cursing herself for picking an argument with the only people she had left. The only people she could still call without a reason, just to talk. "I'm sorry, Mom. I didn't mean it like that. Look, I was wondering if I could come over next week? I have some time left before I start my new job, and I'd like to see you both before I leave."

"You're coming to visit us?" her mother sounded puzzled. "Good God, of course, that would be great. It's just that you haven't been here in a long time, and I need to prepare your room and..."

"You don't have to do anything," Nathalie interrupted her again. "I just need a bed. Hell, I don't even care if I sleep on the couch, or even in the barn. And you don't have to prepare a banquet or bake twenty cornbread muffins for breakfast. It's just me. I could even help you guys out with the chickens and the cornfields." Her mother laughed.

"You? Help on the farm? Don't worry dear. You know I like to take care of *you,* because I don't get the chance very often." She cleared her throat. "Please let me know when you land, and I'll make sure your father picks you up in the truck."

"No need," Nathalie protested. "I'll take a cab. It will probably be late."

"Nonsense." Her mother put on an authoritative tone. "Cabs are a waste of money. Your father will pick you up."

"Alright, thank you," Nathalie said. She would never tell her mother she'd just given away thousands of dollars' worth of purses.

55

"This looks great, guys. Well done!" Lena inspected the final flowerbed along the palace wall. It looked even better than she'd imagined, and for the first time in a week, she managed a smile, reassured that the side entrance would be perfect for the opening party. *If only Nathalie could see this.* She'd been working non-stop since Nathalie had left, and that was fine. Work was the best distraction, she knew that from experience. Gumbo however, was not happy with the situation. He hadn't been to the beach in days, and instead was having to make do with the fenced off area on the lawn next to Lena's car. He barked in frustration when Lena looked his way.

"I'm sorry, buddy. I know you're bored." She checked her watch. It was almost six pm and time to go home. There would be no work on Sunday, and therefore no more excuses to avoid the house. She'd been coming back late at night and had continued to sleep in the annex, so she wouldn't have to face the reminders of Nathalie around the house. Bernie, one of her best gardeners, was calling her name from his truck, where he'd just removed his overall.

His bald head was glistening with sweat, and he left muddy streaks on his forehead as he wiped it.

"Hey Lena! You wanna go for a drink?"

Lena shook her head and walked over to him, rolling her shoulders and stretching her arms over her head. Her body always felt good after a hard day's work.

"Nah, I think I'll head home."

Bernie frowned. "Come on, Lena, it's been ages since we've had a beer together. Plus, you owe me one for dumping Mrs Delevoire on me." He shook his head. "Actually, it's Miss Delevoire now. She's a right mess, that woman. Never satisfied with my hedge trimming, no matter how perfect the result, and always, always asking for you. She drives me mad."

"Alright then." Lena laughed. She decided to forgive him for the nickname he'd given her. Bernie didn't mean any harm, and besides, she knew how difficult Christine Delevoire could be. "But just one and I need to take Gumbo home first. I think he's had enough. I can meet you at Alain's in let's say, two hours? The traffic shouldn't be too bad by now."

"That sounds good." Bernie gave her a thumbs-up. "I'll see you there. Don't stand me up this time."

SOCIALIZING WAS the last thing Lena wanted, but Bernie was right. She hadn't had a beer with him in a long time, and it was important to maintain a good relationship with her freelancers. Bernie was a genuinely nice guy and she wanted him to know that she appreciated what he did for her. She managed a smile as she sat down opposite him, calling the server for two beers.

"Almost done, Bernie. Almost done," she said. "Two

more weeks like this and a little bit of luck with the weather, and we'll have the Royal Gardens ready before the deadline."

Bernie nodded, tapping the table with his fingernails. "We always meet our deadlines with you," he said, "but I've never been on a job as smooth as this one. You've done great work with the planning, Lena."

"Thanks." Lena smiled at the compliment. "I'm lucky to have the best people." Their server handed her a beer and she held it up in a toast. "To many more jobs together."

Bernie held up his glass too. "Cheers to that." He winced after the first bitter sip of his beer and sighed after swallowing the cool liquid. There was a silence. "Hey Lena?"

"Yeah?" Lena frowned at his sudden serious tone of voice.

"Are you alright?" He shifted in his chair, rubbing his shiny forehead. "I mean, you've been quiet lately. You've been keeping to yourself, staring into space over your lunch break. The guys have noticed too and I just..." He hesitated. "Well, I just want you to know that you can talk to me."

"Thank you, Bernie." Lena realized she sounded surprised, and although talking to Bernie was the last thing on her mind, it was sweet and unexpected, coming from him. "That's very kind of you," she said. "But I'm okay. I mean, I'll be okay. It's nothing I can't handle." She gave him a smirk. "I'm Magic Lena after all." She couldn't resist teasing him.

Bernie's eyes widened. "Right," he said. "Magic Lena. Yes, I'm sorry about that. It was only a joke, but it seems to have spread out like an epidemic."

"Don't worry." Lena shook her head. "I know how these things go. Anyway, it got me thinking, and I've decided I'm going to set strict boundaries from now on. No more sleeping with clients and dumping them on you. Seriously, I'm not even going to have as much as a coffee with them."

Bernie sighed in relief. "Thank you. That would be really helpful," he said. "Again, I'm sorry if I caused you any trouble by giving you that nickname." He fiddled with the pile of coasters between them on the table. "There's also something else, Lena."

"What?" Lena frowned. "What's wrong, Bernie?"

"Well, you know when I had the day off to celebrate my anniversary?"

"Yeah?" Bernie was clearly uncomfortable. "Did you have a fight with your wife?"

"No." He looked up at Lena with a nervousness she'd never seen before. "Nothing like that. We had a lot to drink, my wife and I, and we met Nathalie. Your Nathalie." He sighed. "I might have said some things about you, just as a joke. And I shouldn't have."

Lena leaned in closer. "What kind of things?" By now, she had an idea, but she wanted to hear it from him.

"Just some things about your reputation." He looked so miserable that Lena almost felt sorry for him.

"I shouldn't have done it," he continued, "but I didn't see any harm in it at the time. We were just having a laugh."

"So that was you." Lena sat back and watched him suffer in silence for a while. She thought of yelling at him, but what was the point? She was tired of fighting, tired of the draining emotions that were weighing her down. It wouldn't have made a difference what he told Nathalie. She was gone, and Lena was trying to move on. Her expression softened at the sight of his tearful eyes. "I suppose you were only telling her the truth."

Bernie shook his head. "I'm so sorry, Lena. I've been a terrible friend. You're kind and generous and talented. I should have talked about all your amazing qualities instead of making you into some womanizing heartbreaker. I feel terrible about it."

"It's okay." Lena took a sip from her beer. "I'm glad you came clean, Bernie. But as I said, I'm moving on from all of that now, it's not who I am anymore so I'd appreciate it if you would stop mentioning it."

"Of course." Bernie nodded. "Are you mad at me? You must be furious."

Lena shrugged and waved at Alain, who threw his apron behind the bar before making his way towards them. "Looks like we've got company." She managed a smile. "Hey, why don't you buy us all another beer and we'll move this conversation on to a more cheerful subject?"

"Sure. I'll buy you both beers all night." Bernie's face lifted in relief as he rushed inside to open a tab.

56

"There's my Nat-Nat." Nathalie winced when her father hugged her so tight that it hurt her ribcage.

"It's good to see you too, Dad." She handed him one of her suitcases and followed him to his pick-up truck that was parked at least a mile away from Alexandria International Airport. Parking fees were something her father had managed to avoid his whole life, and he wasn't going to give in now. Louisiana was warm and humid, and the discomfort of the hike reminded her of her early school days, when she used to walk for half an hour just to reach the bus stop. There was still the scent of rain in the air, from earlier that day, and the mosquitos were buzzing around her, attempting to eat her alive. Nathalie knew she didn't have to bother with polite chit-chat. Her father wasn't much of a talker, except when it came to the farm.

"How are the chickens?" she asked, when they were finally seated in the car. She rolled down the window, gasping for air. Although it was dark now, the heat and the humidity were still close to unbearable to someone who wasn't used to it.

"Chickens have been a bit rowdy lately," he father mumbled. "Starting to think there might be a fox or a wild dog snooping around, trying to get into the farm at night." He turned onto the Highway 66, but instead of speeding up, he kept on creeping over the road as if he was driving a tractor. Nathalie didn't comment on his driving, despite the five cars behind them.

"Oh, that's not good. Have you seen anything?"

Her father shrugged. "No, but it's been keeping me up, worrying. I might sleep outside in the barn tonight; see if I can shoot the damn creature."

"Okay..." That was the end of the first conversation they'd had in two years. Nathalie watched the familiar road signs pass them. Not much had changed since she had last been here, but then there wasn't much to change either. Small country roads, farms, motels, family-run restaurants and lots of churches with well-kept gardens and cemeteries. Nathalie had always felt like she didn't belong, as if she was a tourist in her own hometown. But today, it was comforting to see some familiarity after staying in a soulless airport hotel for two nights. She came here once, sometimes twice a year. Jack had always accompanied her when she did, ever since they started dating in University. But as their company grew and the years passed, the poor phone signal on and around her parent's farm had made them reluctant to stay for longer than two days. This time around though, there would be no phone calls, no urgent emails or contracts to be drawn up, and no Jack. They passed a restaurant where Jack had taken her for dinner once, on their way back to the airport. He was never keen on her mother's Southern cooking and had insisted on getting some 'real food', as he called it. They had left earlier than planned and dined for two hours while they caught up on their emails over their first two courses, both their laptops in between them on the table. Thinking back to that night, Nathalie realized that romance had died a long time ago. She didn't miss him, yet it was surreal to be here without him. Her father turned onto their drive, just before Pineville, and as they drove towards the house, Nathalie could see the light was still on in the kitchen.

"My baby," her mother said, as she gave Nathalie a long hug. "What's happened to you, Nat? You look so skinny." She looked Nathalie up and down and rubbed her shoulders. "Don't you think she looks skinny, Hank?" she asked, not expecting an answer. Her husband rarely answered, but that was how they communicated. She talked, and if she was lucky, he pretended to listen.

"I'm fine, Mom." Nathalie studied her mother's face. It had only been two years since she'd last seen her, but she looked older, and smaller than Nathalie remembered. Her grey hair was thinning out, and the crow's feet around her eyes were significantly deeper than last time she'd visited. The pink velvet robe her mother always wore at night looked bigger on her now, the color doing her complexion no favors. Nathalie was suddenly overcome by guilt for letting so much time pass, so she hugged her mother once more. "It's good to see you both." Betsy Kingston looked over Nathalie's shoulder when she let go.

"So, Jack isn't here?" she asked in a thin voice.

"No, Mom. I told you, we're divorced. He won't be coming along anymore." Nathalie tried not to sound irritated as she followed her mother into the kitchen and sat down at the wonky dining table that had been in the family for generations. Her stomach turned at the greasy smell that penetrated her nostrils. It always smelled the same in her parent's kitchen. Cornbread, bacon, eggs, catfish or any other fried food they would have, alongside a bowl of corn, cabbage and gravy. The décor hadn't changed either. Nothing in her parent's house was ever replaced, unless it was broken beyond repair. The kitchen was spotless but tired looking, with yellow seventies tiles on the walls, matching the worn-out yellow and brown floral curtains. The plates in the cupboard next to her were still the same plates she'd eaten from when she was younger, just a little bit more chipped around the edges. A drawing she'd made when she was four was still on the fridge, the paper now yellow and stained, held in place by a 'Welcome to Pineville' magnet. As always, it was just an observation. Nathalie didn't feel sorry for them. Her parents were happy with what they had and would never accept her help. Not that they needed it. They weren't poor, just simple people who were content with what they had. But Nathalie knew that she would help them when the time came. When they would have to make the difficult decision to let go of the farm and move somewhere smaller and more accessible to spend the rest of their days. Her mother walked over to the stove and checked on the gravy that was simmering on a low heat.

"Well, it's a shame about you and Jack. Your father and I have been praying for you, and so has the rest of the church community." She turned back to face Nathalie. "Are you hungry, dear? We've already eaten but I've got lots of leftovers."

"Sure," Nathalie lied. She wasn't hungry, but it was the only thing she could do to make her mother smile. "It's always nice to have a home-cooked meal." Her father was in the doorway, looking restless. The topic of divorce was not something he was prepared to deal with late at night, Nathalie guessed. She smiled at him, and he smiled back before picking up the rifle in the corner next to the table.

"I'm going to check on the chickens, make sure they're safe." With that, he was off.

LATER THAT NIGHT, Nathalie stared up at the ceiling from her old bed. The stars she had stuck on when she was twelve were still there, and so were the boy-band posters on the door. The sunlight had faded them, and they were curling up at the corners, as if begging to finally be removed. Nathalie studied the N-Sync poster she had torn from a magazine when she was fifteen and wondered if she had ever really been interested in boys. She wasn't sure. There had been boyfriends, but somehow, she couldn't seem to remember their names. Had she always been like this? Always into women? And did it even matter? She was pretty sure she couldn't fall in love with anyone after Lena, whether it was a man or a woman. Because Lena was different, and right now, it felt as if somehow she was the only one, and always would be. Nathalie felt tears welling up when she thought of her. The disappointment and the hurt she'd seen in her eyes when she told her she was leaving were something she wasn't able to shake from her memories. Lena had been right all along. They should have stopped before it was too late. They had been carried away by their whirlwind romance, without thinking of the consequences. Nathalie hadn't really given the whole woman thing a good thought until now, because everything had seemed right when they were together. Wasn't it strange that she had suddenly fallen head over heels for a woman? Wasn't it strange that Lena was the only person she'd ever truly been in love with? It went deeper than she liked to admit, and the question that kept her from sleeping returned to her thoughts over and over again. Was it worth the risk, giving up everything for someone she didn't know that well? Her brain told her it wasn't but the tight knot in her stomach told her otherwise.

She thought of Lena's grandfather, who had moved from New York to France, to be with the love of his life. He'd given up everything. But what did everything mean to her? And in the end, what did she really have, apart from a new job that would look good on her CV? Nothing.

She thought of the office in Monaco she'd been looking at, imagining herself having client meetings there. Before returning home, to Lena. They would have dinner together, drink, talk, laugh, make love... Home. The word that had always been strange to her was starting to take on a whole new meaning, now that she wasn't where she wanted to be. With *who* she wanted to be. Nathalie looked at her watch. It was four in the morning and she hadn't slept yet. Her parents would get up soon. They'd make breakfast, watch the news and feed the chickens. As soon as the sun was up, her mother would go out into the fields, to check on the corn, the cabbage and the potatoes, and come back with a trolley full of produce to sell in their shop. Then she would bake bread, and maybe some cakes. Her father would gather the eggs and they would open the shop together at nine am precisely. Never a minute sooner, never a minute later. They would sit there in silence like good schoolkids until the first customer finally came in around eleven.

"Oh no, it's Sunday." Nathalie said it out loud without realizing it. The days had passed in such a haze, that she'd lost track of time. It was Sunday. Her parents would go to church and they'd expect her to come along. She was tired, but she knew she wasn't going to get any sleep, so she picked up her phone and started typing a message. Because what did she have to lose?

"Hi Lena, I miss you and I get that you're angry. You were right, we should have stopped after that first night. We should have tried just to be friends before it was too late to go back." She paused, pondering over how to continue. *"But I don't regret anything. I want you to know that you were the best thing that ever happened to me. You made me feel alive, made me realize what it's like to long for someone. To love someone and to be in love."* She thought about deleting that last part but didn't. Now was the time to speak her mind, and it would be much easier over text.

"I would still really like to see you again. We need to talk. XXX Nat."

57

The following morning, Lena woke up with a blazing headache. She opened one eye and looked around the living room. She was on the couch, fully dressed, and it was light, most likely late in the day. Her little get-together with Bernie was only ever supposed to be one drink. Catch up, and then go home. But Alain had joined them, heartbroken after Samantha had left. Lena vaguely remembered him crying at one point, and so she had ordered him another beer and then another, listening to his pain, that wasn't much different from her own. Somehow, it had been comforting to know that she wasn't the only one suffering from a broken heart. She scanned the living room and established the kitchen door was still open. Outside, Gumbo was barking, the way he barked when he saw a squirrel or a bird, picking up food that was left out overnight. She got up slowly, moaning in agony, to check if her car was in the driveway and sighed in relief when it wasn't. *At least I didn't drive back.* There was a pizza box on the table in front of the annex, alongside two empty bottles of beer. She felt the pockets of her jeans. They were empty. *Where's my wallet?* Barely able to walk, she searched the annex and found it on the kitchen table, next to her phone. In the doorway, she instinctively glanced at the French doors to Nathalie's bedroom, when it hit her again that Nathalie was gone. The sadness stabbed her deep in her belly. *I should have said goodbye.* She stopped for a moment, contemplating whether to continue sleeping in the annex or the main house, but Gumbo's bark reminded her that he needed attention and feeding, so she walked out and called him.

"Hey boy. Sorry I passed out. I forgot about the time," Lena said as she kneeled down and scratched him behind his ears. Gumbo didn't blame her, he never did. Jumping up and down, he danced around her before speeding off again, chasing a bird. Lena left the door open for him and put food into his bowl. Then she stumbled back into the living room and crashed on the couch, because the bedroom just seemed too far away. Her phone was still in her hand, indicating she had messages. She sighed and scrolled through them, still with one eye open. When she saw there was a message from Nathalie, she sat up, suddenly a lot more focused. She read it a couple of times, her heart beating in her throat. Coffee. She needed coffee. And she needed to think.

AFTER HOURS OF CONTEMPLATING, Lena put her phone down. This was exactly why she didn't do long distance anymore. Of course, she wanted to see Nathalie. She wanted to hold her, to kiss her, to apologize for walking away. She wanted to look into her beautiful blue eyes, stroke her cheek and tell her that she felt the same, that she loved her. She wanted to make love to her, wake up with her, fall asleep with her. But the past two weeks had been difficult. And now, if Nathalie came back, even if it was just to talk, the pain would start all over again when she left at the end of her next stay. Then her visits would be less and less frequent, and so would her replies to Lena's messages, until she finally met someone else. *Some high-powered businessman. Or woman.* That thought raced through her brain, almost blinding her with rage. There was no point putting herself through this again. No point whatsoever. Lena thought about ignoring the message, but she wanted to do the right thing, and so she replied.

Hi Nat, I'd be lying if I said I didn't miss you too, but as I told you, I really can't do this. I apologize for reacting the way I did, and I wish you all the best in your new job. Lena.

Lena regretted sending it almost immediately, but what else could she have done? She walked into the kitchen and opened the fridge, searching for another drink to numb her sadness for a little while.

58

"The power of the Holy Spirit and the redemptive love and work of our father in..." Nathalie's phone vibrated in her pocket and she suddenly woke up, startled. She took it out and looked around to make sure no one had noticed she was sleeping. The Ministry seemed to last longer than she remembered, and she had struggled to keep her eyes open until finally, she'd fallen into a blissful sleep next to her parents on one of the front pews. The pastor turned his attention to Nathalie as he finished his sentence, clearly aware of her dozing off. "... in heaven, the truth of God's work..." She smiled at him, trying her hardest to look impressed by his speech. She was so tired. When they'd arrived hours ago, she had suggested she stay in the back, but her parents had been sitting on the same pew for thirty years and changing that now would be unthinkable. Her mother had simply laughed and said; "No pumpkin, our seats are over there, right at the front, by the pastor." Nathalie clenched the phone in her hand, contemplating whether to look at it or not. The message she'd sent Lena the night before had kept her waiting for a reply all morning. Finally, she couldn't take it anymore. As the pastor looked the other way, she quickly opened her message and saw it was from Lena. She read it, then she read it once more, before tucking the phone back into her pocket with a trembling hand. Turning her attention back to the pastor, she cried quietly.

"WELL IF IT isn't Nathalie Kingston!" a woman yelled when Nathalie and her parents exited the church. Nathalie looked over at the woman who had called her name and gave her a polite wave. It wasn't the best time to talk to people, as she'd been crying non-stop for the past twenty minutes. But the butcher's wife stormed over, determined to catch up.

"Nice to see you again, Mrs Applebee." She sniffed, fighting to keep her emotions under control.

Mrs Applebee took her into a tight embrace. "Our little lost soul. We've been praying for you, my dear." She smiled. "But by the looks of it, you've found your way back to God."

Nathalie gave her a puzzled look. "I'm sorry?"

"No need to be shy my dear. You're not the first one to cry after being reunited with the Lord. Pastor Fallon has been known to have that effect on people."

"Oh that... I'm sorry. I didn't mean to..." Nathalie wiped her face, suddenly realizing Mrs Applebee was referring to her tears.

"No apologies needed, Nathalie. We're all glad to see you're back. Say, do you remember Eddie?" She turned to the church door, where a tall, dark-haired man of Nathalie's age was talking to some other people. His suit was too big for him, as if he'd borrowed it from his father's wardrobe. "Eddie! Hey, Eddie! Come here and say hello to Nathalie. It's Nathalie Kingston!"

Eddie looked up, smiled and made his way towards them. He gave Nathalie a curious glance-over. "Hey there. It's been a while."

Nathalie shook his hand. "Yeah, it has." She studied the man she'd gone to primary school with, searching for a resemblance to the chinless little boy with the big glasses and frumpy jeans. He'd certainly grown into his looks. His shoulders had broadened, and his jawline was well-defined. His eyes were still kind, but he looked tired and mildly irritated when Mrs Applebee and Nathalie's mother walked off together, leaving them there.

"Please ignore my mother," he pleaded. "I've just been through a divorce. She's been trying to set me up from the second the ink was dry and I'm not sure how much longer I can take it."

"Don't worry." Nathalie looked up at him. "I've just been through a divorce myself. But I'm sure you've heard all about it." She rolled her eyes. "My mother told me the whole church has been praying for me."

Eddie gave her a sympathetic smile. "I knew about it, alright. But I won't bore you with the details of the communal prayer you never asked for." There was an awkward moment, in which they both contemplated whether to stay behind and talk or follow the group of church-goers who were heading back home. "Hey, I don't want you to think I'm prying here," Eddie continued, "but you seem upset. Is there anything I can do for you?"

"No, but thank you." Nathalie shook her head, then spotted the rectangular shape in his chest pocket. "Actually...do you have a cigarette by any chance? I just got a shitty message on my phone and I could really do with one."

Eddie looked over at his parents. They had just turned a corner onto the main road and were almost out of sight.

"Yeah, I do. Just wait till they're gone. My parents don't know I smoke."

Nathalie managed a chuckle and held up a hand. "Same here." She saw her mother turn around and look at them, discussing something with Mrs Applebee. "I can't believe they're trying to set us up. Is that really what they're doing?"

"Yeah. I'm afraid so." Eddie shrugged as if it was no surprise to him. "So where do you live now?" he asked.

"Chicago," Nathalie said. She bore the pointy toe of her heel into the dusty path and kicked a pebble into the grass. "Well, technically I don't live anywhere at the moment. My ex-husband and I have just sold our apartment there. I'm moving to Singapore in a couple of weeks, for a new job."

"Wow." Eddie's eyes widened. "Sounds like you did well for yourself after you moved away from here." He waited until the others were out of sight, produced a pack of cigarettes from his pocket and offered one to Nathalie. "So, what do you do?"

"I'm in sustainable manufacturing," she said, too tired to explain the details. "What about you? I'm surprised you're still here. You were always the one who was desperate to get away. Not that there's anything wrong with living here," she added. "Pineville is a lovely place and all..."

"No need to sugarcoat it," Eddie said. "I wanted to get away all right. But I knocked up my ex-wife Brianne when I was eighteen, so I never went to university. Brianne's father gave me a job in his realtor's office and I'm still there to this day. We have a son, his name is Eddie Junior. He's with Brianne today, that's why my parents made me go to church with them."

"I see." Nathalie said, lighting her cigarette. "I'm sorry about your marriage."

"Don't be." Eddie shook his head as they started to walk

back towards town. "We only stayed together for our son, and that was a mistake. I've been seeing..." He chuckled. "I can't believe I'm telling you this."

"Go on." Nathalie nudged him.

"Well, I've been seeing Darlene for two years now. Darlene Sellors. Do you remember her?"

"I sure do." Nathalie smiled. "Prettiest girl in school. Hell, even I had a crush on her." She winced when she realized what she had just said. Thinking back, she had been quite obsessed with Darlene for a while.

"She still is." Eddie shrugged. "She's a hairdresser, owns the salon in town. But she's also married with two kids."

"Wow. So that's where it gets messy."

"Yeah, you could say that. We got talking one day when she was cutting my hair and it just clicked, you know. I even stayed for another hour after she'd closed up, because I didn't want to leave, and she didn't want me to go either. Have you ever had that before?"

"Yeah." Nathalie looked up at him and cocked her head. "I know what you mean."

"Anyway," Eddie continued, "we didn't want to break up our families, so we saw each other in secret, twice a week, for years. That was a mistake, not to mention wrong. Her husband found out, I still don't know how, and he told my wife before he broke my nose. Then, of course, all hell broke loose and the whole town got involved. I'm only just out of the woods."

"Small town politics." Nathalie mumbled.

"Small town politics," he repeated. "Darlene is finally getting a divorce too. We thought about moving away, but then I won't get to see my son as much as I'd like to. So instead, I guess we'll just stay here and continue to live our lives in this town where everyone knows about our business and my boss hates me because I cheated on his daughter." He sighed. "If he doesn't fire me, because God knows, I deserve that. The pastor is convinced Darlene's marriage can still be saved if they set me up with someone else. Someone available." He gestured from himself to Nathalie and back.

"That's just stupid." Nathalie said, feeling his frustration.

"What I wouldn't give to start over somewhere nobody knows me." Eddie turned to Nathalie as they walked. "It's funny. I've never told anyone about Darlene. I've never seen the point, because the whole town already knows and besides that, it sounds so wrong when I say it out loud."

"It can't be wrong if it feels right." Nathalie waved at the owner of the diner they passed. She recognized his face but couldn't remember his name. "That's just the way life goes sometimes. And we can't all be expected to get it right the first time around now, can we?"

"I guess not. So, what about you, Nat-Nat? Do people still call you that?"

Nathalie laughed. "Only my parents, but it's fine. I don't mind."

"Do you have any kids?"

"No. It was just me and Jack and a whole lot of hard work. And now it's just me." She flicked away her cigarette stub and put her hands in the back pockets of her jeans. "I did meet someone, after Jack. I'm not going to lie, it was the best thing that ever happened to me but I don't think it's going to work out."

"Why not? Eddie frowned. "If you don't mind me asking."

"I don't know. Because of my job, I guess. It's a big risk, giving up everything for someone, and even if I wanted to do that, I think it might be too late."

"Right." Eddie lingered at the junction. "Didn't you just say; 'It can't be wrong if it feels right?'" He held up a hand. "Those were your words, I'm just sayin'."

Nathalie grimaced. "I did say that, didn't I?" She noticed she was standing next to a bench with a sign that she hadn't seen before. "Hey, there's a bus stop here now. I could have done with one of those when I was fourteen."

Eddie laughed. "Yeah, me too. My parents don't like it one bit. They say it brings strangers onto their doorstep." He nodded towards his parents' house. "Talking about parents, I've got to go. Family lunch and all that. It was nice talking to you, Nat-Nat."

"It was nice talking to you too, Eddie. Take care." Nathalie waved at him as she walked into the opposite direction, picking up her pace as she tried to catch up with her parents.

59

Lena had taken to drinking while she cleared out the annex. The bottle of Pastis was next to her on the nightstand as she piled up the boxes she was either going to throw away or keep. She hadn't had time to go through her things before she first started renting out the house, so she'd thrown all her paperwork and personal effects into boxes and pushed them under her bed. But now that she was spending more time in the annex, she was running out of space, and it was time to get rid of anything she didn't need.

She had a vague idea of what was in them, but it still stung when she found old photo albums from her time with Selma in the first box she opened. She slumped down on the floor, leaned against the bed, and refilled her glass before she picked one up and flicked through it. There were pictures of Selma and her on the beach where they used to hang out on the weekends, and pictures of Lena on her birthday with Selma, her grandfather and a tiny puppy that Selma had gifted to her.

"Look Gumbo, this is you when you were a baby." She

held up the album for him to see. Gumbo sat next to her on the floor. He turned his head and stared at her hand instead, clueless as to what she was referring to. Lena smiled, thinking back of the memory. Her grandfather had insisted on calling him Gumbo, and despite finding it rediculous, Lena had given in. That was a good day, she remembered. They'd had dinner with friends and played music all night long while Lena checked on the sleeping Gumbo every ten minutes, making sure he was still breathing. They were both so young then, Lena noticed. She had long, braided hair and a nose piercing back then. Selma had dyed her hair bright red and she wore black, as always, even in the midst of summer. She had her arm around Lena's shoulders and her lips pressed against Lena's cheek. Her grandfather was smiling into the camera, holding up a glass of Champagne. That was Robert alright. Always positive and passionate, and always living each moment as if it was his last, even at that difficult time, when François had just passed away. The only comfort she felt in his death, was that he had no regrets. Lena still missed him every day, but she was finally at the point where she could look at these photographs with fond memories, instead of feeling the pain of not having him around anymore. The next page had pictures of her and Selma holding up the key to their first apartment. Then, more pictures of them having a celebratory picnic on the floor of their empty living room. They'd been happy, and Lena was convinced the love between them had been mutual. She could tell by the way Selma looked at her in the photographs. Lena skipped to the last page, and there was Selma with her suitcases packed. Despite their fights over Selma's departure, they'd been convinced they'd be able to work it out somehow. They'd both promised they would call every day, and that they'd see each other once a month.

Lena would fly to New York, or Selma would come to France. It seemed doable at the time, or at least that's what they thought. Lena put the album on the 'keep' pile and opened the next photo album, containing pictures of her and Selma in New York, the first time she visited. Lena had made sure to keep well away from her old neighborhood, avoiding any places where she could have bumped into her parents. But that hadn't been hard. Selma had managed to get an apartment in Manhattan, and she was living the American dream while working her ass off for a promotion. Even during Lena's visit, she hadn't been able to take any time off, or so she said. For the duration of the week, they only saw each other when she came home late at night, exhausted from a twelve-hour day. They still looked happy, though, sitting in a restaurant in Chinatown, smiling for the picture. Selma had promised she would come to France after that, but she cancelled two days before, claiming she had a big deadline she couldn't afford to miss. So, Lena flew to New York again. And again. In between the visits, it was mostly Lena who initiated contact until finally Selma stopped calling her back. Instead, Lena got a text message from her, saying she was very sorry for not replying, but that she'd met someone else. Lena had been devastated, and flicking over to the first empty page, she remembered the pain and the desperation she'd felt that day, when she broke down on the bedroom floor of the apartment they'd shared together. Until recently, she'd been convinced that Selma was her one true love, that she would never be able to love anyone the way she loved her. She also thought she'd be able to settle for less at some point, that she could be happy with someone else, as long as her expectations weren't too high. But Nathalie had blown her away, proving that there was such a thing as a second chance. Only this time around, it hurt even more.

Lena took another gulp of her drink. Her head was starting to spin now, and although she knew she'd had too much, she reached for the bottle and refilled her glass. Everything about this was so wrong. *Is it me? It must be, because it seems like history is repeating itself.* She turned to Gumbo.

"And now, I'm back where I started, Gumbo. Missing someone who left me for a job. A *job* for fuck's sake. And I can't even blame her this time." She sighed. "I should have known better."

Feeling lonely and in need of some comfort, she scrolled through her phone and dialed Beth's number. It went straight to voicemail. A little later, she got a text back.

Bruce is here. Don't call me this week.

Great. Not even alcoholic Beth had time for her. She scrolled further until she stumbled upon Christine Delevoire's number. She checked the last time she had called her. It was almost nine months ago. Christine had called her many times since then, but she'd never answered. It was funny, she thought in her drunken state, that the only options for booty calls were in her client list. She pressed call.

The phone rang a couple of times until a cold voice answered.

"Lena?"

"Hey, Christine. Yeah, it's me. How are you?"

"How am I?" Christine sounded flat. "Are you seriously calling to ask me how I am? How dare you." She raised her voice. "You never called me back, Lena. Not once."

"I'm sorry, I was busy and..."

"Fuck you, Lena. I thought we had something special,

you and me, and suddenly, you just ignored me and sent that chubby colleague of yours to finish the work in the garden. How do you think that made me feel?"

"I'm sorry, Christine. I thought it was just a bit of fun to you. I never meant to..."

"And then, I found out that you slept with my friend," Christine interrupted her again. "My only friend, as a matter of fact. Farah told me about you. So, what happened? You dumped me for her and then you dumped her for someone else? Is that how it works with you, Lena? Huh?" She sniffed. "I know you're only calling me because you're drunk. I can tell by your voice."

Fuck... Lena kept silent. Christine was furious, and she had every right to be. She could try to apologize again, but it wouldn't make things better. Not for Christine, and not for Farah. Without another word, she hung up and refilled her glass.

60

The chickens were restless again, according to her father, but to Nathalie, they always sounded the same. She'd offered to check on them, so her parents could get a good night's sleep, and was now regretting it as she crossed the yard towards the barn where the chickens stayed at night. She had her father's gun in one hand, and a flashlight in the other, sneaking around the building as if she were a burglar herself. Nathalie didn't have a clue how to use the gun, and wasn't even sure if it was loaded, but it seemed like the right tool for the job. The night was pleasant, and it was warm and quiet. The choir of crickets that always started singing at dusk had gone silent, and the only sound came from a lonely frog, calling from the pond behind the house. Nathalie wasn't scared, but she was cautious, expecting a fox or a wild dog to jump out of nowhere any minute. She checked the broken window next to the barn door. It was too high. There was no way a fox could jump through there, she thought, despite her father's claims. She walked over to the gap in the side wall of the old wooden building. Instead of patching it up, her father had put a plant pot in front of it. Although it looked misplaced, there were no paw prints or any evidence of digging. *He's just being paranoid.* There was no sign of any predators and after having circled the perimeter twice, Nathalie lowered the gun and relaxed, before opening the heavy barn door. The chickens seemed fine. They were quietly congregating in separate areas of the barn, not remotely bothered when Nathalie walked in. She held up a hand in a greeting, then shook her head and rolled her eyes, wondering if she was starting to lose her mind.

She hesitated by the front door as she was about to go back inside. It was three am, but she was wide awake now, and knew she wouldn't get any sleep anytime soon. She looked over at the hay bales next to the cornfields that she used to play in as a child. They were square now, instead of round, but they were still stacked up high like a flight of stairs. Drawn to them, Nathalie let go of the door handle and made her way back into the fields. She pulled herself up onto the first hay bale, scratching her bare legs on the occasional twig. *This used to be so much easier.* Or maybe she was just getting older, less athletic and flexible. That was a depressing thought. When she'd finally reached the top, she let herself fall on her back and looked up at the sky, taking a deep breath. The scent of lavender hit her nostrils, and she closed her eyes, trying to picture Lena's face. It became harder every day. She took the piece of soap out of the back pocket of her shorts and inhaled against it as she allowed memories to flood her mind. She cried, quietly at first. As the memories became more vivid, the pain became sharper and she shook as she let her tears run freely, curled up on her side, clenching the bar of soap in her hands. *What have I done?* Minutes passed, then hours. Nathalie fell in and out sleep, exhausted from the choking emotions that showed no sign of subsiding. She woke up when something rustled in the grass below her. Slowly, she sat up and grabbed the gun as she looked over the edge of the haystack. There he was. *No. It's a she.* A fox crossed the field with four cubs on her heel. They were in the cabbage patch, playing and chasing each other. She put down the gun and tried to be as still as she could as she watched them. It was a beautiful sight. They stayed there for a while until they slipped into the cornfields and disappeared out of sight. For the first time in years, Nathalie appreciated the beauty of her surroundings, and she felt a lot calmer now, gazing up at the millions of stars, glistening in the darkness. The Southern skies were beautiful, just like she remembered. They lay over the flat fields like a dome, ensuring nothing ever changed. *Not here. Not under these stars.* The Church bells would always ring on a Sunday, the seasons would always come and go, and the cornfields would never be replaced by high-rise buildings or shopping malls, at least not in a very long time. But they weren't her stars. Feeling small and insignificant, loneliness struck her. She felt a need to belong, and it wasn't here. She needed an anchor, something to hold on to. *Home. I need to go home.*

61

"Hey Marcus, it's Nathalie Kingston calling." Nathalie paused. "You don't know me, but I'd really appreciate a couple of minutes of your time to discuss some things." Nathalie always called people she did business with by their first name. It put her at the same level, and she'd found throughout her career that people were more likely to engage if she approached them in a more personable manner.

"Okay." Marcus Obermeier sounded guarded. "You're not from the tax office, are you? Because if you are, you can speak to my lawyer."

"No, I'm not." Nathalie tried to be as to the point as she could. People like Marcus rarely had time for small talk. "First of all, there's an office I'm interested in. It's in one of your Monaco developments. Are any of the small ones on the fifth floor still available? I'm particularly interested in the corner office, facing the south."

There was a pause. "No, they're not. Not unless you're on the waiting list." He sighed. "Anyway, you should talk to my sales team about that. I don't concern myself with the details. How did you get this number?"

"Right, of course. I understand." Nathalie had no intention of giving up. "It's just that the corner office is perfect for me, Marcus, and I don't have time to wait for people to drop off the waiting list. I'm kind of in a hurry. I can pay cash if you like. Maybe we could work out a deal, you and me?"

Marcus was silent for a moment before clearing his throat. "I'm listening."

Good. This was good. Nathalie had never been flexible in her business morals in her life but she sure was grateful that Marcus was.

"How about you move me to the top of the list and I pay a years' lease upfront, plus a little bonus for you, huh? Let's say 10 percent? Nobody needs to know." She waited for a reply. "Marcus? Are you still there?"

"Eh... yes. Miss Kingston, was it?"

"Yes, Nathalie Kingston."

"Okay Miss Kingston, I think we can work with that. As long as we can keep it quiet. Can I call you back tomorrow?"

"Yes, that would be great." Nathalie beamed in excitement. It was a big step, but she would do everything in her power to make it work. "But Marcus," she continued. There's another thing I'd like to discuss with you..."

62

"Nat-Nat, are you leaving? Why are your cases packed?" Nathalie's mother looked from the suitcases to Nathalie and back when she walked into her daughter's bedroom. A deep frown appeared between her eyebrows.

"Yeah. I'm leaving. I didn't tell you sooner because I've only just changed my ticket."

"But why?" Her mother shuffled on the spot. "Are they sending you to Singapore already?"

"No, something came up." Nathalie sat down on the edge of her childhood bed. "But I want you to know that I'm going to make more of an effort to come here in future, if you want me to."

"Of course, Nat-Nat. It would be wonderful to see more of you. Why wouldn't I want that?"

Nathalie braced herself for what was going to be the most difficult conversation of her life and patted the space on the mattress next to her for her mother to sit down.

She took a deep breath. "I'm in love, Mom. And I'm afraid you might not agree with my choice of partner."

Her mother shook her head. "I don't understand, Nat. It's great that you've met someone. We all need a man to take care of us in the end, although I can't say I'm not disappointed you didn't stay married to Jack." She took Nathalie's hand in her own and squeezed it. "But I'm trying to come to terms with that, and as you say, it's your life and you're old enough to make your own choices."

"It's not a man. I'm in love with a woman." Saying those words out loud to her mother was terrifying, but she'd thought long and hard about it, and it needed to be said. "She lives in France. That's where I'm going." She nodded towards her suitcases.

"No." Her mother shot her a puzzled look and immediately let go of her hand. "Did you just say... a woman?"

"Yeah, I did." Nathalie turned to her mother but failed to make eye-contact.

"No. That can't be right. My daughter is not a sinner. No Kingston is a sinner and I'll be damned if you become the first."

Nathalie tried to keep calm. It was exactly the reaction she'd expected, but it was still a slap in the face. "I'm not a sinner, Mom. I'm just in love. And there's nothing wrong with being gay." She took a deep breath. "Mr. Ainsworth from across the road is gay and you don't have a problem with that."

"No, he's not. How can you say that?" Her mother sniffed. "Mr. Ainsworth is a respected member of our church community. He's married with two children."

"He's still gay." Nathalie felt bad for dragging Mr. Ainsworth into her mess, but she needed any ammunition she could get to try to get through to her mother.

"Stop saying that word, Nathalie. Even if he were, which he's not, he wouldn't act upon it."

"Yes, he would, and he does," Nathalie said matter-of-factly. "He's been having an affair with the postman for as long as I can remember. It's not a secret, a lot of people know about it. I saw them talking to each other outside church on Sunday, and believe me, they're still very much an item. Now what kind of life is that? I don't want to live in secrecy."

"You're lying." Her mother turned her head, avoiding her gaze. "Mr. Ainsworth is no…"

She can't even say the word. Nathalie let out a deep sigh.

"And neither are you," Betsy continued with tears in her eyes.

"Don't you want me to be happy?" Nathalie didn't raise her voice. She stayed as calm as she could, knowing it was the only way.

"Of course, I want you to be happy. You're my daughter, my own flesh and blood." Her mother closed her eyes, holding on to her chest as if she had trouble breathing. "But not like this, Nathalie. Not like this. If you only give me a bit of time, stay a bit longer, I can find you a handsome young man with a…"

"I'm leaving," Nathalie interrupted her. "I've told you what I wanted to get off my chest and I'll leave you to think about it. We don't need to talk about it ever again, that's up to you. But I'm not going to make a secret of my love life either. You can pretend this conversation never happened. However, if someone here asks me, I'm going to answer honestly, because I'm not ashamed." She stood up and gathered her bags. "I've left my French number on the kitchen table. You can call me anytime if you want to talk and I'll visit you soon, if you want me to."

"Is your father driving you?" Her mother asked in a thin voice.

"No, I've ordered a cab." Nathalie moved her bags to the front door. Her mother lingered behind her, unsure of what to do or say. "I thought you and Dad might want to talk. So, either you can tell him, at some point, or I will." She gave her mother a sad smile before heading out. "I hope to see you soon, Mom. Oh, and tell Dad he's just being overprotective about the chickens. There's nothing out there."

"Wait," Her mother walked over to her and took her into her arms, hugging her like it was their last goodbye. "Please think about what you're doing. I'll be praying for you, Nat-Nat."

Nathalie released herself from her mother's grip and kissed her on the cheek.

"I don't need to think about it. But I think you should."

63

Lena looked over the bedroom once more, feeling accomplished. It looked presentable again, with fresh flowers on the nightstand and a new pair of slippers next to the bed. Bit by bit, she'd erased every trace that Nathalie had left behind. Her food in the fridge, a wineglass with her lipstick marks, left out on the terrace, and a piece of paper with phone numbers and notes scribbled on it. It was all gone. She could have hired a cleaner. It was a big house, and making it look spotless wasn't an easy job. But she needed closure, or at least some kind of ritual to rid herself of the memories of Nathalie that wouldn't seem to go away, no matter how hard she tried. Lena had waited for weeks until she finally felt like she could handle it. Now, there were clean towels in the bathroom, soap and shampoo in the shower, and she'd bought a new set of bed linen for the bed in the yellow bedroom. She'd cleaned all the other rooms too, just in case her new tenant preferred to sleep upstairs or wanted to have guests over.

"At least this one is a man," she said to Gumbo. "So Mommy doesn't have to worry she'll do anything stupid this time." Her heart sunk when she spotted a hairpin in the plant pot next to the bed. She picked it up and examined it. It was Nathalie's. Regret flushed through her, just like every other time she'd been reminded of her. It still hurt, all the time. *Forget about her. Just let it go.*

She walked into the kitchen and threw the hairpin in the bin, before pouring herself a generous glass of wine. Then she went to work, preparing a welcome meal for her new guest. Having a branch in Monaco, he would potentially come back if he liked the house, so she wanted to give him the best welcome she could.

Marcus Obermeier from Austria had seemed like a nice enough man in their correspondence. Lena had been honest with him and told him she lived in the annex. He said he didn't care. Marcus just wanted somewhere to stay for three weeks while he closed his latest real-estate deal in Monaco. Somewhere discreet, where he would be able to bring 'a friend' from time to time, as he put it. Lena guessed he was referring to his mistress, but she hadn't pried. Just in case, she made sure she had enough of the chicken stew for two, a bottle of chilled white wine in the fridge, and candles on the kitchen table and outside, on the terrace. It was starting to get dark now, and she lit a couple to create some atmosphere.

AN HOUR LATER, the buzzer for the gate sounded throughout the annex. Fresh out of the shower, Lena slipped into a pair of shorts and put on a white linen shirt before she rushed outside towards the driveway. She smiled when she saw the car pull in. The Jaguar was an excellent choice, she thought, listening to the tires screeching as it came to an abrupt halt next to her Porsche. *I think I like this Marcus already.* The door swung open, and as Lena pulled her face into a welcome smile, she realized it wasn't Marcus who stepped out of the car.

"NATHALIE?" Lena stared at the woman who was walking towards her now, failing to comprehend what was happening. Nathalie was still as beautiful as she remembered. Her hair was bouncing over her shoulders as she walked, and she was dressed casually, in sneakers and a short summer dress. *Not again. Please don't do this to me again.* "What are you doing here?" Lena took a deep breath, unsure whether to keep her distance or to take Nathalie into her arms. "I've got a tenant coming, right about now."

"Marcus?" Nathalie said. "He's not coming." She didn't look smug, or amused. She looked humble and nervous as she closed the distance between them. "I've arranged alternative accommodation for Marcus, so this is my rental for the duration of his booking." She looked up at Lena. "Believe me, he's more than happy. I got him a place with a butler and he's the kind that likes to show off. He even promised to give you a five-star rating as it's technically still under his name." She paused. "So, you can either ignore me, shout at me for doing this, or hear me out."

Lena didn't know what to say as she looked into the blue eyes that would surely mess her up all over again. It was dangerous, she knew that. It would open a door to a whole new level of pain. One that included false hope, disappointment and so many more sleepless nights. But she couldn't look away. Nathalie showing up was the last thing she'd expected, but it was also the most beautiful surprise. She felt so much pain and joy and excitement to see her again, that she was afraid she might break down.

"Please hear me out," Nathalie begged again when Lena didn't answer. "I just want to talk to you." She swallowed, and Lena could see tears in her eyes. "I've missed you. God damn it, I've missed you so much, Lena. Every day was a struggle, knowing that you were here, and I was on the other side of the ocean. You were out here, living your life, probably moving on without me. The thought of you forgetting about me was unbearable, and I imagined I'd slowly fade from your memory one day and you'd say; 'Nathalie? Who was that again? Oh yes, of course. She was one of my tenants and we had a thing back in the day.'" Nathalie shook her head. "And that would be all." She looked up at Lena. "And that's not acceptable to me. Because I think we belong together, Lena. I believe I was meant to come here and meet you. I was meant to get to know you and lose myself with you. So please just listen, because I need to tell you this."

Lena's shoulders dropped. There was no way she would walk away again. She had missed her so much.

"Okay." Lena's hand trembled as she reached out for Nathalie's. "Let's sit down." Nathalie took her hand and followed her towards the direction of the pool, where they took a seat next to each other on one of the sun loungers. Lena shivered at the contact when Nathalie's arm brushed against hers. She thought of letting go of her hand, but she couldn't. Not now, when she was finally here.

"I turned down the job in Singapore and I've put down a year's lease on an office in Monaco," Nathalie said, getting straight to the point. "Marcus Obermeier's development." She turned to Lena. "You know, your tenant who was supposed to arrive today?"

Lena frowned, letting the words sink in. Then her expression softened as relief washed over her.

"You're moving to Monaco?"

Nathalie shook her head. "No, I'm moving to France, but I'm starting my own business in Monaco, consulting on environmentally friendly manufacturing. It wasn't easy, I had to move my entire capital here, but it's all done now, and I've got my paperwork sorted. My temporary work permit will arrive next week." She took Lena's hand. "Look, I don't expect you to take me back here and now, and maybe it's too late, but I would really like to start over if you'll give me another chance. I know it's a risk, moving here, but the fact is, I love France, and I feel like this is a place I could finally belong." She pursed her lips, searching for the right words. "I've missed you so much that it hurt. Every day without you seemed pointless." She paused and took a deep breath in an attempt to hold back her tears. "Even if you don't want to do this, I've got to start making a home for myself somewhere, and all I know is that it's never going to be Chicago or Singapore. I've been happy here."

Lena squeezed her hand. "You're really moving here?" Her eyes met Nathalie's for a brief moment. They were filled with emotion, welling up when she lowered her head, staring down at their entwined hands. "Wow."

"If you don't want me here, I can stay in the guesthouse in town for now," Nathalie continued, "I'll be looking at some properties this week. I decided to put all my stuff up for auction in Chicago, so I'll be starting from scratch." She managed a smile. "I kind of like the idea of a fresh start. It's like you said; life is an empty sheet right now, and I'm in the lucky position to paint anything I want so why use the colors that I'm bored with? I want to be here, with you. And if it's too late, well... I still want to be here."

Lena's face broke into a smile. "I don't want you to move to town," she said, her voice unsteady. "I want you to move in here, with me. Unless it's too soon..."

Nathalie held her breath at the words she'd been dying to hear. She wiped away a tear and turned to Lena, taking her other hand.

"Really? You'd want me to move in with you?" I mean, I'd love nothing more, but you know what you're saying, right?"

Lena nodded and closed her eyes as she lowered her forehead against Nathalie's.

"I love you, Nat." There was a silence. "I wasn't sure if I could love again, but I love you more than I've ever loved anyone." Lena's wall had lifted, and she finally allowed herself to feel. It was liberating to let her tears run freely, and to finally say what she wanted to say. She took Nathalie into a tight embrace, burying her face in her neck.

"I love you too." Nathalie smiled through her tears when she spoke the words, sinking into the embrace. They held each other for minutes, until Nathalie looked up, searching for Lena's lips. She'd been longing for them, craving her kiss since the day they'd parted. "Kiss me," she whispered.

Lena took her face in her hands and brushed her lips lightly against Nathalie's, drawing a quick breath from her mouth.

"I've missed you so much, Nat." She took Nathalie's bottom lip between her own before pulling her in, deepening the kiss. Nathalie felt Lena's warm mouth on hers, then her tongue as she tilted her head and parted her lips. She moaned, running her hand through Lena's hair, down to the back of her neck. The warm sensation that spread through her core only grew stronger when Lena lowered her down on the sunbed and sank on top of her. Her hunger for Lena's kiss and her touch came back tenfold, leaving her desperate for more.

"God, that feels good." Nathalie sighed and turned her

head as she let Lena devour her neck. She felt Lena's teeth scrape over her skin, her wet mouth on her ear as she listened to her ragged breathing. The sound of it made Nathalie want her even more, and she arched her back in delight when Lena moved a hand under her dress, up her thigh and around her waist to unclasp her bra at the back.

"Take it off," Lena said, sitting up and straddling her. Nathalie barely had time to take off her dress and her bra before Lena's lips and hands were all over her again. She'd never felt more wanted in her life. Lena touched her with such conviction, such passion. The feeling of her warm hands was almost too much to bear. Lena bit down on her nipple, softly at first, before taking it into her mouth.

"I need you," she said in a hoarse voice. Then she moved back up to face Nathalie and kissed her long and deep. Nathalie moaned, wrapping her legs around Lena's hips that were thrusting into her. She moved her hands underneath Lena's shirt, but Lena grabbed her wrists and pinned her hands above her head in a tight grip. "Soon." Her eyes were dark and full of anticipation. "Let me have you. Please."

Nathalie took in a deep breath and nodded when Lena slipped her fingertips under the edge of her panties, still holding her wrists with her other hand.

"Can you feel how much I want you?" she whispered, spreading her legs. Lena smiled as she moved her hand further down, stroking the sensitive skin between her thighs before slipping a finger into her wetness. She bit her lip and closed her eyes in delight as she moved into Nathalie, adding another finger when Nathalie lifted her hips, begging for more. She kept Nathalie's wriggling hands in place, teasing her with slow strokes. She looked more aroused than Nathalie had ever seen her, moving into her in a slow, steady rhythm while she moaned quietly each time her fingers went a little deeper.

"I can feel it. God, you're so wet." She opened her eyes and watched Nathalie drown in ecstasy, crying out when she penetrated her faster and faster, until she couldn't hold back anymore. She finally let go of Nathalie's wrists, allowing her to pull her into an all-consuming kiss while she sent her over the edge, holding her fingers deep inside of her. She felt Nathalie's contractions, the trembling of every limb. She heard the release in her voice and saw the intensity in her eyes. It was beautiful.

"Fuck, Lena." Nathalie sighed, her chest heaving up and down. "Only you can do this to me." She pulled Lena in and kissed her again.

"Only you can make me do this," Lena said. She was still inside of her, pulling out slowly before she pressed her hand down between Nathalie's legs, drawing another gasp from her mouth. She let her fingers run through Nathalie's folds, up to her stomach and over her breast, resting her hand there while she licked her lips.

Nathalie looked up at Lena's aroused expression, overcome with a need to get her out of her clothes as fast as she possibly could. She traced Lena's back, skimming the top of her waistband before she moved her hand inside, marveling at the softness of her bottom. She squeezed it, and looked up at Lena with a cheeky smile.

"I want you out of these clothes within the next thirty seconds because I have plans for you."

64

The pool water was refreshing after hours of heavenly lovemaking in the heat of the night. Nathalie had her arms around Lena's neck and her legs wrapped around her waist as they kissed. She felt physically exhausted, but full of energy at the same time. Lena held her tight, moving towards the deeper end of the pool. It was dark, and the candles by the poolside painted a perfect picture over the garden of *Villa Provence*.

"I'm so glad you're here," Lena said in a soft voice. "It's more than I ever dared to hope for."

"I'm glad too." Nathalie stroked her cheek and placed a kiss on her nose. "I still can't believe I'm here again." She smiled. "So, we're really going to do this, huh? You and me?"

"Yeah. You and me." There was no doubt in Lena's mind. She wanted Nathalie with every fiber of her being. "Are you nervous about starting over? A new life, setting up a company in a country where you don't speak the language? Where you don't know anyone, apart from me?"

"Of course I am." Nathalie leaned back and dipped her

head into the water before raising her gaze back to Lena. "I'd be lying if I said I wasn't nervous. But I'm also hopeful, and I feel like I can do anything with you in my life. I think I'll settle in pretty quick." She sighed, taking in Lena's face. She was gorgeous. "I'm going to take French lessons and I've given myself a one-year deadline to be able to speak basic French. Enough to get around and make small talk, anyway."

"Ambitious lady. That means we'll have to practice some more together." Lena frowned, suddenly more serious. "Did you tell your parents? About us?"

Nathalie nodded. "Yeah. I told my mom. It didn't go down very well." She shrugged. "I thought about not telling them, just leaving them in ignorance. I don't see them that often anyway, and I'm sure I'd be able to wriggle myself out of their desperate matchmaking attempts." She smiled. "But then they wouldn't know the most important thing about me. And the most important thing about me is that I love you. I wanted them to know that."

"I get that." Lena traced Nathalie's mouth with her thumb, holding her face in her hands. "So, are you still on speaking terms?"

"Yeah. I think we are. They'll probably dodge the subject for all eternity but that's their choice, and I've made mine. I'll still visit them, and we'll talk about chickens and cornbread. Anything but *that*." She laughed. "I wouldn't be surprised if the whole church is praying for me again. The whole situation is beyond annoying but still, I'd like you to go there with me someday. I don't want to lose the ties, even though I have no connection with my hometown whatsoever. I want to show you where I grew up, where I'm from. Is it strange that I feel that way?"

"Not at all." Lena smiled. "I'd love to see where you grew up. Just give your parents some time. Just because mine never came around doesn't mean yours won't."

"Have you ever thought of going back to New York? To visit your parents?" Nathalie asked.

Lena shook her head. "No. They never contacted me, so I assume they feel like they're better off without me. My mother never begged me to stay when I told her I was moving to France either. But I came to terms with that a long time ago."

"I have another question." Nathalie seemed nervous as she fiddled with a strand of her hair. "I don't want you to think this is important to me, or feel pressured, but I've had some time to think while I was at my parents, and I was just wondering if…" She hesitated. "Well, I was wondering if you want kids. We never talked about the subject. Is it something you've thought about?"

Lena chuckled. "That's a loaded question. What if I give you the wrong answer?"

"There is no wrong answer."

"Okay. In that case, I suppose I would like to have a family one day. But if it doesn't happen, that's fine too. What about you?"

"I never wanted kids," Nathalie said. "But I feel different with you. It's the weirdest thing. I've even thought about what a great parent you'd be and I can picture us with kids."

"Really? You think I'd make a great parent?" Lena arched an eyebrow and smiled.

"Yeah. I do." Nathalie took a tighter hold of her. "But I'd like to enjoy this first, for a few years at least. Besides, I need to focus on the basics right now, like setting up my company and learning French."

Lena laughed. "Why not start straight away? Tu as faim?"

Nathalie frowned. "What?"

"Are you hungry?" Lena asked again, this time in English.

"Oh, right." Nathalie laughed. "I'll have to remember that. Tu as faim, you said?"

"Uhuh. Great pronunciation already."

Nathalie rolled her eyes. "Yeah, right. But to answer your question in English for now, yes, I'm starving. I haven't eaten since lunch on the plane, and I won't deny that my appetite's been fed by getting a taste of other things..." She winked.

"You poor thing." Lena shot her an amused look. "I'm so sorry, I didn't even offer you anything. Give me ten minutes and I'll heat up the food. I made some earlier."

"Oh, believe me, you offered me more than enough," Nathalie said, laughing. "But wait." She reluctantly let go of her grip on Lena and headed for the steps. "I'll do it. I'm starting over, so I might as well get into the habit of cooking. I'm determined to become as French as I possibly can." She grinned. "But you're welcome to help me because for now, I have no idea what I'm doing."

They both got out of the pool and were drying themselves off, when they heard barking coming from the annex.

"Shit. It's Gumbo." Lena rushed over to open the door. "I completely forgot he was still in there." Gumbo came tearing out and headed straight for Nathalie.

"Hey boy, I've missed you. I'm so sorry we forgot about you." She bent down to greet him but to her surprise, he jumped straight into her arms. "I think he missed me too," she said in a sweet voice, kissing his nose. "Are you coming into the kitchen with us, Gumbo? I'll make you some food too." Gumbo barked at the word 'food', and they laughed as they walked back to the main house with Gumbo sprinting ahead of them. Nathalie took Lena's hand, and savored the moment. She was finally home.

EPILOGUE

It was late August and the roads were congested with vacationers in rental cars and campervans, making their way to Italy. In high-season, Lena rarely drove to Monaco at any other time than five in the morning, especially on a Saturday. But today was an exception, and having left plenty of time for the journey, she was in no rush. She looked at Nathalie from the passenger's seat and grinned.

"You look sexy, driving in that dress."

Nathalie gave her a flirty smile from behind the steering wheel and hiked up the hem of her red satin dress as she accelerated, revealing a tanned thigh.

"Oh yeah?" She nodded towards the campervan with the Dutch number plate in the fast lane that was holding up the traffic. The driver's head was turned, staring at Nathalie until the beep of a car horn finally made him jump and speed up. "I'm not one for tooting my own horn, but I think he might agree with you."

Lena laughed. "I think every single driver here will agree with me." She shifted a hand underneath Nathalie's dress, trailing her fingertips between her thighs. Nathalie bit her lip and shivered, trying to keep her focus on the road.

"Do you mind if we stop by the office on our way back? I forgot to bring some paperwork yesterday and I'm working from home next week, so I'll need it."

"Sure." Lena watched her pull a strand of hair back, securing it behind her ear. Nathalie's hair was pinned up. Her red lipstick matched the color of her sleeveless cocktail dress and her simple sandals. She looked effortlessly beautiful, Lena thought. "I haven't been to your office since you got the keys. I'd love to see what you've done to the place." She squeezed Nathalie's thigh and smiled. "Anyway, I doubt I can wait until we're home to get you out of that dress, so the office will have to do. You're killing me, Nat."

Nathalie stole a fleeting glance at Lena while she took a turn into Monte-Carlo.

"Same here. You look sexy as hell." Lena wore a white shirt and a pair of formal black trousers. She seemed relaxed, leaning back in her seat with her feet up on the dashboard. "I'm proud of you, Lena."

"Thanks, but you haven't seen it yet." Lena checked her watch for the time. "I'm feeling a bit nervous," she said. "I know there's nothing else I could have done to make it better, but it's still nerve-wracking. My garden will be all over the newspapers tomorrow."

"Don't worry, it's going to be great." Nathalie pulled into the long drive that led up to the formal gates of the Princely Palace, where they got out and handed the car over to the valet. They were greeted by representatives who led them to the red carpet that circled the wall into the garden.

"Oh God, I didn't see this coming." Nathalie stared at the line of reporters, snapping pictures of the guests. She swallowed hard and hesitated.

"Come on." Lena took her hand and waved at the lady who had been her main contact throughout the project.

"Lena, thanks for coming," the older, white-haired lady shook Lena's hand and turned to Nathalie. "And you must be Nathalie. It's a pleasure to meet you. I'm Pippa." She gave them both a warm smile. "Now, there's nothing to be nervous about, it's all very straightforward. If you don't mind, I'd like you both to go over there to have your picture taken." She looked from Lena to Nathalie and back. "How may I refer to your relationship?"

"Partner," Lena said. "Nathalie is my partner." Despite the sudden nerves, Nathalie felt warm and fuzzy at hearing the words. She pinched Lena's hand as they walked towards the reporters alongside Pippa.

"After that," Pippa continued, "I'll introduce you to the family. They're very pleased with the result and they're looking forward to thanking you personally for all the hard work."

Nathalie felt awkward, standing in front of twentysomething reporters, but when Lena put an arm around her and pulled her in, she couldn't help but smile. Just before they were about to leave the carpet, Lena turned to her and stole a kiss, leading to even more frantic clicking of the cameras.

"I'm sorry," she chuckled. "But I love you and I want the whole world to know that you're mine."

"THAT WAS INTENSE." Nathalie sighed in relief and took a seat next to Lena on a bench, accepting a glass of Champagne from one of the servers. "I'm glad the formalities are out of the way, so I can finally take in your creation." She looked over the pristine lawn and the grand flowerbed, showcasing the Royal Crest. The fountain was the showstopper, with a smooth piece of marble in the middle, cut into a spiral with five arms that moved the water around. "I can't believe you did all of this. It's incredible."

"It wasn't just me," Lena said. "Unfortunately, I couldn't bring the team today, but they've got tickets, so they can take their families next week, when it's open to the public again. I've got two for Alain and Samantha as well, she's flying over to see him on the weekend."

"Really? Again?"

"Yeah. Alain is smitten with her." Lena winked. "I love teasing him about it. I guess neither of us expected to be in this position so soon. You know, tied down, taken, tamed."

Nathalie laughed. "No, I suppose you didn't, but neither did I." She ran a hand through Lena's hair. "I'm so happy, Lena. I…"

"Do you guys mind if I take a picture?" One of the photographers asked, interrupting her.

"No, it's fine." Nathalie put an arm around Lena, and they both smiled as they held up their glasses in a toast.

"It's a shame they're everywhere," Lena mumbled. "I don't think there's a single place here where we can make out like a couple of reckless teenagers."

"Exactly my thought." Nathalie's gaze wandered down to Lena's lips. She had to gather all her willpower not to press her mouth against them. "But we'll have all the time in the world later."

Lena smiled and kissed Nathalie's forehead. "All the time in the world sounds like a dream. That's all I've ever wanted."

AFTERWORD

I hope you've loved reading Beyond the Skyline as much as I've loved writing it. If you've enjoyed this book, would you consider rating it and reviewing it on www.amazon.com? Reviews are very important to authors and I'd be really grateful!

ACKNOWLEDGMENTS

I would like to thank Claire Jarrett and Laure Dherbécourt for beta reading and editing, and making this a better book. It's been a real pleasure to work with you both. You don't know each other, but you are a dream team.

Also, a huge thanks to the talented photographer Julia Caesar for letting me use her photograph on the cover.

And last but not least, thank you Aleks, my wonderful wife of five years, for supporting me in my writing. I'm trying to be a good housewife :)

ABOUT THE AUTHOR

Lise Gold is an author of lesbian fiction. Her romantic attitude, enthusiasm for travel and love for feel good stories form the heartland of her writing. Lise's novels: 'Lily's Fire'(2017), 'Beyond the Skyline' (2017), 'The Cruise' (2018) and 'French Summer' (2018) are the result of a quest for a new passion, after spending fourteen years working as a designer. Lise lives in the UK with her wife.

ALSO BY LISE GOLD

Lily's Fire

Beyond the Skyline

The Cruise

Printed in Great
Britain
by Amazon